# THE DEAD OF WINTER

## JAMES H LEWIS

THE DEAD OF WINTER

by James H Lewis

*For Mark Smukler, public media guru, who first suggested I incorporate the Pittsburgh Potty in a story.*

RUDY WAS the product of a mixed marriage, a fact of no concern to his parents since they were too. His face and body seemed composed of spare parts. His hair, a mix of white and brown, was wiry and close-cropped. A pair of deep-set brown eyes overlooked a pointed nose that ceaselessly probed the air, and his ears stuck up like sails. Though he was small and compact, he had powerful legs and could outrun anyone or anything in the neighborhood.

Cindy, who ran behind him as they made their way out of the apartment complex on Old Mill Road, didn't care. She knew he lacked breeding, but bristled when her girlfriends call him a mutt. She loved this combination of Shetland sheepdog, miniature pinscher, and whatever else had invaded the yards of his forebears over the years.

At the moment, the seven-year-old wasn't thinking about her companion, who pulled her along at a clip that belied his appearance, but at a sense of anticipation she ascribed to the first scent of spring in the air. The dog pulled her along as he tore down the road from their apartment.

The last vestiges of snow lay piled on either side, forcing her to walk in the roadway. This was something her mother had instructed her not to do, but Rudy had a mind of his own this morning. Runoff formed rivulets that gathered into a stream. She tried to dodge the worst of it, but her running shoes kicked up spray that crept up her jeans from her ankles to her knees. Her father would be furious, and Cindy wondered whether she could slip them off and shove them into the washer before he returned from work.

They reached the bottom of the hill, where the road crossed North Branch Creek and joined the busy highway that shared its name. Cars raced along it at fifty miles per hour and more. "C'mon, Rudy," she said. "Time to turn back."

The dog stopped in his tracks and went into alert like a pointer, something she'd never seen him do before. "C'mon, boy," she repeated. She tugged at the leash, but Rudy strained against it with such force she feared he might rip her arm from its socket. She switched the leash from one hand to the other. Sensing a moment of freedom, the dog took off, plunging down the slick embankment toward the culvert that passed beneath the bridge.

"Rudy, come back," she yelled, but the dog didn't respond, barking at a snowpack that lay alongside the stream. He looked up at her, then returned his attention to the white mound, which bore a dark crust from the mud thrown up by passing automobiles.

Cindy burst into tears. "Darned dog," she said. "I'm in trouble now." She scrambled down the bank after him, losing her balance and sliding down the ice-covered vegetation. Her jeans were soaked; mud caked the back of her legs and her bottom. Reaching the animal, who continued to shift his attention between her and the snowpack, she grabbed his leash and yanked on it.

"Move!" she called. "Now!"

The dog barked, strained at the lead, and scratched at the icy patch. "What is it?" she said, curious to see what had his attention. He dug furiously at the frozen surface, frantic to get at something trapped under a pile of broken wood. *A piece of fencing?* she wondered.

Something round and pale green jutted out from the icy debris, so light she wouldn't have noticed it if the snow weren't so dirty. As she leaned forward to study the object, Rudy relaxed, content now that his human had taken charge. Fishing gloves from her coat pocket, the girl scraped at the snow, clearing a path around the spherical object, then noticed it was attached to what looked like a small branch.

She drew back in terror as she realized she was looking at a bare heel, an ankle, and God only knew what more hidden in the snow.

---

TEN MILES TO THE EAST, another dog was out for a walk, being led rather than the other way round. Howie, a white Westie, dawdled, sniffing at every patch of newly exposed grass he could find. The woman who led him was four times Cindy's age, and unlike the young girl, thought not of the first stirrings of spring but of mud season.

She was of medium height, but her erect posture created an impression she was two inches taller. She concealed tight blond curls beneath a knit cap that bore the emblem of the US women's national soccer team. Two prominent features dominated her triangular shaped face. One was a prominent nose that would have gained more notice were it not for deep-set cerulean eyes so piercing they arrested the attention of anyone who met her.

Lydia Barnwell had adopted Howie after his owner, a fellow police officer and her former lover, was killed during a domestic disturbance four months earlier. The Westie had gone into depression, and the late officer's parents had forced him on her. At first she'd resisted, but as she pulled him out of his doldrums, she found an equal measure of comfort. Lydia had grown so attached to him she'd just bought a two-bedroom house halfway up a hill in Carnegie, which she was working to bring into the $21^{st}$ century.

On most days, she enjoyed these morning walks, for they wiped everything else from her mind. For twenty minutes, she didn't mull over pending investigations, fret about her testimony in an upcoming court case, or worry about her safety. She and Howie just walked together, enjoying or cursing the weather, depending on what it was doing to them.

But not today. Days after the new year, she'd joined the Allegheny County Police Department as a detective. It was a lateral move from the small police force she'd served in Boyleston, but the pay and benefits were better and, more important to her, provided the opportunity to work on tougher cases.

Or so she'd hoped, but it wasn't working out that way. In the two months since making the change, she'd been assigned to work under other detectives, handle small robberies, or, as one of the few bilingual officers on the force, question Spanish-speaking victims and suspects. Rather than advancing her career, she'd taken a step backward.

This morning, resentment burned within her, upending her one carefree moment of the day.

As Howie buried his muzzle in the soil at the base of a fire hydrant, her cell phone rang. She answered it with her last name.

"Sorry to disturb you on your day off," detective sergeant Glen Carpenter said, "but a child has discovered a body in a culvert in North Fayette. The locals have secured the site, and the crime scene investigators are on the way, but we need you to take charge of the investigation."

"Any sign of foul play?" she said.

"We won't know that until the medical examiner has examined the body. It may be nothing more than the victim stumbling on an icy patch and falling off the road." He said he'd text the location to her phone and rang off without apologizing for ruining a day on which she'd intended to start redoing the upstairs bathroom.

*Thanks a lot*, she thought. *Another routine assignment.*

At the moment, Lydia Barnwell wished she'd never left the Boyleston force, but although the position she'd vacated remained open, returning was out of the question. She had mixed business with pleasure, and her role there would never be the same.

---

Lydia took her personal car, since returning to headquarters off Greentree Road would have taken her in the wrong direction. She also carried what equipment she'd need in her trunk. She wound north on Chartiers Avenue, joined I-376 at Campbell's Run Road, and exited on Route 30 toward Weirton, West Virginia. Within minutes, she'd left behind the blight of malls and big box stores: Home Depot competing with Lowe's; Costco vying with Sam's Club; Target versus Walmart; an Ikea, Macy's, and a T.J. Maxx; banks seeking deposits and hawking loans; hotels, car rental agencies, and long-term parking lots surrounding Pittsburgh International Airport; and a slew of restaurants dishing up every cuisine from China to Mexico, Italy to Japan, Tex-Mex to country cooking, and ubiquitous fast-food drive-ins serving burgers, pizza, and tacos.

Turning off the highway was like entering another world, a pastoral panorama of rolling hills and verdant valleys, brooks flowing into streams lining the road. Even on a day when gray clouds boiled and frothed on the horizon, Barnwell was captivated by the bucolic scene and vowed to return once the weather changed. Only later would she discover that area homes faced frequent subsidence caused by abandoned coal mines and that behind the hills, energy companies had drilled into a former strip mine to extract natural gas through hydraulic fracking, injecting thousands of gallons of fresh water into the Marcellus Shale, its foul rivulets flowing into the streams she found so inviting.

Orange cones narrowed North Branch Road to a single lane. Patrol officers from North Fayette Township directed traffic, allowing one lane through at a time. Lydia wished she'd returned to Greentree for a cruiser, for her unmarked vehicle was indistinguishable from every other car on the road. Turning on the warning blinkers only annoyed other drivers.

She sat in traffic for seven minutes, enduring three stoppages, until she reached the officer directing traffic. After studying her ID, he held up oncoming cars until she could cross the bridge onto Old Mill Road. She passed another line of cones, parked on the side, and walked back to where the crime lab van was parked.

Barnwell flashed her ID at the county patrol officer, whose name on the aluminum clip on his pocket identified him as Patrolman J. Mullins. He leaned forward to get a close view of her badge, then raised his eyes to her face. "You're the new one," he said.

"Detective Barnwell," she said. "What do we have here?"

"A body in the culvert," he said, pointing toward the bridge that crossed the creek. "Been there for some time, from the looks of it. The CSI team has just started." They'd traveled farther to reach the scene, but in their well-marked van hadn't been forced to sit in traffic.

She asked who'd discovered the body. "A young girl," Mullins said. "Her mother called it in. Name's Thorson."

"Where is she?" Barnwell asked.

"We took her information and sent her home. She lives in one of the apartment buildings up the hill." Barnwell looked around, spotting a row of townhomes to the west of the bridge and three apartment buildings overlooking the scene from above. She took down the information and posed a few questions about how the youngster had found the body, but Mullins had told her everything he knew.

"Who was first on the scene?" she asked.

Mullins pointed to a female officer from North Fayette who stood inside a guardrail observing the technicians. "Name's Foster," he said. "She'd climbed down to examine the body. I hope she didn't screw things up."

"Why would you say that?" the detective asked.

"Being local and all."

Barnwell bristled. "North Fayette is a professional

force. Twenty well-trained officers let by an experienced chief. I'm sure she knew what she was doing."

Did the officer know Barnwell had joined the county from one of the smaller forces that dotted the area? Some were staffed by amateurs and part-timers, but not North Fayette. Barnwell didn't care whether his disdain was directed at the township's police force or because the first to arrive was a woman. She was having none of it.

She introduced herself to the patrol officer, noticing as she approached she was a light-skinned Black woman. Was this another reason Officer Mullins had been so contemptuous? She identified herself as Nadine Foster and proved to be more forthcoming than Mullins had been. She described how Cindy Thorson's mother had called 911 in near hysteria.

"Her daughter told her she'd found a body, but Cathy—that's the woman's name—didn't believe her, so she came down the hill to look for herself. I don't know how she made it down the bank. It's overgrown with weeds, and the runoff makes it slippery. But somehow she did, found a foot sticking out from beneath some leaves, and called dispatch as she stood there."

The officer arrived minutes after the call. "Our headquarters is just up the road, so I got here before Mrs. Thorson was even out of the culvert," she said.

"Did you examine the body?" Barnwell asked.

"No. I only got close enough to confirm what the mother said and radioed you folks. I didn't want to disturb the scene."

"You did well, Officer," she said, feeling a smug sense of satisfaction that Foster had, indeed, followed procedure. Barnwell returned to her car and opened a packet of white paper protective gear, knowing that the booties, bottom of the suit, and gloves would become muddy messes by the time she reached the body.

As she started down the bank, her feet slid out from beneath her. Only by crouching and extending her arms did she regain her balance. She crept the rest of the way by walking crablike, maintaining purchase with the sides of her boots. Barnwell approached the medical examiner's investigative team and introduced herself to the white-coated figure bent over the body. "Is there anything you can tell me?" she asked.

The investigator peered over her shoulder and smiled. "Brandy Timmons," she said. Barnwell recalled her from the case in which David Kimrey, her former lover, had been slain, but with her head enveloped in the white bonnet, hadn't recognized her. "The photographer finished moments ago, so I'm just getting underway." Timmons wiped a sleeve of the white gown across her forehead. "It's a white male, approximately 5-10. That's all I can tell you now, except he was nude. Not a stitch of clothing."

"Strange," Barnwell said. "Any wounds or other signs of trauma?"

"I can't tell yet because he's lying face down, but nothing on his back, at least."

"How long has his body been here?"

"We won't know until the autopsy, but I'd say weeks rather than days. Give me half-an-hour, and I may have more."

Barnwell thanked her, made her way up the bank, and approached Mullins, the county officer. "I want you to head up the hill, cross the road, and go to the first residence you find. Ask whether they've seen or noticed any strange activity here over the last few weeks."

"Do you have anything more to go on?" he asked.

"Not yet, but residents will have seen all this commotion, so let's question them before they start telling themselves stories." She had seen memories fade over time, and embellishments overtake facts.

Mullins wasn't happy, but walked toward his patrol car to do as he was told. Barnwell turned toward the North Fayette officer. "I'm heading up the hill to talk to the mother," she said. "While I'm gone, you're in charge."

"Understood," Officer Foster answered, puffing out her chest.

***

THE APARTMENT where the child lived was in the topmost of the three recently constructed buildings. Barnwell rode the elevator to the third floor and pushed the doorbell. Seconds later, a man answered. He appeared to be in his early thirties, had brown hair and eyes, and his delicate features were almost feminine. His trousers appeared to be part of a uniform, but he wore a sweatshirt emblazoned with the logo of the Tennessee Titans. "Mr. Thorson?" Barnwell said.

"Ben," he answered. "And you are...?"

"Detective Lydia Barnwell, Allegheny County Police Department. May I come in?"

"I guess," he said and drew back from the doorway, "but my wife says she's told you everything we know."

Through the hallway, Barnwell saw a woman standing with her back to the window, observing the conversation. The furnishings were by Ikea, and the walls were bare, creating an impression of impermanence. "Mrs. Thorson," she said, striding into the room and extending her hand.

"I've already told your officers how she found the body.

She wasn't supposed to be there. I've told her not to go that far. I was doing laundry, and she promised she was just walking the dog." She kneaded her hands and cast an inquiring look at her husband. Barnwell wondered if the explanation was meant for her or for him.

"I'd like to speak with your daughter. Cindy, is it?"

The pair exchanged glances, some private conversation passing between them. "Is it necessary?" the husband said.

"She found the body. I need to know how she came to discover it, if she saw anything else at the site, how close she came..."

"We don't want to involve her any more than she already has," Ben Thorson said. "There's nothing she can tell you."

Before Barnwell could respond, his wife said, "We don't want her name in the paper or her picture on television. These are dangerous times."

"We won't release her name, and news media never identity minors," Barnwell said. "I have to ask her a few questions for the record. That's all."

"She found a body," he said. "Cathy reported it. What more can we tell you?"

Barnwell trained her gaze on him, and he looked away. "What do you do for a living?" she asked in a calm voice.

"What difference does it make?"

"Please answer my question. Where do you work?"

"At the airport," he said.

"And what do you do there?"

Thorson glanced toward his wife, then gave up. "I'm a shift manager with the TSA. I left work to deal with this. I'll need to get back soon."

Barnwell gave him the slightest of smiles. "If I were to come through security this afternoon and set off the metal detector, your people would want to search me, correct? And if I resisted, you'd pull me aside until I submitted, even if it meant I missed my plane."

"Yes, but I don't see—"

"I'm about to do the same thing," she interrupted. "I can't act with impunity, as you can, but I can get a court order allowing me to question your daughter. Once I have it, I can keep you from your work while I question her and take my sweet time about it." She finished with a sharp nod of her head.

"All right," he said, "but we want to be present."

"Of course." Barnwell glanced at Cathy Thorson, who continued to fold one hand over the other as though washing them. The detective cocked her head toward the woman as her husband left the room, but she averted her eyes.

Thorson returned with his daughter, glaring at Barnwell as he led her into the room that served both as a living and dining area. He tried to direct the girl toward the end of the dinner table and to place himself alongside her, but Barnwell intervened. "Sit by me, Cindy," she said. "How old are you?"

"I've just turned seven," she answered, casting a sidelong glance at her father. Was she seeking his permission to speak? Barnwell didn't like the vibe she was getting.

"You're our hero," she said with what she hoped was a reassuring smile. "If it weren't for you, it might have been some time before we discovered the man lying there."

"It was a man?" the youngster said, her eyes widening.

"Yes, but that's all we know right now. We'll have to find his family and learn what we can about him. That's my job." At last, Cindy returned Lydia's grin. "Tell me how you found him."

Cindy shifted in her chair, twisted a stray lock of hair, and turned toward her parents for reassurance. "It wasn't me who found him. It was Rudy."

"That's her dog," Thorson said.

"He was tugging at his leash so hard, I lost control. He tore off and splashed into the stream."

"A thousand times I've told you to stay in the complex," her mother said, turning toward her husband. "I was washing sheets. I can't watch her every minute."

"No harm done," Barnwell told her. "As I said, it's fortunate she found him." She turned back to the girl. "Now, Cindy, your dog went down the embankment, and you followed?"

"I couldn't leave him there," she said, as though answering an allegation.

"Of course not," Barnwell said. She was about to add that, had she let the dog go, he might have disturbed the body, but thought better of it. "So you followed him and … what then?"

"Rudy was digging at something. I tried pulling him back, but he wouldn't stop. So then I saw it."

"Saw what?" Barnwell asked. "Tell me exactly what you found."

"A foot," the girl exclaimed as she recalled her discovery. "I didn't know what it was at first. Just a round greenish thing. It was only when I looked closer that I saw the ankle."

"Did Rudy uncover it?" Cindy squirmed and again turned toward her father. "I'm hoping you did," Barnwell said.

"Yeah, that's what happened. I spotted this round thing underneath a pile of wood. Rudy kept digging at it, so I scraped some leaves away. Then I made out an ankle."

"And what did you do then?" Barnwell asked.

"I ran home. I grabbed Rudy by the collar and made it up to the road and ran to get mom."

"Good for you," Barnwell said. Turning to Cathy, she said, "And what did you do?"

"I didn't believe her at first, but she insisted, so I walked down the road. We left Rudy home."

Barnwell nodded. "Good thinking."

"I made Cindy stay on the bank while I climbed beneath the bridge." She glanced at her husband and turned back. "I'm afraid I scraped some more leaves away, just to be sure."

"Of course," Barnwell said. "You didn't want to waste our time sending out a false alarm."

"That's what I thought." A look of relief passed over her face. "But once I was sure, I called 911 from my cell phone. Then we waited for the police."

"And you didn't see or touch anything else?" she asked. The woman shook her head. "Did you notice any cars passing as you looked? Anyone stop or display unusual interest?"

"I didn't notice," she said. "I was so busy. Cindy, did you see anyone?"

"No, ma'am," the girl said. *Ma'am*, Barnwell thought. *A well-disciplined child.*

The detective closed her notebook. "You're a brave little girl, respectful and bright. You did well."

The girl beamed, turning to her father as though seeking his approval. Barnwell thanked them and rose to leave. She looked around, seeking an excuse to separate Cathy Thorson from her husband. "Walk me out, please," she said.

"I'll do it," her husband said.

"I want her to show me where in this building we can

see the bridge."

"You can't," he said.

Barnwell took on a firmer tone. "You should return to work. I'm sure they need you. Thanks again for your help."

Thorson shrugged with obvious reluctance, but allowed the two women to pass through the front door. Barnwell walked her to the end of the hall, but all the entrances were closed, and there was nothing to see but the exit sign. Barnwell reached in her pocket, pulled out a business card, and scrawled her personal number on the back. "Keep this somewhere safe. If you think of anything else, or you need help," she said, emphasizing the last three words, "call. Any time, day or night. Just call."

Cathy Thorson nodded and shoved the card into the pocket of her slacks.

Barnwell returned to the site with her jaw locked in a grimace. Reviewing the exchanged glances between the couple and Thorson's resistance to questioning their daughter, she suspected he was domineering, even abusive. Would Cathy be brave enough to reach out to her if the need arose? Lydia hoped so. She'd encountered too many women trapped in unhealthy relationships, particularly those who lacked independent incomes, which appeared to be the case here. The husband worked, the woman stayed home to care for their child. She wondered if Cathy had her own means of transportation and made a mental note to find out.

At the moment, Barnwell had no time to devote to the issue. Mullins stood alongside the metal guardrail, peering at the scene below. "Anything?" she asked.

"There was no answer at the house on the left, but I awoke the man in the one to the right. He wasn't happy."

"And?" she said, uninterested in whether she was brightening the day of a potential witness.

"He claims he hasn't noticed anything, but he works nights, so if your mystery man down there went into the ditch after dark, he wouldn't have been around."

"He lives alone?" she asked. Mullins's blank look showed he'd neglected to ask.

Shaking her head in disgust, she stepped away, standing to one side as the evidence team placed the corpse in a body bag. Brandy Timmons approached, her white protective gear caked in mud. "Let me slip these off, and we'll talk."

Barnwell followed the investigator to the van and held her arm as she removed the booties, then stepped out of the snowman's suit. Only when she'd finished and knotted her dark brown hair at the back of her head did she speak. "He appears to have been a young man, late twenties or early thirties We'll be able to narrow that down after the autopsy. There are no identifying marks or tattoos. Nor is there any sign of trauma in the usual sense. No bullet or knife wounds. No bruises about the face or body."

"But?" Barnwell said, having caught the woman's qualified response.

"Two things," she said. "First, he didn't fall into this ditch. He was deposited here."

"How can you tell?" Barnwell said, fixing her blue eyes on the woman. Her pulse quickened. This was no drunk falling into a stream and drowning. Something more was involved.

"Scratches along his back and buttocks are consistent with his having been dragged. In addition, I found plant debris in his rectum that appears to be identical to that found on the slope. I'll test to be sure, but I think the person who left him here had him wrapped in a blanket or tarp. He either fell out or the individual pulled him out for the last few yards to hide his body."

She paused as she rubbed her hands together to warm them up and watched the evidence team slip and slide as they maneuvered a stretcher up the embankment. "Whoever did so covered the corpse with pieces of broken fence. The big snowfall we got in early February covered the body, and when the hard freeze came a few days later, it turned to ice."

"So he's been here since at least February 7th," Barnwell said. She could pinpoint the date because she'd had to dig her car out after the storm.

"And not much before that. I hope we can fix the date fairly closely."

Barnwell was always impressed by what the forensics team could learn from a corpse. They were a group of trained scientists who saw their work as a calling. They investigated every death involving trauma in the county. The Division of Forensic Laboratories tested latent prints, trace evidence, drugs, toxicology, and DNA. They even did environmental testing, analyzing food and air samples not only for the county, but for the state of Delaware. Examiners like Brandy Timmons trained for years before being allowed to touch evidence.

"You said there were two things," Barnwell said.

"You're going to love this. Take a look."

She led the detective to the evidence van, where the forensics team was lifting the gurney containing the body bag into the rear. "Hold on a minute," she told them. She donned another pair of white gloves from her pocket, unzipped the bag, and revealed the victim's ankles. "See those marks?"

Barnwell bent over to study them. "Bruises," she said. "Black and blue." She straightened up and looked at the examiner. "What am I seeing?"

Timmons continued unzipping the bag, revealing a hand encased in plastic. "I've bagged both wrists. I'll explain why in a moment. But notice how the hair has been stripped from his wrist?" She inclined her head to look up. "This man's arms and legs had been bound with tape of some sort."

Barnwell suppressed an urge to smile. The department had sent her out on a routine matter, something of little consequence. A man who'd stumbled into the ditch in the darkness while under the influence of drugs or alcohol. Nothing with which veteran detectives need concern themselves. Let the new gal handle it. But this was something more. "What's your guess? Was he kidnapped and murdered?"

"Or died from natural causes after a night of rough sex," Timmons said.

"S&M?" Barnwell said. "I can't imagine tying both his arms and legs."

"I can," Timmons said. "In this job, we see it all. The coroner's team may be able to tell after the postmortem. There's one more thing, however."

Timmons stood up, stripped off the gloves, and wiped her forehead with her hands. "I said ice covered the body, but beneath that layer, a trickle of water continued to flow in the stream. Because he was lying face down all those weeks, the skin on his face has fallen away. The same thing happened to his hands, which is why I've bagged them. I hope we'll be able to take his fingerprints, but...." She curled the edge of her mouth and shrugged, conveying her uncertainty.

"Thanks," Barnwell said. "I know you'll do your best."

How had the man died? Barnwell wondered as the van pulled away. Why were his wrists and ankles bound? Who had dragged his body down the bank and into the stream? Why this place, in full view of residences on both sides of North Fork Road and only a quarter mile from a police station?

And more to the point, who was he?

CHAPTER TWO

BARNWELL DROVE the quarter mile to North Fayette Township Park, which housed a baseball and softball field, community center, volunteer fire department, and the combination township office and police station. Chief Martin Lawson assigned Officer Foster to her. Barnwell called for two county officers to join Mullins. The chief helped establish a makeshift incident room at the community center, a stunning glass and brick building with a cantilevered roof whose glass window afforded a sweeping view of the North Branch Valley.

She assigned Office Foster to the townhomes, and the other three to each of the buildings above the Old Mill Bridge. "Knock on the door of every unit," she told the officers. "Ask if anyone saw activity around the bridge during a night in early February. Record every detail, no matter how small: how many were involved, what sort of vehicle they drove, the date, as close as they can recall it, and anything else that might help us."

Mullins piped up. "Wouldn't we be better off identifying the body first? Then we'd know where to look."

She stared at him for a second, trying to think of a snappy comeback, then realized to do so was to engage him in a decision that was hers to make. "We'll do it my way, officer. Thank you." Nadine Foster suppressed a smile as Barnwell put Mullins, who'd been testing her, in his place. "That's it, then," she said. "If you find a witness, radio me, and I'll join you."

When they'd gone, she expelled her breath as though she'd been holding it. There was a name for what troubled her: impostor syndrome. Deep down, she recognized her fear of being exposed as a fraud had no basis. Lydia had traveled a long road to reach this point, graduating cum laude as she earned a pre-law degree from Duquesne University and passing the Municipal Police Officers' Basic Training Program with honors. She'd then waited months until she found a position as a patrol officer with the Boyleston police force.

She'd endured over a year working under Chief Jason Russell until he was arrested for stealing from the department. Once Karol Novak replaced him, Barnwell prospered. She studied and passed the detective's exam. Chief Novak gave her what amounted to a battlefield promotion after she helped unravel a twenty-year-old murder case in which the wrong man had been convicted and sentenced. Her work on two subsequent cases brought her to the attention of county detectives Glen Carpenter and Lyle Jeffrey.

Now here she was, three months into a dream job as detective for the second largest county in Pennsylvania. Yet the men with whom she served—and most were men— doubted her abilities. She had received nothing more than chickenshit assignments since joining the force.

She'd begun doubting herself. Gone was the support of Chief Novak, who had redirected her with a gentle hand when she made a misstep, never criticizing her. At Boyleston Borough, she'd been part of a team. At ACPD, she was all alone in the ring, with spotlights trained on her and everyone in the crowded arena waiting to see if she'd fall on her face.

Lydia Barnwell would not let that happen, nor would she allow anyone to see her sweat.

SHARON EASTERLING KNEW BETTER than to speed on North Branch, not with the police station a hundred yards from the road. She'd been stopped before and let off with a warning. One day, she'd get a ticket. For the past six weeks, however, she'd flown northeast along the two-lane stretch as she headed to work, her eyes focused on the road ahead, not daring to look to her left.

When she passed Donaldson Road, saw the sign warning her of single lane traffic ahead, and encountered the long line of vehicles awaiting their turn, a knot formed in her stomach. Was the hold-up due to construction or something else? If the latter, she knew what that something was.

She drummed her fingers on the steering wheel, eager to pass through and leave this place behind her. She turned on the radio, punched buttons, listening for soft rock. Something by The Eagles, maybe, or Fleetwood Mac. Finding nothing to suit her, she turned it off again.

Sharon was nearing fifty, but until recently hadn't looked it. Her dishwater blond hair was dark at the roots, and dark circles arced beneath her eyes. Her heart-shaped face was puffy. The lines around her mouth drooped, and her eyes sported the tracks of crow's feet. As she idled, she pulled down the visor and painted her mouth with lipstick. She smeared it past the upper border, let out a loud curse, and began wiping it away when the driver of a pickup behind her leaned on his horn.

"All right, damn it," she said, dropping the lipstick to the floor and tapping the accelerator a bit too hard. She caught up with the SUV ahead of her and inched forward as the northbound traffic crawled past the orange cones single file.

As they neared Old Mill Road, she turned toward the left, saw the activity at the bridge, and emitted an involuntary sob. Returning her attention to the road, she hit the brake, avoiding the bumper of the hatchback by inches. She rested her forehead on the wheel and shivered. The driver of the pickup blared at her again. To spite him, she remained motionless, but as his trumpeting grew more insistent, she saw a uniformed officer staring at her.

In her panic, she hit the accelerator again. The officer studied her vehicle as she cleared the intersection and inched past the long lane of traffic waiting its turn to head southwest. Once she'd cleared the line, she pulled to the side of the road and let the pickup pass. The driver gave one last blast and enveloped her in a cloud of black smoke.

BARNWELL HAD little to do while the teams went door-to-door in the apartments and townhomes on Old Mill. She spent a half hour listening to the channels on her police radio and running over the questions she'd asked herself earlier in the morning. Chief among them, who was the dead man and why had someone picked this spot to dump his body? She found the latter question perplexing. This was a rural area of Allegheny County. There were dozens, perhaps more than a hundred places to conceal a corpse. Choosing this spot along a busy road, in full view of residences and within shouting distance of the police station, made little sense.

Minutes before noon, Officer Foster's voice crackled over the radio. "I've found something. You'd better hear this for yourself." She gave the unit number, and Barnwell was on her way. Five minutes later, she pulled up in front of the townhouse and climbed the stairway alongside the garage. The North Fayette officer opened the front door before she knocked.

"This is Horace Tillman," she said. Barnwell nodded toward the man and passed her ID under his face. He appeared to be in his late sixties, just under six feet, and slender. He had a ruddy complexion, a thin mouth, and was nearly bald, a ring of gray hair around his ears and neck with an oasis of white strands that stood erect on his crown. Barnwell couldn't help staring at the thicket of hair, expecting it to topple over at any moment.

"Tell the detective what you saw," Foster said.

"Not much," he said. "I was looking out at the snow to see if it was getting as heavy as they'd predicted. They're usually wrong, you know? This car crosses the bridge, parks alongside the road there, and two or three people get out. What made me notice was they killed their headlights when they turned off North Fork. It struck me as odd, you know?"

"What kind of car was it?" Barnwell asked.

The man scratched the back of his neck, then pulled the stranded tuft of hair erect. *Is he trying to make it grow?* she wondered. "I dunno," he said. "I didn't see it too well."

"Sedan, hatchback, SUV?" she prompted.

"Not an SUV, but like that, I think. Smaller than full-size, you know?"

"Make? Model?" she asked. "Color?"

"I didn't notice. It was too dark."

This was getting nowhere. "You said there were two or three occupants. Can you describe them? Male or female?" He shook his head. "Did they take anything from the car?"

"They opened the trunk and hauled something out, but I didn't see what. I lost interest. Whatever they were doing, they weren't trying to break in to one of these places, so I just went back to the game."

"What game?" she said. "Do you recall who was playing?"

He looked confused. "No. It was just a college basketball game. I watch whatever's on. Does it matter?"

"I'm trying to fix the date," she said. "It could be significant."

"I already told you that," he said. She said nothing, but raised her eyebrows to pose the question. "The night of the storm. Back in ..."

"February 6th," she said. "It began snowing about nine that night and continued until noon the next day."

"There you go," he said.

Barnwell spoke into her radio. "All units. Check with the management of the apartment buildings. See if they have surveillance cameras and, if so, whether they've preserved videos from the night of February 6th."

She asked a few more questions, but Tillman had nothing more to share. It was as he had said. He'd looked out the window to check how hard snow fell, seen a car pull up, noticing it only because the driver had killed the headlights before parking, decided it had nothing to do with him, and gone back to watching TV. But she couldn't resist asking one more question: "Did you think to report this to the police?"

"Why?" he said. "Whatever they were doing was none of my business, you know?"

She wished she'd had a buck for every time she'd heard that. Trying to get surveillance tape was a fool's errand. Six weeks had passed, and most servers recycled the videos after two weeks, a few after four.

But at least she now knew when the body had been dragged down the bank and concealed beneath the bridge. It wasn't much, but it was something.

***

SHARON WAS LATE FOR WORK. Again. She apologized to her supervisor, telling her she'd been caught in traffic, which was true. "I'm sorry," the woman said, "but this makes the third time in the past few weeks. We're not over-staffed here. We each have a role to play, and ...."

The woman droned on for two minutes, during which Sharon could have been working at checkout, arranging larger items in the basket and bottom of each cart to speed the scanning process.

"I'm sorry," she repeated, choking back tears. "It won't happen again."

"No, it won't," the boss lady said. "This is your last warning. Do you understand?"

Sharon nodded, saying not a word, but the supervisor wasn't satisfied. "Do you understand?" she repeated.

"Yes, ma'am."

"Then get to work."

She took her place behind the cashier and began organizing each customer's items, giving each a warm greeting and smile as she'd been taught, even though she longed to cry out, "What are you doing here? Why do you need all this crap? Go home!"

At two, she took her mandatory fifteen-minute break, but instead of grabbing a slice of pizza as she usually did, she huddled in a corner at the rear of the break room, tapped a contact on her phone, and cupped her hands over the mouthpiece. When the party answered, she spoke just above a whisper. "They've found him."

The woman at the other end didn't ask to whom she referred. She knew the answer. "I'm surprised it's taken this long."

"What are we going to do?" Sharon asked, shaking so hard she had to lean against the wall for support.

"What do you think?" the woman answered. "We're doing nothing. They found him. It was bound to happen. They'll spend days trying to identify him. Once they do, they'll not find a thing to trace him back to us."

"But Moira—" Sharon said.

"Don't worry about her. She can take care of herself. They may question her, but they can't pin anything on her besides the one lesson. Trust me, she won't involve us. The cops will be at a dead end."

Sharon began to speak, but choked. "You need to get hold of yourself," the woman said. "We've been through all this. We only tried to scare him. The bastard had that coming and more. He died, and we did nothing to cause it. Case closed."

"They'll find the house," Sharon said.

"They'll find nothing." The woman's harsh voice softened. "You need to calm down. All we did was leave his body for someone else to find. Nothing more. We've taken every precaution. Once they learn he died of natural causes, they'll figure he croaked in someone's bed, someone who couldn't afford to be connected to him. They'll search for her—or him. The guy always gave off a funny vibe."

She seemed to consider that while Sharon held her breath. "Because he wasn't murdered or anything, they'll lose interest. Trust me."

Sharon squeezed out an okay, but didn't convince herself.

"The only person who can make this into a bigger deal is you."

"My break is over," Sharon said. "I have to clock in."

"You do that," the woman said, adding in a soothing voice, "Just ... relax."

AT MID-AFTERNOON, Lydia returned to ACPD Headquarters in Greentree. She refilled her water bottle from the purifier tap, sat at her desk with her ankles crossed, and logged on to the National Criminal Information Center, which maintains a list of all missing persons reported by any law enforcement organization in the country.

She found no reports of a tall white male missing in Allegheny County. Because North Fayette borders Beaver County, she widened her search and again came up empty. She found three reports of men matching the description elsewhere in Western Pennsylvania, one in West Virginia, and two more in northeastern Ohio, but all had been found.

This was not unusual. Most missing persons turn up within days. Many run off on their own to avoid unpleasant family circumstances, shack up with a lover, or go off on a bender. A few disappear for good. Family members may tell police their loved one would never do so, but after countless hours of police work, they are often proved wrong.

Teenagers often run away to escape an unstable home. They soon discover life on the road is worse. Young women find themselves exploited, often trafficked by someone they've met online. Young men may turn to robbery or worse, ending up in jail or turning to gang life. Many of these young people succumb to drug use, sickness, or malnutrition. Too many become murder victims.

The worst cases are missing children. Youngsters are abducted by a family member, a father who's been denied parental rights or a grandparent intervening when they decide their own children are incapable of caring for them. All too often, however, sexual perverts take children off the street, sometimes in broad daylight.

Nothing galvanizes not just law enforcement, but entire communities than the threat to a child. Lydia knew this firsthand. Two years before, she'd worked the case of Rose Fallon, whose mother reported her missing from a thrift shop in Boyleston. She had injected herself into the search for Rosie over the objections of the ACPD detective in charge, Lyle Jeffrey. She'd cracked the case, which had not had a happy ending.

She and Chief Novak had allowed Jeffrey to claim credit for that one, and he had not forgotten When Barnwell solved the case of a murdered real estate agent a year later, he'd helped bring her onto the county force.

Now, she was working her first real case here, but the NCIC provided no help. After an hour of searching, she found no report of a missing person matching the sketchy description Brandy Timmons had provided.

She closed the screen, took a swig out of her water bottle, and reached for her notebook. She let her mind wander for a few moments and began writing, posing the same set of questions that had bothered her earlier in the day. Her thoughts returned to Cathy Thorson. The young woman had seemed distressed that her daughter had wandered off the apartment's property and ventured down Old Mill Road. "A thousand times I've said to stay in the complex," she'd said. In explaining why she didn't want Cindy's name reported by the media, she added, "These are dangerous times."

At first blush, this seemed nothing more than standard parental caution, but as Lydia recalled the look on her face as she'd spoken, she saw something deeper at work. The reason, she figured, was her husband. Ben Thorson had both Cathy and her daughter under his thumb. Lydia had felt it throughout the conversation.

She opened the NCIC database again and searched for any record of his arrest or conviction. Again, the computer remained mute. Still, there was something there. She was sure of it.

Lydia recalled Thorson's odd reaction when she'd asked where he worked. Was it her imagination, or had he cast a glance at his wife before answering?

Besides investigating crimes of violence in smaller municipalities across the county, ACPD is the law enforcement agency for all county property, including Pittsburgh International Airport. Barnwell looked up the ACPD roster and called District 1 Inspector Mort Whelan. After identifying herself, she said, "I need a favor."

———

Assistant medical examiner Tyrell Brown reached Lydia by phone late in the afternoon, telling her he'd completed the autopsy. "Some aspects of this death remain a mystery, but let me tell you what we know."

He filled in details of the dead man's description. "He was 5-11 in height, weighed 165 pounds, and was in his late twenties or early thirties.. He was slender and in good health, appears to have worked out regularly. His last meal was a peanut butter sandwich, which he'd ingested about two hours before his death. There was no trace of alcohol in his system, but as for drugs, that will take some time."

He paused and drew in his breath. "His vital organs were in excellent shape. His lungs were clear, and he didn't smoke. There's no sign of coronary artery disease or a previous myocardial infarction. This makes the cause of death quite interesting."

"Heart attack?" Barnwell asked.

"How did you figure that out?"

"From the way you built up the story."

"That's why you're the detective," the pathologist said with a chuckle. "Although his arteries had no accumulation of plaque and he showed no evidence of an MI in the past, his heart stopped beating."

"Caused by...?"

"That we don't know. We have to remember those bound wrists and ankles. Perhaps it resulted from a sex act gone wrong. He may have died of fright; it's been known to happen. He may have received an electrical jolt of some sort, though there's no evidence of that. Or he may have been poisoned."

Brown paused, as though expecting Barnwell to interrupt. When she did not, he said, "We'll run toxicology tests, but that can take weeks." Barnwell knew that, despite how they were portrayed on television, there is no single toxicology examination, but a series of tests, as scientists in the lab chase down one possibility after another.

"Now comes the bad part, what we don't know. We couldn't get his fingerprints due to skin slippage." Brown launched into a lengthy explanation of differences between the two layers of skin, dermis and epidermis. "When a body's been in the water for that long, enzymes separate these layers, causing a loosening and sloughing of the epidermis. That's what happened here. His outer skin fell off. I have no way of reconstructing it."

The investigator on the scene, Brandy Timmons, had warned her of this possibility. Barnwell kicked the edge of her desk in frustration.

"We have plenty of DNA samples, though, and if his are on file anywhere, we'll identify him. That also takes time, and we use it as a last resort. So we'll first try to identify him through dental records."

Lydia respected these scientists enough not to tell them how to do their business.

"One more thing about this skin slippage issue," the examiner continued.

Barnwell waited, becoming accustomed to Brown's dramatic reveals. "It also affected most of his facial features, but the structure was intact. Your subject was one good-looking dude. Quite handsome."

"That's something," Barnwell said, forming a mental picture of an attractive man about her own age who took care of his body. She would check with local health clubs and gyms, though dozens dotted the county.

"Do what you can," she said. "Meanwhile, I'll work my end." She thanked him and hung up, knowing that too much time had already passed, and each passing day made it more difficult to determine who had held this man, who had left his body to rot, and why.

---

Moira Buller wiped her face on a towel as she escorted her client past rows of exercise machines. Sweating people gasped and grunted as they worked on biceps, triceps, quadriceps, and other body parts. Moira kept her expression neutral as she threaded her way across the studio floor. The manager of the fitness facility had scolded her for rolling her eyes and sneering at some of the more hopeless of the club's denizens. "At least they're trying," she'd said, "and they pay us well."

Moira had been unaware her face conveyed the contempt she felt for some of these people. Like Ralph and Walter, who showed up every morning, donned swimsuits, and sat at the edge of the pool trading high school stories as the older women worked out in water aerobics. Glory Days, as The Boss had sung. Who did they think they were fooling? Merely checking in at the gym did nothing for you.

"Same time next week?" she asked as they reached the front desk. The woman agreed, and the attendant booked the next appointment. Moira thanked her and checked her schedule. Nothing for another hour.

She scanned the bodies laboring away across the facility. Older women crowded the pool. Old geezers vied with young moms for space on the machines, some coming only to gawk at the young bodies and remember the good old days. At 4:30, working people would arrive, and the pace of activity would accelerate. Moira had one more client this morning, then would return home until late afternoon.

She entered the small changing rooms reserved for

female employees, opened her locker. and stripped off her tank top. Reaching for her phone, she saw she'd had two calls from the same number. Moira looked around. She wasn't supposed to use her phone here, but she was alone at the moment and didn't want anyone overhearing this conversation. She punched the screen, and her call was answered almost immediately. "What's up?"

"Hold on a minute," Annette Henley said. Moira could hear her fumbling in the background, and knew she was leaving her desk and looking for a quiet place to speak. It took half a minute before the woman, now out of breath, said, "It's Sharon. The bitch is coming unglued."

"She called me twice yesterday," Moira replied. "I was on the floor, so couldn't take her calls. What's she saying?"

"She's panicking, convinced they're going to trace the body back to her. I told her there's no way, but she keeps going back to the same thing. I told her to put a sock in it, but that didn't work. Then I tried sweet-talking her."

That must have been something, Moira thought. Annette was the project manager for a construction company. She worked around men all day, was as rough hewn as any of them, and had a mouth to match. Moira didn't know her well—hadn't met either of them until two months before—but had seen her volcanic temper spew lava and language.

"She's searching the internet, looking into kidnapping charges," Annette continued. "Can they tell when some-one's looking for that sort of thing?"

Moira didn't have to ask who "they" were. "I don't think so," she said, though she wasn't sure. "I hope she's not poking around on that neighborhood site. We'd agreed to get out of it."

"I didn't think to ask her, but it wouldn't surprise me. She won't accept that we did nothing to him."

"We did, though," Moira said.

"But we didn't kill him. We put the fear of God into him, but we weren't anywhere near him when he—" Annette broke off without finishing the thought. "She could bring us down."

"I know," she said. Another trainer entered the room. Moira cupped her hand around the phone and said in a low voice, "What do you want me to do?"

"Talk to her. Reassure her. Get her under control."

"Hi, Nancy," she said to her colleague, who glared at her. "I'm just finishing." In a brighter tone, she said, "Of course. I'm sure I can help. Let me get my schedule, and I'll call to set up a time."

"What the fuck are you talking about?" Annette demanded.

"Because I'm in the locker room now. I'll call you back as soon as I get dressed."

"Oh, I get it. Someone's there."

"That's right," Moira answered.

"Good, because if you can't shut her up, I will."

Moira shuddered and glanced at the fellow trainer who was stripping to enter the shower. "I don't recommend that," she said. "You could hurt yourself. Let's work on it the next time you're here."

"You heard me," the voice came back over the phone. "Either you fix her, or I will."

With that, she disconnected, leaving Moira breathing in quick gasps as though she'd been working out.

AFTER LYDIA TOOK Howie for his late afternoon constitutional, she began preparing chili, browning ground beef while she sautéed onion, garlic, and green pepper in a large pot. Her kitchen window looked out on the back yard, a small stretch of lawn interrupted by a neglected garden. In the spring, she'd plant green beans and tomatoes, lay out pots of basil, parsley, and rosemary, even though a neighbor had warned her she'd be feeding the deer that roamed unmolested through the community.

The days were getting longer, but no brighter. She sighed as she looked out at the overcast sky. She'd been raised on military bases in sunnier climes—Italy, Japan, and many years at what was now Joint Base San Antonio. Pittsburgh, the story went, had only sixty days of sunshine a year. This was overstating the case somewhat, but this winter had been dreary. She longed to feel the sun on her face, sit on her deck in a pair of shorts, her long legs splayed in front of her as she drank the one beer she allowed herself, watching the sun set. Anything but this slow fade from gray to black.

Lydia opened two cans of kidney beans and tomatoes and emptied them into the pot, added a bottle of pimientos, and stirred in a tablespoon of mild chili powder. She added a teaspoon of hot chili power, dipped the teaspoon into the bubbling mixture, and tasted it.

It was spicy enough for her, but she knew her guest. She'd lived in the house less than two months, and while Calvin Mayfield, along with two other Boyleston officers, had helped her move in, this was the first time she'd cooked dinner for him. Perhaps she'd invite him to stay. If so, it would be only their third night together, the first having followed the death of David Kimrey by only days. While she and David hadn't been together for many months, she'd viewed that night with Calvin as a betrayal.

They'd been nervous around each other for weeks, pretending to other members of the Boyleston Police Department their relationship remained strictly professional. This had fooled no one, particularly not Detective Mark Ewer, who had blasted it all over headquarters. Lydia's decision to pursue the ACPD job had been motivated, in part, by her need to separate her business and personal lives. Her one-night stand with the man who would have become her boss hadn't caused her to flee, but it made her decision easier.

And where was the man? She replaced the lid, turned the heat to low, and wandered into the front room. She was assaulted by flashing red, white, and blue lights that painted the room in Fourth of July colors. But this was no holiday. Without donning a jacket, she opened the door and almost tripped down the stairs to the squad cars parked at angles on her street. Neighbors stood on their porches, gawking at the display. "What's going on?" she said.

"We had a report of a suspicious man in the neighborhood," an officer said.

She looked at the figure bent over the hood of a police vehicle with his hands behind him. "What's he done?" she demanded, not bothering to mask the shrill edge to her voice.

"That's what we're trying to determine," the officer said. "We got a call about a prowler."

"That prowler, as you put it, is my friend. His name is Calvin Mayfield, and he's chief of police of Boyleston Borough."

The officer stared at her for a moment, then looked back

at the man bent over the hood. "Do you have some identification?" he asked in a muted voice.

"Do I need it?" she demanded. "I live here. I own this house."

"Just show him your badge," Mayfield shouted.

She glared at the officer, turned on her heel, and returned seconds later, flashing her ID. "I want your name and badge number," she said.

"Leave him alone," Mayfield said. "Don't make things worse."

As the officer removed the plastic cuffs from Mayfield's wrists, Lydia turned and glared at the onlookers. "I'd like to know what racist pig called this in." No one answered, a few looking nervously at those standing on adjoining porches, the rest retreating to the comfort and anonymity of their homes. "Well?" she said.

The officers apologized to Mayfield, who waved them away. "You're doing your jobs," he said. "I get it."

"I do not," Lydia shouted.

"C'mon," he said, cupping her elbow with his hand and guiding her to the door. "It's not their fault."

Lydia was still shaking when they entered the house. "You fixed this up nice," he said, looking around the front room.

"How can you be so calm?"

Mayfield looked down at her, taking a deep breath as his presence filled the room. He spread his arms out in a gesture of helplessness. "Because I'm used to it," he said. "I'd told them who I was, and they were listening. Another fifteen seconds, and they would have let me reach for my ID. Then this firebrand came roaring out of her house..."

He tried to grin, but she wasn't mollified.

"Lydia," he said, taking her hands in his. "This goes on

all the time. I don't want you to think it doesn't anger me, but it doesn't help. I've learned that. They got a call and had to respond. You and I would have done the same thing. Given another minute, they would have recognized they'd been set up."

Lydia shook her head, wiping tears away on her sleeve. "I hate this," she said.

"Welcome to my world."

"How do you stand it?"

"I have no other choice," he said. "I go about my business and live my life. I hang out with decent people and ignore the rest. Except for lawbreakers. Those I can't ignore."

Lydia shook her head and threw up her arms in frustration.

"If you have some better idea, I'm open to it," Mayfield said. "Meanwhile, something smells pretty damn good."

CHAPTER THREE

MORNING CAME TOO SOON, but when Lydia rolled over and looked out her bedroom window, she decided not to complain. The sky was azure, and even with her windows closed, she heard birds chirping. Her prayers had been answered, and not just by the change in weather.

Calvin had left around midnight, and while one part of her wished he'd spent the night, she made no objection. Lydia valued her independence and wasn't ready for the compromises a long-term relationship demanded. For the moment, she was content to have him come and go.

Her outlook should have reflected the change in the weather, but Lydia couldn't shake her resentment over last night's incident. Who had called the cops on a well-dressed Black man emerging from a late-model Toyota? Calvin had blown it off, saying someone was just being careful, but she was less forgiving. A "neighbor," if the term applied here, had harassed her guest and made her private life a community event. *Welcome to the neighborhood, Lydia.*

Was this what still rankled her, she wondered as she filled her Moka with ground coffee, or was it the racism itself? Put another way, was her concern more for Calvin or herself? She told herself it was the former, but wondered whom she was kidding.

The coffee maker stopped bubbling. Lydia removed it from the heat, heated milk in her frother, and poured herself a latte. She filled Howie's bowl with dog food and her own with cereal. After they finished, she left her cup and bowl in the sink, donned a pair of jeans and a wool shirt, and hooked the dog's leash onto his harness. His tail drummed a beat as she stepped off the front porch. At the edge of the sidewalk, stalks of crocus reached for the sunlight. A robin pecked at the ground, an early bird getting a worm. "It's a myth," she told the bird. "There are plenty of worms around. You don't have to be up early to find them." Howie looked up at her, but had no comment.

The turn in the weather was a harbinger, she told herself. She wouldn't allow one nosy neighbor to ruin a day filled with promise. She had a new job and, finally, a case worth her talents. This was a new beginning.

THIRTY MINUTES LATER, a summons turned the blooms to straw. "Inspector Morris wants to see you," the department's assistant said. As Barnwell continued toward her desk, she said, "I'd go up there now."

Andrew Morris commanded the department's investigative division. Eighty detectives and their support personnel reported to him probing homicides, narcotics distribution, human trafficking, missing persons, robbery, arson, burglary, child abuse, sex assaults, and white-collar crimes. What could he want with her?

Lydia bounded up the flight through the stairwell,

carrying her water bottle with her, and entered Morris's office. She'd met him once, the day she was hired. Apart from seeing him stroll through the detective division, she'd not spoken to him since. He was a burly man, not fat, but husky, with a square jaw and a full head of prematurely gray hair he kept trimmed to within a half-inch of his scalp.

Morris's assistant told her to go on in. She found him sitting behind his desk with Detective Lyle Jeffrey occupying one of the three chairs arrayed in an arc before it. Lydia smiled, then scowled, sensing that this was no ordinary get-acquainted meeting. She took the offered seat and clasped the water bottle between her thighs with both hands.

"You pulled three county officers and one from North Fayette into an investigation of a missing man yesterday," Morris said.

Barnwell nodded her head, her tight curls bouncing. "I did, sir."

"Why?"

She drew back, surprised at the question. "I'm trying to determine who he is and why he died."

"The report lists his death as a heart attack," the inspector said.

"Yes, sir, but he was a young man, in perfect health, with no sign of heart trouble. We need to know what caused the attack and why his body was left by the side of a road."

"Detective, two teenagers were shot dead in Braddock this weekend. A man's body was found in an abandoned building in McKeesport. We've had a slew of drug arrests, the robbery of a filling station in Homestead, and a rape in Munhall. Add that to dozens of similar incidents over the past month and you understand why I'm concerned. You commandeered all these resources without seeking prior authorization."

He turned from her to Jeffrey, as though seeking confirmation.

"I understand, sir," Barnwell said, "but it's not just that the man is unidentified and his corpse was found in a culvert. Someone dumped it there. A witness saw two or more people park along the bank on the night of February 6th and pull something from the trunk. The man was naked; he had no identifying marks; and his ankles and wrists had been bound."

Looking toward Jeffrey for support, she said, "It's a suspicious death, and too much time has elapsed already."

"You may be right," Morris said, "but his death may have resulted from natural causes. A sexcapade gone wrong, and his partner—or partners—panicked." Lydia wondered how long he'd been storing that word away, looking for the opportunity to unleash it. "Five officers, including yourself, spent half the day questioning nearby residents. It's a question of proportional response."

She leaned forward to explain this was how they'd located a witness to the night the body had been left. Jeffrey warned her away with an almost imperceptible shake of his head. "Yes, sir," she said. She uncapped her water bottle and took a long drink to conceal her anger.

"Now what's this about an inquiry to Inspector Whelan?" Morris asked.

Lydia lowered her water bottle and capped it. "I asked him to question the TSA about one of their employees."

"Why? How does this relate to the unidentified body?"

Barnwell took a deep breath and raised her eyes to the ceiling as though seeking divine intervention. "The father of the youngster who found the body gave me a rough time about interviewing her and was reluctant to tell me where he works. I saw signs he's abusive, so I checked him out."

"Abusive? Has his wife issued a complaint?"

"No, sir," she said, "but she was intimidated by him. She kept apologizing for letting her daughter wander off the apartment grounds."

Morris shrugged, as though any woman might have done the same. "But he has no connection to this body?"

"None that we know of."

Morris leaned back in his chair and gave her what passed as a smile. "You're new here. We normally give a new detective some time to get acclimated before handing them a case on their own."

"Sir, Detective Barnwell served two years with the Boyleston force," Jeffrey said. "She helped solve two homicides." While Lydia appreciated the intervention, saying she'd "helped" on these cases understated her role.

"I've read her file," Morris said dismissively. "But we have our own procedures here. In a small organization like Boyleston, you can act with relative independence. Perhaps you have to," he added, studying Lydia for her reaction.

"We have dozens of detectives, all working cases of varying importance. We can't have everyone vying for resources and getting in each other's way. Nothing would get done. You see?"

Lydia did not, but murmured, "Yes, sir."

"Good," he said, rising. "I'm sure you'll do well here, given a bit of guidance. You and Carpenter brought her in," he told Jeffrey. "Take her under your wing,"

"Will do," he said.

Lydia paused at the door, ignoring Jeffrey's gentle hand on her back. "May I ask one thing, sir? What did TSA tell District 1 about Ben Thorson?"

Morris scowled as though she hadn't heard a word he'd said, but shrugged. "Thorson? Yes. He's no longer employed there. Hasn't been for several weeks."

Lydia stiffened, every fiber absorbing this information and claiming vindication. "Did they say why, sir? Did he resign? Was he fired?"

Morris batted an imaginary fly with his hand. "No. They didn't tell us, and I wouldn't have expected them to."

SHARON GNAWED her knuckles as she watched a TV reporter standing beside the culvert on Old Mill, reading notes on her smartphone. "Allegheny County Police have not yet identified the victim," she said, "but it's believed the man died during the snowstorm on February 6th."

The video switched to images taken the day before of crime scene investigators working below the bridge. "Police found no identification on the body, which was unclothed." As the report showed scenes of officers going door-to-door through the apartment buildings, she said, "Officers from the county and North Fayette spent the morning questioning nearby residents, but without success. Anyone with information is asked to call ACPD headquarters."

Sharon raised a mug of lukewarm coffee to her lips, but her hands shook, sloshing the liquid down the front of her sweater. She appeared not to notice, put the cup down, and reached for her phone. She tapped one of her contacts and stood at her kitchen counter as the number rang and went to voice mail. She hung up and dialed again, her eyes darting about the room as she waited for the party to answer. When it went to voice mail again, she squeaked out a quick message. "Call me. We need to talk."

Running her hand across her mouth, she paced back and forth between her kitchen and living room. She glanced at her phone again and stabbed at another contact. The number rang once, twice, a third time before Annette Henley, not concealing her weary tone, answered. "Hello, Sharon. What is it?"

"We have to talk. They're going to door-to-door at the apartments."

She was met with an exasperated sigh. "Of course they are. And what have they found? Nothing. You need to take a chill pill."

"Maybe they're just saying that. Suppose someone saw us?"

"If they had, they'd be at your door, wouldn't they? You need to get hold of yourself. The only person who's going to give us away is you. Go about your business like nothing's happened, and you'll be fine. We all will be."

Sharon whimpered, her breath coming in quick gasps. "I rang Moira, but she didn't answer."

"Don't call her," the woman said, her voice raised as she articulated each word. "The less we speak to each other, the better. Get back to the way things were before we met. Go to work. Come home. Make dinner. Sleep. Get up the next morning like nothing's happened, because nothing did. We did nothing to him. Got it?"

"We kidnapped him," Shirley said. "That's a federal offense. I looked it up."

"You what?" The voice was shrill now.

"I Googled it."

"Get off the internet. Stop obsessing over this. First, we did not kidnap him. He came voluntarily. Second, the Feds don't get involved unless you take a person across a state line. We did nothing to this man," she said, then added, "At least not compared to what he did to us."

"I don't know," Sharon said.

"I do. You're making trouble for yourself and for both of us. Calm down. Take some time off. Go on vacation."

Sharon snorted. "Using what for money? I can barely afford groceries." She was met by silence. "Are you there?" she said.

"Of course I am," Annette said in a softer tone. "Look, they don't even have a name for this guy. When they do, how could they connect him to us? They'll be looking for a man named Brad, but we knew no one by that name. Mike, Carl, and Jerry. That's who we dealt with. So even when they identify him, they'll be at a dead end."

Sharon considered that for a moment. "Perhaps you're right."

"I am right. So go about your life. Don't go poking around the internet. And don't call Moira." She paused a moment. "You're scared, but you don't need to be. Got it?"

"Yeah," she said after a moment. "Thanks."

BARNWELL SLAMMED her water bottle on the desk and collapsed into her chair. "You were a lot of help."

Lyle Jeffrey let the slightest of smiles escape his lips. "I seem to recall attesting to your experience."

"He said I wasn't fit to sleep with the hogs," she fired back. "But you stuck up for me. You said I was."

"Feel better now?"

"Not at all. Are you going to give me some guidance now? Take me under your wing?"

He ignored her barb. "Morgan is under a lot of budget

pressure. How much, I don't know. He doesn't share the details, thank the Lord. But he's been encouraging us to close cases more quickly and preaching about needless expenses, so you know it's coming from somewhere."

Barnwell sat with her arms folded, staring at him. "He doesn't know you yet, so when he sees you calling in patrol officers and requesting help from another division, he doesn't know whether you need all you're asking or are just cutting corners. Give it time, and he'll come around."

Lydia took a swallow from her water bottle while she considered the response. She was not without self-awareness. If anything, she spent too much time questioning her competence and her reaction to perceived slights. After David Kimrey's death, she'd agonized over whether she was responsible for his death. On the evening before he'd lost his life responding to a domestic disturbance, he'd attempted to reconcile with her. Lydia rebuffed him, and when he'd asked for a hug "for old times' sake," she'd refused. Had he died trying to prove himself?

And now this. Had she overreacted to the discovery of the body? Called in too many horses? Carpenter had sent her on what he thought was a routine case. When she'd discovered there was more to the man's death than what first appeared, should she have alerted him? Had her satisfaction at finding herself in charge of a homicide investigation clouded her judgment?

Hell, no, she told herself. "Meanwhile, what am I supposed to do?" she now asked Jeffrey. Reviewing the facts in the case, she said, "I have an unidentified corpse whose body was left to rot by person or persons unknown. Evidence suggests he'd held against his will. Beyond that, I have nothing. *Nada. Niente.* How am I supposed to solve this?"

Jeffrey questioned her about the steps she'd taken to identify the man. She described her search of the NCIC, local reports of missing persons, and requests to the public for information. He wrinkled his brow and studied the surface of his desk. "If you have any better ideas, I'm listening," she said.

"I don't know what more you can do until you get a positive ID."

"And that could be days, even weeks," she said.

"Hopefully sooner," the detective sergeant said.

Barnwell closed her eyes, letting her anger ebb. "Let's think about what we know," she said. "Someone drove to the intersection of Old Mill and North Branch Road on the 6th of February, pulled a body from the trunk of a car, and dragged it down to the stream bed, hiding it under some rubble. Why would anyone do that?"

"Because they didn't want to be connected to the man's death." Jeffrey said. "Let's assume his heart attack was caused by—what did Morgan call it?"

"A sexcapade," she said, smirking as she did so.

"Right. So maybe he was having it on with a married woman. If her husband found out, there'd be hell to pay. So she had to get rid of the body and had to do so quickly. She got a friend to help her, put the body in the car, and drove to the first place she could find."

"Whoever it was must have panicked," Barnwell said. "If you want to conceal a body, there are better places along the road than near a police station and beneath dozens of apartments."

"I've only been in that area a few times," he said, "but I seem to recall the North Branch lies behind trees most of the way."

Lydia nodded. "So maybe they didn't have the time or manpower to find a better—" She stopped, lost in thought.

"What?" he said.

"It was the night of the snowstorm," she said. "They may have set out to find a place to dump the body when it started dumping snow. Driving was treacherous that night. They didn't just panic. They found themselves with no other choice. If they'd slid off the road, the police might have had to rescue them. They couldn't risk their finding a body in the trunk."

"Worse yet," Jeffrey said, "they might have had to abandon the car, and a tow truck would have impounded it."

"Exactly," she said. "Whoever left that body lives somewhere near the bridge, a mile or two at most."

"How do you figure?"

"They had to get back to wherever they came from. I'll check with North Fayette to see if there were any calls for help or abandoned cars that night, but if not, they didn't live far."

"Okay." Jeffrey said as she made a note to herself.

Barnwell leaned back in the chair and painted the air with her pen. "And what about Ben Thorson? He claims he's a supervisor at TSA when he's not."

"Are you changing the subject now?"

"Am I? I don't know. There may be no connection, but it's curious, isn't it? A child finds a dead body, and when we try to question her, her father puts up a fight and tells us a lie. I'd like to know why."

"You should ask him. If you want company, I'll come along."

She clamped her mouth shut, her face a mask of determination. "I probably will," she said, "but first, I want to know why he's no longer with TSA. If he spins another yarn, I want to call him on it."

"I can't help you there," he said, "and I wouldn't go calling District 1."

She snorted. "I've learned that lesson, but there has to be a way. I intend to find it."

---

"Would your chief allow you to take on an assignment for me?" Lydia said into her cell phone.

"I don't see why not," Nadine Foster answered. "What does it entail?"

Lydia stood outside ACPD headquarters on Parkway, basking in the warmth of the unexpected sunshine. "It involves asking a few questions without raising suspicions."

"Undercover work?" the North Fayette officer said.

"Something like that. It deals with the father of the youngster who discovered the body. He's telling me a tall tail, and if I pursue it, I'm crossing a bureaucratic line."

"Sounds fun," she said. "Let me ask the chief and call you back."

Lydia disconnected and went for a brisk walk around the parking lot. She would have given anything to hear birds reveling in the spring day, but their sounds were drowned out by the traffic on Parkway West.

What she was asking was risky. If someone found Foster was poking around where she, Barnwell, had been told not to look, Inspector Morris would be pissed. So would Jeffrey. She might be suspended, could lose her job. But Barnwell had to know why Ben Thorson had left his job before she confronted him with his lie.

She was about to reenter the building when her phone

rang. "I didn't tell Chief Lawson the whole story," Nadine said. "I just said you needed help questioning witnesses."

Lydia smiled. She'd found a fellow devious spirit.

"But he's okay with it," she said. "So, what do you need?"

Lydia turned and walked away from the building, keeping her back to the windows as though someone watching might overhear. She explained what she wanted.

"That's no problem," Foster said.

* * *

Lydia returned home at 5:30. Howie jumped up on the leg of her slacks and whined. "You need to go out?" she said. "It's early. Okay."

She leaned down to tie the leash to his harness, but the Westie continued to whimper.

"What is it, boy?" she said. She hadn't had the dog that long, but was already attuned to his moods. Something was bothering him, and it wasn't just a full bladder.

She dropped the leash and wandered through the living room. What was causing him such an upset? She made a circuit of the dining room and kitchen, finding nothing amiss.

Howie stood at the base of the stairs, trailing his leash. He looked up, sounding like a squeaking door. She followed his gaze and, in the thin light seeping through the window on the landing, saw a shadow reflected against a wall. Something hanging, swaying, out of place. She took one step. Then another. The object came into view.

Lydia leaned against the railing as she peered upward. She couldn't believe what she was seeing. Her chest tightened. Her breath caught in her throat.

A long rope was tied to the upstairs banister, at the end of which was a hangman's noose.

---

THE SAME CARNEGIE police officers who'd accosted Mayfield the night before arrived within minutes of her call. Lydia was still shaking, although whether in fear or anger, she couldn't have said. She led them into the house and pointed up the stairs. "There," she said. "I found this when I walked through the door."

"And it wasn't there when you left the house?"

Lydia gave the officer a contemptuous stare but didn't answer. "I guess not," he said.

He and his partner took photos of the noose, then called for an evidence team from the county, since Carnegie didn't have one of its own. They checked the doors and windows while Lydia waited, her arms crossed, a glum look on her face.

It took fifteen minutes for the evidence team to arrive. They questioned her about what she'd touched when she came home. Lydia told them she'd spent the weekend giving the house a deep cleaning, but couldn't recall whether she'd wiped down the railing and banister. They began dusting for prints.

She left them to their work, taking Howie out for his evening walk. As she turned from Boquet onto Trimble Street, she cast a suspicious eye at each residence. Someone had broken into her home, how she didn't know. Whoever it was had left a message. She was not welcome here. Not as long as a Black man visited her.

She turned up Cherry Way behind St. John Lutheran Church and continued around the block. Howie stopping at every bush, hydrant, and signpost to investigate who had preceded him, then lifting his leg to announce his presence. The sun was setting as she rounded the block. A woman stood on her front porch, peering down the street at the police cars blocking the street. "What's going on?" she said. "Is someone hurt, do you know?"

She identified herself as Anna Molnar. She was in her early forties, with long, black hair that flared in the breeze. "Someone broke into my house," Lydia said.

"Oh, no," Anna said. "Did they take anything? We've had some car break-ins, but this is the first I've heard of a house being robbed."

"I don't think so," Lydia replied. "Instead of taking something, they left something."

The woman screwed up her face. "Like what?"

"A message. My friend and fellow police officer is Black. Someone left a hate message."

"No," the woman said. "Who would have done such a thing? We're not like that."

"Someone is."

A boy who looked to be about ten years old burst through the front door, sucking a lollipop. "Tommy, someone's broken into this lady's house. Who would have done a thing like that?"

The boy shook his head. "No one from around here," he said.

Lydia wasn't having it. "Someone called the police when my friend showed up last night. They tried to have him arrested."

"That's disgusting," the woman said. "We're neighbors here. We look after each other. Live and let live, that's our motto."

Howie chose the moment to empty his bowels. Lydia

took a green plastic bag from her jacket, inverted it on her hand, and bagged the mess. "I'm sorry," she said.

"No need," the woman replied. "We have a dog, too. They have to go somewhere." She asked where Lydia was from, and she explained she'd moved two months ago from an apartment in Boyleston.

"My first house," she said. "My dad was an Army colonel. We lived all over the world, but never had a place of our own. I was looking forward to this, but someone doesn't want me here."

"I can't think of who would do such a thing, but I'll ask around. If I find out who did this..."

She left the thought unfinished. Lydia thanked her and turned to leave. "What kind of dog is that?" the young man asked.

She smiled, reached down, and stroked his fur. "He's a West Highland Terrier. They call him a Westie. He belonged to a friend of mine, a fellow officer who was killed last year."

"Over in Boyleston?" the boy said.

"Yes, that's the one."

"I hear he was a good guy."

"That he was," she said. "Thank you."

She returned to her house, smiling despite her anger at what had been done to her home.

The Carnegie officer met her as she entered the front door. "We know how he got in," he said. He led her down to the basement and pointed to a half window at the top of the concrete, above the washing machine. "The lock was rusted," he said. "Whoever got in didn't have to break the glass. He just pushed on the frame until the latch gave way and clambered down over your washer."

"Did they find prints?" she asked.

"Yeah, the county's wrapping up. They got plenty. If this person's on file, we'll find him. Meanwhile," he said, "you'll want to secure that window and check the latches on the others."

Lydia thanked him and led the patrolman upstairs. The two officers from the county's evidence team were just packing up, and she thanked them as well. "We'll have a report on your desk in the morning," one said.

Both teams prepared to leave the house when another squad car pulled in behind them. Calvin Mayfield emerged, leaving the motor running and his door open. He bounded up the stairs toward them. "What's going on?" he said. "You hurt?"

"I'm all right," she said. "It happened while I was at work."

She wanted to find her own way to tell him what had occurred, but the Carnegie patrol officer saved her the trouble. "Someone broke in and hung a noose from the second floor."

Mayfield's mouth dropped open. He looked from the officer to her and back again.

Lydia wasn't imaging it. Calvin's deep black face turned gray.

CHAPTER FOUR

NADINE FOSTER'S uniform allowed her to talk her way through airport security. She rode the shuttle train from the main terminal to the gates and parked herself in the food court. Passengers queued in front of counters selling burgers, pizza, chicken sandwiches, Asian food, doughnuts, and pretzels, none of which appealed to her. They cast anxious glances at their watches, struggled with wheeled luggage, and tried to calm unruly children. Or did not, in one case, allowing the brat to scream and race between tables unattended.

Nadine ordered a latte, took a table, and waited. She watched as the occasional TSA agent or pair of agents came, ordered food, and either sat and ate or departed, bags in hand. None were what she was looking for.

Twenty minutes after she'd landed, a trio of Black agents ordered burgers, sprawled at a table meant for four, and began wolfing down their meals.

Nadine sidled over to them. "Mind if I join you?"

One of the two men looked up and smiled, happy to have an attractive sister slide in next to him. Nadine introduced herself to the trio, and they did the same. Her admirer identified himself as Joe. She made small talk for a few minutes, asking how busy they were on this March morning and listening as they described how, just minutes before, another rattlebrain had tried to go through security with a loaded handgun. They'd summoned airport police, who, having determined he had a concealed carry permit, seized the weapon and sent him on his way.

"What brings you here?" Joe asked.

"Trying to gather some information," she said.

Her questioner drew back. "What sort?"

"This is strictly unofficial," she said. He threw a suspicious glance at his companions, who returned them. "We've tried to go through channels, but you know how it is." She rolled her eyes heavenwards, at whatever brass hat had blocked a perfectly reasonable request. "It's about one of your supervisors. Former supervisor," she corrected herself.

The three stared at the table without commenting. The lone woman wrapped the paper that had contained her sandwich together and stuffed it in the bag.

"I'm not trying to get him in trouble. I just need to know why he left," Nadine said.

Joe raised his eyebrows in inquiry.

"Benjamin Thorson," she said.

"He's left?" Joe said. "I thought they just suspended him while they investigate. Have they fired him?"

"Not that I'd heard," the female member of the trio said. "They asked me a bunch of questions last week: what I'd seen, what others have told me. I didn't think they were through yet."

"What are they after?" Nadine asked.

Joe leaned back, folding his papers as the woman had done. "What's he done?"

"Nothing that I know of." She searched for the right explanation and decided the truth might suffice. "We came across him during a missing person investigation. We have no reason to believe he has anything to do with it. But when we asked him where he worked, he said he was a TSA supervisor and had left work to talk to us. That wasn't true, and we'd like to know why he'd tell us a story."

The three looked at each other. The woman shook her head.

Nadine looked directly at her. "If you ask someone what's in their handbag, and they tell you nothing when you know damn well there's something, you clear it up so they can be on their way and you can go on with your job. It's the same here."

Joe relented. "It's not about him," he said. "It's his brother."

---

SHARON EASTERLING FINISHED RETURNING the couple's purchases from the belt back to their carts. She began lining up those in the next basket when she felt a tug at her sleeve. Turning, she found Moira Buller staring at her, her mouth locked in a grimace. "Take a break," she said in a harsh whisper. "We need to talk."

"I'm not due for another half-hour," Sharon said.

"Take it now," Moira ordered.

The cashier turned on the two of them. "You need something?" she asked Moira.

"I need to talk to my sister here. It's a family matter."

"Okay," she said. She called a supervisor, who made double-time to the register. "Sharon here needs a break. Something going on in her family."

The supervisor glowered at Sharon. "Five minutes," she said. She motioned for another worker to take her place as Moira led Sharon toward the break room.

"Not here," Sharon said. "You're not allowed in." She led the woman out the exit, and they stood together as shoppers left with loaded baskets and new arrivals pulled carts from the lines.

"You can't just come in here like this," Sharon said. "I'm in enough trouble already."

Moira pointed a finger at her chest, forcing Sharon to take a step back. "You," she said, spitting the word at her, "need to stop whining. No more calling Annette. You're making trouble for yourself and the two of us."

"I'm worried that—"

"We had a plan," Moira hissed, pushing Sharon back along the line of carts. "It's worked out better than we hoped. It took them six weeks to find him. We thought we'd be lucky if we got just one. You know what they say? The longer it takes police to solve a crime, the less likely they are to solve it? We've put a month and a half distance behind us. Now you're screwing it up."

Sharon shook her head, fighting back tears. "I only — It was my house. The two of you—."

"We're in this together," Moira said. "If they identify one of us, the others will follow. That TV show, The Weakest Link?" She shoved her index finger against Sharon's breastbone again. "That's you. Stop panicking and stick to the plan. Or else."

Sharon's eyes were like saucers. "Or else what?"

"Problem here?" a voice asked. They turned to see one of the male workers trying to slide a long row of carts into the space where they stood.

"None at all," Moira said. "Problem solved. Right?"

Sharon nodded and turned toward the entrance, wobbling on trembling legs.

---

My place or yours? This was the question Officer Foster posed to Lydia in the early afternoon. Barnwell, certain Inspector Morris wouldn't appreciate her continuing to poke around at the airport, didn't hesitate. She logged out and headed west on I-376, driving the thirteen miles to the North Fayette police station.

Nadine poured herself a cup of coffee, while Lydia refilled her water bottle and sat across from her in the spartan interview room. "I found three TSA officers willing to talk," she said. "They were suspicious at first, but they're brothers and sisters, so they came around."

Lydia had seen it before. Black witnesses would share information with Black cops that no white officer could shake loose. It was a bond forged through blood and bloodshed.

"Two months ago, the airport's federal security director notified your folks about a rash of thefts at a security checkpoint. When ACPD reviewed the security footages, they spotted three TSA agents working together whenever thefts took place. In one sequence, an agent opened the zipper of a small bag, extracted a wallet, and stayed with the bin as it moved down the conveyor belt. He pushed it through the scanner, pulled it out at the other end, replaced the wallet, then thrust his hand into his pocket."

"Oh, yeah," Lydia said, recalling the arrests District 1 had made shortly after she joined the force.

"In another," Nadine said, "two agents appeared to be talking as one pointed to a bag inside a bin. The other opened it as it emerged from the scanner and pocketed something. He looked up at his partner, nodded, and smiled."

"So Ben Thorson was one of the three?" Lydia asked.

"No. You'll see how he figures into this in a minute. On January 18th, they arrest these three. They appear before a magistrate for the preliminary arraignment the following day. Two weeks later, a pair of them show up for the formal arraignment, but one, Brad Walker, doesn't. He disappears. Every law enforcement agency in the county is on the alert, but we haven't found him."

Barnwell remembered the case. The three had been taken into custody days after she joined the ACPD, but since Division 1 was handling it, she'd paid little attention.

"And here's where it gets interesting," the officer said.

Lydia leaned her chin on her fist as Nadine smiled, enjoying the drama. "This Walker character turns out to be the half brother of ..." The patrol officer held out her arms, inviting a response.

"Ben Thorson," Lydia said, "their supervisor."

"You got it. That's all my agents could tell me, although once they opened up, they had no end of speculation. They think Walker was the ringleader of the group, but they're divided on what role Thorson played. One thinks he was aware of what was going on and let it happen, another thinks his brother duped him. Thorson's suspended pending the outcome of an investigation. One of the three was re-interviewed a few days ago, so it's still underway."

Barnwell took two long swallows from her water bottle, closed her eyes, and leaned her head back. What did Thorson know about the scheme? Where was his brother now? Was Thorson hiding him?

Was this why he'd lied about still working at TSA? No,

that didn't follow. The District 1 officers had already made the connection. So had the district attorney. Thorson had no reason to claim he was still working there when authorities knew he was not. "Something's missing," she said, "and not just the brother."

Nadine muttered in agreement, but didn't derail her train of thought.

What, if anything, did this have to do with the unidentified body Ben's daughter had found beneath the bridge? When she'd tried to interview the girl, his behavior had set her on edge, leading her to look into his background. Now that she knew his story, what did she have?

"I hope I'm not being pulled in the wrong direction," she said aloud, "but I'm going to confront him with the fact he misled me and see what he has to say."

Besides, she thought, what more can I do while the forensic labs complete their tests and give me some answers?

"Can I come along?" Nadine said.

"Sure," she said with a smile. "You've earned this." She needed a witness to this discussion, and using the North Fayette officer might keep this excursion off the books.

Sitting at Nadine's desk, Barnwell logged on to the ACPD intranet and boned up on the airport investigation. Brad Walker's partners were in talks with the district attorney, both claiming Walker had organized the operation. One said they took turns serving as lookouts along the line and seizing money and IDs from bags. They pooled everything they took and divided it evenly, but Walker, he claimed, had kept driver's licenses and credit cards. Neither could tie Ben Thorson to the scheme, although one said Walker claimed they had "protection." When asked what that meant, Walker had refused to say.

"That must be why they're still investigating after all these weeks," Lydia said. "They suspect Thorson served as their lookout, but they can't prove it. They'd love to interrogate Walker, but he's on the lam."

Armed with their new information, Barnwell drove the quarter mile to Old Mill Road. Foster rang the doorbell, and a woman's voice called, "Just a minute."

It was a bit more than that before Cathy answered the door. The smell of cleaning products—Pine-Sol, Lydia figured—assaulted them. Her hair was a tangle, and she wore a faded sweatshirt and sweatpants. "Sorry it took me a bit," she said. "I'm cleaning."

"Is your husband home?" Lydia asked.

Cathy stood half behind the door, gripping it as though barring their entrance. "No," she said. "He's at work."

"No, he's not," Officer Foster said.

Lydia saw a flicker of concern pass over the woman's face. Alarm? Uncertainty? She placed a hand on Foster's arm, not about to reveal to Cathy what they'd learned. "We checked before we came," she lied. "He's not there right now."

Cathy brushed her hair back with her wrist. "Then I don't know where he is," she said. "I'm sorry."

"Can you reach him by phone?" Lydia said. "We need to speak to him."

"I suppose so. Hold on a sec."

She began closing the door, but Lydia said, "Do you mind if we come in?" and advanced on her before she could refuse. As the woman backed away, the two officers stepped around a two-sided pail on the floor, half of it filled with what looked like a cleaning solution, the other side containing a few cups of dirty water.

"Where's your daughter?" Barnwell asked as Cathy reached for her phone.

"In her room," she said. "Studying."

Lydia nodded and glanced about the living room, noting again how austere it seemed. It was as though the couple had just moved in and had yet to unpack. Cathy retreated into the galley kitchen, turned her back, and held the phone to her face. She cupped her hand over her mouth, but Lydia heard her say, "That police officer's back. She wants to talk to you."

She listened for a moment and said, "I don't know. She didn't say."

Another pause and she handed the phone to Lydia without another word. "Mr. Thorson, I'm here with an officer from the North Fayette Police Department. We need to ask you a few questions. Can you come home?"

She heard an intake of breath. "Can we handle this over the phone?" he asked. Before she could respond, he said, "No. Let's meet somewhere. How about ..." Another pause. "There's a Panera Bread at Settlers Ridge. Can you be there in fifteen minutes?"

"We're on our way," she said.

As she returned the phone, Cathy turned her back and reached for something beneath the sweatshirt at her waist. *Is he tracking her?* she wondered.

As though reading her thoughts, the woman looked up, her face contorted in anxiety. "You have him wrong," she said. "He's a wonderful husband and father and a good provider. We're a happy family."

Lydia betrayed no emotion. "I'm glad to hear it," she

said. She wanted to continue the conversation in Ben's absence, but there was no time.

---

IT USUALLY TAKES twelve minutes to drive from Old Mill Road to Settlers Ridge Shopping Center, but when the pair reached the interstate, they found themselves in rush hour traffic. It took sixteen minutes to reach the restaurant, but they made it before Thorson.

Nadine ordered coffee, while Lydia settled for apple juice. She had long since rejected the police officers' habit of all-day caffeinating, confining herself to a single shot from her Moka coffee maker in the morning.

Ten minutes passed. Fifteen.

"Maybe he got caught up in the traffic," Nadine said.

Lydia considered the thought, then recalled the urgency with which he'd insisted they arrive in fifteen minutes. "He wanted us out of their apartment," she said. She kicked herself for allowing Thorson to dictate the terms of the interview. "I should have insisted he come to your station."

At that moment, Thorson ambled in, dressed in the same work pants he'd worn two days before, only now, in deference to the warmer weather, he wore a black t-shirt picturing Johnny Cash with an upraised middle finger. As he slid into the vacant chair Barnwell had placed between them, Barnwell was again struck by his soft features. With a wig, padded behind, and falsies, he could have starred in a drag show.

"What's this about?" he demanded. It was the first question he should have asked when she'd spoken to him over the phone, strengthening her suspicion that his fifteen-minute deadline was a ruse to get them away from his wife.

"When I spoke to you Saturday morning, you told me you work at TSA," she said. "That's not true."

He gave the slightest of shrugs. "I'm sure you've done your homework. I've been laid off."

"Suspended," she corrected. "They think you helped your brother run that theft ring."

"Well, I didn't." He barked out the response, causing an older couple at a nearby table to look up. "I've told you people, I had nothing to do with it. My only sin was helping that shithead get hired. He's been nothing but trouble his whole life, and now he's brought me the same."

"What's the relationship between you two? You're half brothers...?"

"Different fathers," he said. "My dad ran away when I was three. Mom married a man she'd met at work." He rose and approached the counter, returning with a plastic glass filled with water. "Hayden Walker was another user. She had terrible taste in men. I don't know why she married him. Needed the financial support, I guess. Maybe she was trying to look after me. Whatever her reason, it didn't work out."

He toyed with the glass, and Lydia sensed there was more to the family story. But that wasn't why she'd brought him here. "Why did you lie to me?" she asked.

Again, the slight shrug, accompanied by a snort. "Isn't it obvious?" he said.

"I think I know, but you tell me."

His glare was filled with contempt. "I didn't want her to know, of course. She still doesn't."

"You've been out of work for weeks, and you—"

"I'm not out of work. I found a job at a shipping warehouse just off the airport property. We send stuff out on cargo planes and receive boxes and crates bound for local companies. It doesn't pay as much as the TSA, but it covers the bills. Carnegie Distribution Center," he added. "You can check it out. I'm sure you will."

"Why wouldn't you tell Cathy what's happened? Don't you share this kind of news with one another?"

Thorson again fixed her with a look conveying disdain, but didn't speak for several seconds. Barnwell wondered if he was concocting another story. "I work outside the home. She works in it. She doesn't check with me about what she's making for dinner, and I don't share news about work, good or bad."

He seemed to consider the answer. "Truth is, I don't like to upset her. It's not that I've lied. She hasn't asked, so I haven't told her. Simple as that."

"You lied to a police officer. That's an offense."

"Okay," he said in a more conciliatory tone, "Cathy hates him. If she knew what he's done...." He swirled his glass as though it contained wine. "He's borrowed money from us. A bit here, a bit there. He never returns it. He always has something big coming up. Going to make a million. It never amounts to anything. She made me promise to steer clear of him."

His voice became softer as he looked past them, as though something of interest was happening in the parking lot. "So, yeah, I've kept this from her. Brad getting me suspended from my job? She'd be furious. As long as I bring home a paycheck, there's no reason to upset her."

"His picture was all over the local news the day he was arrested and again when he skipped bail."

"She doesn't watch the news," he said. "Nothing but stupid game shows."

Barnwell realized Thorson was steering the conversation off track, just like he had done to get them out of his apartment. "Where's Brad?" she said.

"I have no idea."

"C'mon. He didn't show up for his formal arraignment. We're unable to find him. He's hiding out somewhere. He's out of work, so someone's helping him."

"Not me," he said.

Lydia gave him a piercing look. She'd seen many witnesses crack under her blue-eyed gaze. Thorson seemed to wilt, dropping his smart-ass demeanor. He leaned toward them and lowered his voice, affecting an air of confidentiality. "As God is my witness, I don't know where he is. I had nothing to do with those thefts. If I could help you, I would. I hope you guys bring him in and make him tell the truth."

"He hasn't called you? Texted you?"

Thorson shook his head.

"Would he go home to—where are you from?"

"Outside of Louisville, but Mom's long gone. And his father? I've no clue what's become of him." He shrugged and looked off into the distance. "Brad wouldn't go there. The man is a brute."

"All right," she said. "But if I find you've lied to me again—about Brad, your job, or anything else you've told us —I'm bringing you in. Got it?"

Thorson nodded, his face glum. He remained in place as the two officers cleared the table and left.

---

After collecting her own vehicle, Lydia drove to ACPD headquarters, wrote a report, and signed out. Even with the return to daylight saving time a week before, darkness approached as she headed home. She considered stopping for something to eat, but her mind was too full of disconnected threads from the day's revelations to bother. She would forage in her refrigerator and, if that didn't work, call for a pizza.

She pulled to the curb before her house and took the four steps to her narrow porch, stumbling as her foot connected with an object. She opened the front door, turned on the porch light, and saw what looked like a large shopping bag. Howie pawed at it, ignoring he hadn't been outside for twelve hours.

Lydia placed the bag on the kitchen counter, attached Howie's leash, and took him for a walk, guided by the flashlight she kept on the shelf above the fireplace. "We've had quite a day," she told him as they made the rounds of the neighborhood. "Ben's been suspended from his job while his bosses look into whether he helped his brother steal from passengers. He lied to me to hide it from his wife. His brother's gone missing, and he claims he doesn't know where he is. Do you think he's telling the truth?"

Howie raised his leg for a time and looked up at her as he considered the question. They completed their tour of the block and returned to the house. Lydia lifted the Westie and snuggled with him for a moment, but he wriggled out of her grasp and bolted toward the kitchen. He stood at attention, his tail wagging, as she opened the bag.

A card lay on top. She opened it and read, "Welcome to the neighborhood. We are sorry someone harassed you. Good people live on this street."

She smiled to herself. All day, she feared she'd made a mistake buying in this community. Here was proof she'd made the right choice. She removed the rest of the contents: a box of cornbread muffins on top, two small containers beneath it containing mashed potatoes and green beans, and at the bottom, a whole chicken in a plastic container. Someone had gone to a lot of trouble to make amends.

Lydia looked at the note again. Though unsigned, it had to have come from Anna Molnar. "That was so sweet of her," she told Howie, who seemed to agree.

She had a rule: no people food. But it seemed selfish not to allow him to share in the bounty. She cut up a few slices of thigh meat, buried it in his bowl of dry food, and fixed a plate for herself as he devoured his dinner, almost in a single bite.

"Then there's the dead body," she said, continuing her conversation. "I wish I could get some answers from the medical examiner." She remained convinced the body had been dropped beneath the bridge in haste. The winter storm was moving in, forcing someone to act quickly. The culvert provided a convenient spot—near enough to the road to make the task easy, but concealed from public view for at least a day or two, time enough to cover one's tracks. Lydia was equally convinced whoever had done so lived nearby. They'd meant to take the body farther away, but as the blizzard moved in, they couldn't afford to get caught in the storm.

"Two mysteries, my friend," she said to Howie. She dropped her fork onto her plate with a clatter, sat with her folded hands nestled against her mouth, and thought. "I get it," she told the dog. "It fits. It makes perfect sense."

Lydia grabbed her purse and reached for her cell phone, looking for a number that had called hers two days before. "Hello, detective," Tyrell Brown said, alerted by caller ID. "You're working late."

"I'm sorry to disturb you," Lydia said.

The pathologist excused her. "I'm not doing anything

but watching a boring movie. I needed an excuse to turn it off."

"Have you identified the body?" she asked.

"No," he said. "No clothing and no distinguishing marks. No tattoos or piercings. He'd broken his right arm when he was younger, but so do lots of kids. He also had a couple of fillings in his late teens, but nothing major, so dental records got us nowhere."

"DNA?" she said.

"That's next. We test everything else before we take that step."

The county's DNA lab was certified by the FBI and therefore had access to their national database. Lydia knew that took time and resources.

"I may short-circuit the process," she said. "I think I've identified our victim, and if I'm right, I also have a suspect."

CHAPTER FIVE

LYDIA WAS certain the unidentified body was that of Ben Thorson's brother and resolved to probe Brad Walker's background while awaiting DNA confirmation. She was so eager to get underway, she dragged Howie from one intriguing redolence to another during their morning walk. As they rounded the last corner and walked down Boquet Street toward the house, Tommy Molnar popped out of his front door, slamming it behind him. He greeted her with a timid, "Hi."

"Shouldn't you be in school?" she said.

"Spring break," he explained. "A lot of kids have left town this week, but we're staying put."

Lydia had spent much of her childhood on military bases and couldn't recall anything special about the week around Easter. To make Tommy feel better about missing out on adventures his classmates were having, however, she said, "That's what we did." In truth, her father's assignments had allowed her to see much of the world from the time she was little. One of her earliest memories was growing up on a base in Okinawa. Despite little interaction with Japanese children, she'd picked up a bit of the language. Then had come Korea, Italy, and Spain, each exposing her to new cultures and languages. She'd become fluent in the last two and even learned a bit of Swedish during two weeks with a girlfriend during *midsommer*. Lydia doubted Tommy got much beyond the Monongahela River.

"Do you need help walking your dog?" he asked.

At first, she didn't get what he was asking. Howie was a small dog and didn't need two people tugging on his leash. Then she understood. "You'd like to take him out once in a while?"

"Yeah, when you're busy doing the cop thing," he said. She didn't have to think about the offer. "That would be great," she said. "How much would you charge?"

Tommy shrugged and looked confused. "I'm not asking for money. I can take him when I walk Ginger."

Lydia remembered his mother mentioning they too had a dog. "I understand, but if you're going to provide a service, you should be paid for it. That's how the world works."

They haggled a bit, with Lydia offering more than the boy wanted to take. They finally agreed on three dollars per walk. Lydia led him to her house, gave him a handful of green poop bags, and asked if he could begin this evening. "By the way," she said. "Did your mother leave those groceries last night?"

"Yeah, she wanted to repay you for all the trouble you had. The other night, you know?"

"Please thank her for me. It was incredibly thoughtful. I'll find a way to return the favor."

"She's at work right now," he said.

Lydia got the picture. Anne Molnar was a single mother who worked to care for her ten-year-old son. The boy was on his own after classes and during school vacations. She wondered how long this had been going on. Giving him the dog-walking job would teach him some responsibility and keep him out of trouble.

And it freed her to spend as much time as she needed on this case.

Brad Walker's apartment was on the second floor of a three-story building off Parkway West, a straight shot toward the airport. The apartment manager heaved a deep sigh when she identified herself, telegraphing his exasperation. "You folks have been through it already."

"They may not have been looking for the same thing I am," Lydia replied.

He led her upstairs and stepped aside, leaning against the beige colored hallway wall. She stepped onto faux wood flooring that led to a combined living and dining room. Both were covered in a beige carpet whose color mirrored that of the hallway. Lydia estimated the room at sixteen by twelve feet. She'd been through many such flats before and expected to find a coat closet inside the door, but there was only an entrance to the galley kitchen. Whoever had designed these units had cut corners, though she doubted they'd also trimmed the rent.

The room was in disarray. An aging sofa with what looked like a coffee stain sat against one wall, a pile of clothing at one end. An overstuffed chair faced the window whose half-closed white curtains opened onto a deck over-looking a swimming pool. In a corner alongside the window, a large screen TV teetered on a flimsy wooden stand. The walls were bare, no photographs or artwork. A printer rested on a small table, but she found no sign of a computer, the forensics team having removed it. A charging cable dangled on the counter looking into the kitchen, but she found no phone. While the county might have seized it, it was more likely Walker carried it with him when he disappeared. An aluminum and glass coffee table held an empty pizza box, two empty beer cans, and a coffee mug encrusted in brown gunk.

"Someone needs to clean this up," the manager said from the narrow hallway, "but your folks have told me to leave it alone. For when he comes back," he added.

Lydia grunted to show she'd heard. She doubted Brad Walker would ever return, but kept this to herself. She slipped on a pair of gloves and lifted the pile of clothing, looking for anything that might be concealed beneath it, but found nothing.

Dirty pans and dishes filled the sink. The walls of the microwave were splattered with a variety of foods and sauces, most of them the hue of tomato. She opened the basket of the coffeemaker, which was filled with used grounds covered in gray mold. Lydia wrinkled her nose at the fustiness enveloping the kitchen.

The manager stood in the great room with his arms folded, watching her every move. "What sort of person was he?" she asked.

"Was?" he said.

Lydia stopped herself from reacting. "He hasn't shown up for several weeks now," she said.

"Yeah. You folks let him get away."

"What was he like?" she repeated.

"I don't watch people's comings and goings," the manager said. "I don't have the time."

"He paid his rent on time?" she asked.

"I don't handle the money. It all goes through the company." He frowned and stared at the rug, which also sported a large stain near the TV. "They told me he was late a couple times, but he always caught up. He's behind now, of course. You'll have to ask the office for details."

The man had nothing else to offer. "You can go now," she said. "I'll let you know when I've finished."

"And then you can release it? The company wants me to clean it so we can rent it. He won't get his deposit back," he added, looking around at the damage.

"It's not up to me," Lydia said.

The man harrumphed, turned on his heel and left. Barnwell entered the bedroom. The bed was unmade, and a pile of clothing lay alongside the dresser. "It wouldn't kill you to open the drawer," she said to herself. She did so, pawing through underwear, socks, two bathing suits, and a drawer full of short-sleeve polo shirts.

Lydia opened the nightstand drawer and found a pair of wired earbuds, which she suspected no longer fit anything, bottles of aspirin and other nonprescription painkillers, and a keyring with no rings attached. "C'mon," she muttered. "Let's see some signs of life."

Beneath this detritus, she found a photo of who she took to be Walker, sitting alongside another man at an outdoor restaurant. There was a body of water behind them, but no trees or vegetation to suggest where it might have been taken. What struck her was Walker's resemblance to his brother. He was aggressively handsome, a cleft chin in a square face, wavy brown hair and light brown eyes. She assumed the half brothers had inherited their looks from their mother.

Lydia turned to the pile of dirty clothes and searched the pockets of his jeans and cotton slacks. She found wads of used tissue, receipts from restaurants and bars, a discount coupon for ice cream and mayonnaise, and a ticket stub from the theater across the interstate. She sighed in exasperation and was about to enclose the scraps of paper in an evidence bag when she spotted something written on the back of one of the bar tabs. Ten numbers separated by two hyphens. A phone number. She transferred the number to her phone and stuffed the receipt into the bag.

"You boys missed something," she said. "Always go through pockets." She left the apartment, satisfying herself that the lock behind her had engaged.

Brenda Lingenfelter entered the break room and poured herself a cup of coffee. It had been a busy afternoon with long lines at the checkout stands. People with carts full of food for the Easter holiday stood eight deep, having decided to check out all at once. Every crew member had been pressed into service. Just as suddenly as they'd swarmed the registers, the crowd disappeared. Some of the crew returned to their duties. Others took delayed breaks. Brenda and seven others continued to ring up the few stragglers who remained.

When it came time for her break, she slumped at one of the white tables, her eyes swimming with images of items she'd passed through the scanner. Ever since Thanksgiving, her dreams had been of endless lines of shoppers waiting to check out. Their numbers stretched halfway back through the store. She awakened with a start as a recurring nightmare unfolded: a large bulky item—it always changed—wouldn't scan, and she struggled to wrestle with it while the customer became impatient.

Burying her head in her hands, she said, "I am so damn tired." No one answered, since she was alone in the break room. She was fifty-eight, too young to retire, not that her savings would bring her enough to live on. She stared into a future of endless days working and sleepless nights.

She finished her coffee and went into the bathroom, pushing open the door of a stall and closing it behind her. Halfway through relieving herself, she heard someone sobbing in the next cubicle. At first, she ignored it, but as the sound continued, she thought, "I think I have problems."

Brenda pulled up her slacks and flushed the toilet, thinking the sound might make the woman's crying stop. It only intensified. She approached the stall, tapped on the metal door, and said, "Are you all right in there?" It was a ridiculous question, because the woman was clearly in distress, but Brenda didn't know what else to say.

Getting no answer, she rapped again. "Is there anything I can do to help?" The moaning only increased.

"Can I get someone for you?" she asked.

"They're going to kill me," a voice said.

"Who? Who's trying to hurt you?"

"They both are. But I didn't do it."

With that, the woman's weeping turned to wailing, and Brenda became alarmed. "Hold on," she said. "I'll find help."

But from whom? The woman was having an emotional breakdown. No one in the store was equipped to deal with something like that. She ran from the bathroom and found two other employees had taken over one of the white tables. "Get the shift supervisor," she said, her voice trembling. "Someone's having a problem."

The two men looked at her, but did nothing. "Get the supervisor," she shouted.

One of the two swung his legs over the table and rose to his feet, while the other peppered her with questions. Brenda returned to the bathroom where the woman's loud cries had subsided into weeping. Brenda heard her gasp for breath and tried talking to her in a soothing voice.

It took two minutes for the shift supervisor to enter the room. "What's going on?" she asked.

"Someone in the stall is having an attack," she said. "She was hysterical when I entered, but she seems to have calmed down a bit."

At that moment, they heard a crash inside the stall. The shift supervisor leaned down. "Call an ambulance," she said. "It's Sharon. She's passed out and fallen off the commode."

Brenda reached in her back pocket, pulled out her cell phone, and dialed 9-1-1. Five minutes passed, during which the supervisor climbed under the door and unlocked it from the inside. Ambulance attendants flooded the room. They examined the fallen figure and administered oxygen.

"What made her so upset?" the supervisor asked.

Brenda held the words in her mouth for a moment, then let them out in a rush. "She says someone's trying to kill her."

The supervisor shook her head and muttered, "This has gotten out of hand."

LYDIA SAT AT HER DESK, tapping her forehead with the eraser end of a pencil. She'd just ended a phone call with the assistant DA prosecuting the airport theft case. What she'd told her suggested a sequence of events, but some elements made little sense. She wished Chief Novak were sitting in the next office. Months before, she would have taken the problem to him. He would have listened, not making any suggestions, but posing questions that would force her to come up with answers. Novak was no longer here. He was now a civilian, and she had a new chain of command to follow. The problem was that, so far, none of the other detectives had taken her seriously. Just last week, she'd asked one a question about county procedure. He'd shrugged and walked away.

She'd have to chance it. She knocked at Jeffrey's door and found him bent over his computer. "I hate to interrupt."

He turned and looked up, tossing a pencil on his desk. "Come on in," he said. "I'm at a dead end on an armed robbery. I've spent a half hour sifting through arrest records in similar cases and can use a break."

Barnwell took a seat, laid her notebook on the edge of his desk, and smoothed her slacks with both hands. "I think I've identified that dead body."

"You think?" he asked. "Has the crime lab confirmed it?"

Once more, she felt her judgment was being challenged before she could complete the thought. "No. They're still checking DNA. I hope to hear something later today. It's..." She stopped herself on the cusp of spitting out the word intuition. "...old-fashioned detective work."

Jeffrey nodded, but didn't smile. "Tell me," he said.

"Ben Thorson, the father of the girl who found the body, lied by telling us he was a TSA supervisor. He even hid this from his family. We now know why."

"Who is 'we?'" he asked.

She was unprepared for the question. Would the conversation turn on how she'd done her job? She stammered for a moment, then said, "The North Fayette chief assigned one of his patrol officers to help me. She went to the airport and found a group of TSA employees willing to talk."

Jeffrey held up both hands as though in surrender. "And?" he said.

She recounted what Nadine Foster had uncovered. "The DA charged three TSA officers with first-degree misdemeanor theft," she said. "The morning after the arrest, they appeared before a magisterial district judge for preliminary arraignment. They must have had one hell of an attorney, because the magistrate released them on their own recognizance. The assistant DA pushed back. She was trying to combine these smaller thefts into one, so she could up the charge to Felony 3. The judge didn't budge, and the three walked."

Jeffrey sighed and nodded, as though this were an old story. "One of the men is named Bradley Walker. He's Ben Thorson's half brother." At this, Jeffrey dropped the pretense of quiet listening. He frowned and leaned toward her. "The TSA suspects Thorson was a silent member of the ring, but they can't prove it. They've suspended him while they investigate."

"And that's why he lied to you?"

"There's more," she said. "After the preliminary arraignment, Walker disappeared. We've searched for him for weeks, checking his apartment, friends, and neighbors, putting out an APB for his vehicle. We can't find him." She paused for a moment before delivering the punch line. "I believe he's the man we found in the culvert."

"And your evidence?"

She explained her thinking. "Right age and ethnicity, same body build, and the time he disappeared tallies was when our unidentified man died."

"Okay," Jeffrey said with a slight shrug, "but it could be a coincidence."

"Walker may be the only member of the gang who could tie Thorson into the operation," she replied.

"So you're suggesting Cain killed Abel?"

"It's possible. If Walker had talked, he might have implicated him. Thorson could have silenced him."

"Makes sense," Jeffrey said. "But you're way out on a limb here. We don't even know Walker was murdered. The ME says he died of a heart attack."

"They found no evidence of heart disease, however. They're running toxicology tests, but we know how long that can take."

Jeffrey nodded. It could take weeks to identify substances in a body. Technicians can sample blood and tissue, even bone and cartilage, subjecting them to a series of tests, each of which takes time, until they find something that doesn't belong.

Now that Lydia had him hooked, she revealed what still bothered her. "Someone restrained the victim for a period of time. If Thorson wanted to silence his brother, why would he do that? To get information from him? What sort? If he were in on the thefts, what more did he need to know?"

"If it comes to that, we'll ask him," Jeffrey said.

"And where did he hold him? Not in his apartment with his wife and daughter in the next room." She shook her head, her blond curls bobbing with the effort as she realized she was less sure of her case than she'd been fifteen minutes before. "Finally, why drop his corpse in a location so close to where he lived?"

"Your witness says he saw two or three people pull

something from the car," Jeffrey said. "Perhaps they were Walker's TSA partners."

"It might help if we could talk to them," she said. "If they know whether Thorson was part of the operation, it could give us a motive. And if they helped him move the body…"

"The last I heard, they've stopped talking," he said. "But I'll check."

Lydia grinned. This was the help she longed for and had missed since joining the force. "They had to hold him close by," she said, repeating her conviction the snowstorm had forced Walker's abductors to dump his body where they did. "This might be why his wife warned her daughter not to go near the bridge. Thorson may have given her firm instructions."

"If he's abusive, as you suspect," he said. "It fits."

"I've discovered one more thing, but I don't know if it's significant. I went through Walker's clothing and found this number." She opened her mobile and turned it in his direction. "When I was with the Boyleston force, we had no option but to call the number to see who answered, but since we have a digital investigation team …"

"I don't want to get ahead of ourselves," he cautioned. "It could be the number for a bar, a doctor's office, or something similarly innocuous. Let's confirm the ID first."

Lydia agreed. There was a danger in going in too many directions at once, particularly when all she had was conjecture.

"What else are you working on?" he asked.

"Detective Carpenter wants me to help interview a Hispanic suspect today. You know the drill. I sit there and listen, act like I don't understand the language, and if the individual gives himself away in Spanish…"

"All right. Do that today. Meanwhile, I'll ask the crime lab to speed things up. If we get a positive ID and determine the cause of death, we'll pull Thorson in."

———

SHARON SANK INTO HER CHAIR. Although she was the only person in the room apart from her supervisor and the store manager, she tried to appear inconspicuous. Her hip hurt, the result of an automobile accident two decades before that had taken her husband's life. After multiple surgeries, she still walked with a slight limp. Some days, she didn't notice the discomfort. Others, like today, it retaliated for what the drunk driver had done to her.

"You've been with us three years," the manager said. "For most of the time, your work has been exemplary."

She waited for the word she knew would follow. "But your performance has suffered in recent weeks."

"I know," she said, "and I can do better."

The manager continued as though she hadn't spoken. "You've been late four times, you're getting sloppy, and cashiers are forced to cover for you."

"Double checking your work," the supervisor said. "Finding items you've missed in the bottom of carts. Even some in the baskets themselves. When cashiers have to double check your work, it slows things down. Lines back up. Members become impatient."

"I know," she repeated, her voice sinking. She bent over the desk, folded her hands as though in prayer, and rested her forehead on them. In a strained voice, she said, "I'm sorry. I've had a lot on my mind."

"And this business yesterday," the manager said. "I wasn't there, since it was in the ladies' room, but I'm told—"

"You suffered a complete breakdown," the supervisor said, "bawling and hallucinating someone was out to kill you. Half the female staff came to help. Everything ground to a halt."

"This isn't our primary concern, of course," the manager continued. He folded his own hands and leaned toward her. "We care about your health. We're concerned the job is taking a toll on you."

"Please don't," she said. "I need to work. The settlement from the accident—all I have left is my house."

"As you know, we're a generous company. You have a retirement program..." Which didn't kick in until she'd worked here for five years, she thought. "...paid leave, and healthcare benefits."

She spread both hands out in supplication. What did all this matter if she was being fired?

"We want you to take some compassionate leave. You have lots of sick days."

"Over two weeks," the supervisor said.

"Get some counseling," the manager continued in what seemed to Sharon a tag-team match. "We can recommend a professional who's helped other employees. I'll refer you to her." He plastered his most reassuring smile on his face. "When she's cleared you to return, we'll discuss your future."

"Sir, I really don't need this. There's nothing wrong with me."

"It's for the best," he said.

"Something happened a few weeks ago," she said, trying to block the pleading tone from her voice. "I can't say what. But it will pass, and when it does, I'll be fine."

He reached in his pocket and pulled out a pair of reading glasses, mounting them on his face even though he could see her clearly. "This isn't just about you," he said. "We must consider the wellbeing of all our employees."

"They were really upset," the supervisor said.

The manager shifted in his chair, overriding her interruption. "We try to maintain a positive work environment. Retail carries enough tension without subjecting our team members to, uh, personal issues."

Sharon took a handkerchief from her pocket, wiped her eyes and nose, then twisted it in her hands. "And after I see this..."

"Counselor," he said.

"After I see her, I can return to work?"

"That is our goal, but let's see what she recommends. We want what's best for you, whether it's here or in a less stressful line of work."

He rose and extended his hand. "Good luck. Few companies offer the benefits we do."

Sharon didn't thank him. She made no reply, leaving the office, emptying her locker, and lowering her head as she left the warehouse store for what she feared would be the last time.

---

It's easier to find something when you know what you're looking for. By midafternoon, Terrell Brown called from the medical examiner's office. "Your hunch was right," he said.

"Brad Walker?" Barnwell asked.

"We had his DNA from his arrest for the airport thefts," he said. "It matches that of the body left in North Fork Creek."

She asked what would follow. She knew the process in theory, but either Calvin or Chief Novak had managed it at

Boyleston. Brown explained that since his office had confirmed the identification, there was no need for a family member to view the body, "unless they wish to do so."

"When are you releasing the body?" she asked.

"Not until we complete the toxicology tests."

She asked when that might be, but Brown didn't know. "It's up to the lab," he said. "With all this gang-related killing, they're stressed."

She took the news to Jeffrey. "Nice work, detective," he said.

It was the second time today he'd acknowledged her work. She felt a trace of self-confidence returning. "Are we ready to pull Thorson in?"

He held up a finger. "Not yet. Let's first get the cause of death. The ME's lab director is expediting the tox analyses."

"Should we tell him we've identified the victim as his brother?" she asked.

Jeffrey leaned back and folded his arms over his chest. "No," he said, after several seconds' thought. "I'll ask the ME to withhold releasing the ID until we get the labs. Meanwhile, see if you can find where they held him. Search the area around Old Mill Road. The more I think about it, the more I buy into your theory it was somewhere nearby."

"Wouldn't it help to get his phone records?" she asked. "The Technical Services Unit might pinpoint his last location."

Jeffrey massaged his chin. "Good idea. I'll get them on it. Meanwhile, lead the ground search. I'll assign patrol officers to help you." Barnwell scribbled notes as he laid out the procedure. "Start with abandoned buildings, warehouses, that sort of thing."

"There aren't many out there," she said. "It's mostly new residential construction."

"Check it out anyway. If you come up empty, we'll begin a house-to-house search." He leaned forward, punching the air with closed fingers. "I want to know everything we can before we bring Thorson in. If he tries to lead us up an alley, let's have been there ahead of him. If he was in on these airport thefts and escaped responsibility, he's a shifty dude. Let's be ready for him."

She scratched her chin as she looked down. "What if the toxicology report turns up nothing?" she said. "What if, after all this, he simply had a heart attack?"

"Kidnapping is a first-degree felony," Jeffrey said. "Even if he's only charged with unlawful restraint or false imprisonment, it's a first class misdemeanor. That carries a maximum five-year sentence. Add in tampering with the corpse, and he's likely to do time."

She was grateful he'd eased her doubts and provided the support she craved. Returning to her desk, she found a message to call the crime lab. She returned the call, listened to the information the examiner had for her, and hung up, dissatisfied.

---

CALVIN ARRIVED at 6:30 in his official vehicle, alerting anyone who wanted to make an issue of his presence they would deal with a police officer. He placed a paper shopping bag on her kitchen counter and wrapped her in his arms. "How're you doing?" he asked.

"The plot thickens," she said as she removed tubs of green beans, mashed potatoes, and a turkey breast from the bag. Placing the bird on a cutting board with a recessed rim to catch juices, she carved as she spoke. "The ME has identified the body as Brad Walker."

"So your hunch was right," he said.

"It was more of an educated guess." She served their plates and poured two glasses of wine from a bottle in the refrigerator as he carried their plates to one end of the table.

Spotting something at the opposite end, he said, "What's this?"

"A gift from David's father, a jigsaw puzzle of the national parks. I've just started. I'm still finding the corners."

Calvin's eyes crinkled as his face broke into a grin. "First a dog, now this. He really likes you."

She looked down at Howie, curled up at the foot of her chair. "That he does. It was at his insistence that David tried to resume our relationship." She paused and shook her head as though trying to shake the thought out. "Let's discuss something else."

As they ate, she took him through the latest developments. "We won't notify his brother until we have a cause of death. Then we'll bring him in for questioning."

"Why are you so certain he was involved?" Mayfield asked.

While he listened, Lydia recounted the threat Walker's testimony posed to Thorson's future. She detailed the problems she saw with the case—the fact his body had been left almost at Thorson's front door, which she ascribed to the panic caused by the winter storm, and the question of where Walker had been held during his captivity. "We'll start searching in the morning," she said. "I'm getting help from the North Fayette police department again. We'll knock on every door if necessary."

Mayfield, who'd gobbled his dinner down in what seemed like one bite, raised his eyes to a point over her head. "There's still something missing, isn't there? If the storm made it difficult to carry the corpse to a more remote loca-tion, why not just wait? What was the rush?"

"Something must have compelled him to act right away. Perhaps wherever Ben was holding him was no longer be available." She paused with her fork in the air. "Could it be something to do with the storm?" She shook her head and let out an exasperated sigh.

"And you don't yet know what killed him," Mayfield said. "It could be natural causes, like the post mortem found. Thorson is holding him for some reason. His brother has a heart attack and dies." He tapped his wineglass on the table as he thought. Lydia rose to refill it, and Mayfield raised his voice to follow her. "If he'd kidnapped him, he couldn't call the police to report his death. He'd have to get rid of the body."

"My thinking, too," she said as she emptied the bottle into both their glasses. "There's stuff we don't know, but when I expressed my doubts to Jeffrey, he brushed them aside. He's convinced Thorson is behind it."

"So you were undermining your own case," he said, chuckling. Then he grew serious again. "You're assuming Thorson was part of the airport theft ring and acted to prevent his brother from testifying against him. You don't really have much except the family relationship, do you?" He rose from his chair and moved to the end of the table, pushing pieces of the puzzle around as they talked.

"Another odd thing," she said. "Thorson has expressed no curiosity about his brother's whereabouts. Walker failed to appear for his formal arraignment. Thorson knows we're searching for him. Yet, when I confronted him about lying to us and told him we had discovered their connection, he didn't ask about him."

"You suspect that's because he knew where he was?" Mayfield asked.

She raised her glass and peered at its contents. "It makes sense, doesn't it?"

Mayfield raised his head, still pushing pieces around at his end of the table. "If I'm his attorney, I make the case that if he were responsible for his disappearance, he'd make a big show of asking how the search was going. He's told you they were on the outs. Maybe he hasn't asked about him because he doesn't give a shit."

Lydia twirled her empty glass, then stacked their plates and carried them to the kitchen. Calvin was right. There was too much they didn't know. He rose, took the dishes from her hands, and scraped what remained into the garbage, placing the plates into the dishwasher. "Meanwhile," he said, "what does the crime lab have to say about your intruder?"

Lydia snapped her head up, brought back from turning the Ben Thorson problem over in her head. "I forgot to mention it. They called just as I was leaving. They're unable to match the fingerprints with anything on file. From the size of the prints and the narrow opening of the window, they can tell it was someone of small stature. There's nothing else to go on. We may never know."

"But at least you've fixed the problem," he said. And she had. The front and back doors now had double locks, and a maintenance firm had repaired the broken latch and installed grates on the three ground-level basement windows.

They turned in early and spent an hour making love. When he left at eleven, she showered and tried to fall asleep, but it wouldn't come. She arose and made herself a cup of herbal tea while she sat at the kitchen counter. *What am I doing?* she asked aloud. *Do I feel something for Calvin, or is this just for sex?*

After her split with David, she'd vowed never again to form a romantic relationship with a fellow cop. Yet in the wake of his death, she and Calvin had spent the night, thrown together by mutual loneliness. Not only had their affair not abated when she left the Boyleston force, it had intensified. They now met at least once a week, one or the other of them calling to ask, "Are you hungry?" The code words had little to do with food, but their encounters always began that way.

Sitting at her counter, dipping her tea bag in and out of the hot water, she wondered whether this was headed anywhere. Neither had raised the question. They just … *were.* But she sensed they had reached a fork in the road. Days before, she'd said she wasn't ready for a formal relationship. Now, their series of one-night stands left her feeling empty, even slimy.

Her hesitation had nothing to do with race. Growing up abroad and in the integrated world of the US military, she didn't have to confront the worst aspects of racism. When her father returned to the US, racism slapped her in the face. As she began studying it, she'd decided those who denigrated any one group acted out of insecurity.

Calvin Mayfield was an honorable human being, dedicated to his profession and kind to all he knew. She could tell he loved her. That was all that mattered.

Her father might have a different reaction, but that would have little to do with Calvin's color. He simply disapproved of every decision she'd made since coming of age. With his wife gone, Richard Barnwell had refused to assume the responsibilities of parenthood. Forced to raise herself, Lydia had shrugged off her father's neglect and frequent disparagement. When she had the chance, she'd left him behind, which was how she'd ended up in Pittsburgh. What he thought no longer mattered. What she thought did.

She rose, placed her empty mug in the sink, and turned out the light. As she passed the dining room table, she saw he'd identified the four corners of the puzzle and positioned them at the edges of what would become a rectangle. *I need to keep this guy around,* she told herself.

Lydia would either invite Calvin to move in from his grimy one-bedroom apartment, or she would bring the affair to a close. She returned to the kitchen, placed her cup in the dishwasher, and turned it on. Before dousing the lights again, she considered the questions he'd posed about the investigation. If it wasn't the result she wanted, the process was. He had become, in many ways, her partner.

Deciding she would ask him, she stretched out on her bed, pulled the blanket over her, and fell asleep.

CHAPTER SIX

RATHER THAN DRAWING a two-mile circle on a map, Lydia used Google maps to measure the distance from Old Mill to every road leading to it. This eliminated busy Route 30 to the north. "Shouldn't we include it?" Nadine Foster asked.

Barnwell considered the point. "Does it make sense that someone would have driven here during a snowstorm when there are so many more available spots along that highway?"

"Perhaps you're right," the North Fayette officer said.

"I'm not sure I am," Barnwell replied, "but we have to start somewhere using what resources we have."

That included the same three county patrol officers and Foster's North Fayette colleague who had joined her the day Walker's body was discovered. Working in pairs, they would start to the west of the site, one team along North Branch, another heading north on Donaldson Road, the third south on Whittengale. If they came up empty, they would turn east in the afternoon.

Barnwell took Jerald Mullins, the county officer who had bucked her authority days before, to cover North

Branch. She split the local officers between the other two teams and assigned them to search the back roads. North Branch Road, which lined the creek of the same name, ran past several older homes, a few of which were stately, and an orchard. Barnwell stopped at the latter and spoke to the owner for a few minutes. He said he and his wife had remained home throughout the winter and had seen no suspicious activity on their property.

North of the orchard, they came to a speedway, surrounded by a chain link fence. The pair got out of the car and patrolled the perimeter, spotting no buildings in the infield but a locked area under the grandstand that held offices and snack bars. She contacted the owner by cell phone. He told her he'd visited the property at least twice a week and seen nothing. "Vandals used to steal signs off the fence ringing the track. I guess they were decorating the walls of their garages, but nothing so far this year. I'll come out if you want, but I assure you, no one's been around since we plowed the track after the last dirt race in October."

Barnwell took his word for it and backtracked along Kelso Road to North Fork. Mullins, who'd sat in sullen silence to this point, said, "This is a wild goose chase." She was tempted to respond that they wouldn't find a goose unless they searched, but didn't give him the satisfaction. They continued south and came upon a kennel. The owner gave them the same story.

At noon, they returned to the North Fayette police station and compared results. No one had spotted a goose, wild or domesticated. She was convinced Brad Walker had been held somewhere nearby. *But I may have it wrong*, she thought. She recalled what the crime lab technician had said about rough sex. Perhaps, after all, this was a case of S and M gone wrong.

With nothing else to go on, she told them to continue the search. After a quick lunch at a bar and grill on US 30, the three teams headed to locations east of Old Mill.

It was almost three when Foster radioed her. "We've found something." On McKee Road, near Pittsburgh Technical College, she'd located an abandoned heavy equipment rental facility. Barnwell and Mullins arrived within five minutes. "It's been out of business for months," Foster explained. "They rented heavy equipment to contractors, but got in over their heads. The bank repossessed all their equipment, and the owner shuttered the place in August." She led Barnwell to the metal gate, intended to secure a long storage facility with a white roof and blue metal walls. Foster pointed to the padlock, which had been sawed through. "We waited for you before going in. Do we need a search warrant?"

"Do you know who owns it?"

"The bank now," she said.

Donning a pair of rubber gloves, Barnwell studied the broken padlock. "Do we agree there's probable cause of a break-in?" The others muttered agreement. "Then we're required to investigate."

She removed the padlock and swung the gate wide enough so the four of them could enter the property. Approaching an entry alongside the garage door, she saw someone had drilled the lock through, leaving the door slightly open. They stepped inside. Barnwell reached for the light switch, but, as she suspected, the electric company had pulled the plug. The officers pulled flashlights from their belts and scoured the interior. As they did so, something fluttered above them. Foster raised the beam, revealing a nest nestled in a metal joist. "How did they get in here?" she said. "What do they do for food?"

"The crack in the door is all they need," Barnwell said. She led the others up one side of the garage and down the other. Apart from bird droppings and scattered paper, they found nothing. No abandoned desks or chairs, no file cabinets, no sign anything had ever been stored there.

They ventured outside again and circled the building, finding a concrete pad and a fuel pump. With no power to the facility, Barnwell couldn't tell whether the underground tank still contained fuel, but she doubted it. What the bank hadn't taken, vandals had. More to the point, the team found no sign anyone had been inside since the garage had been stripped. Neither a homeless person nor a person, now deceased, held against his will.

***

BARNWELL RETURNED to headquarters at four, battling incoming traffic on Parkway West. She found a message from the digital investigation unit telling her the phone number she'd found in the pocket of Brad Walker's jeans belonged to a woman named Moira Buller. The investigator provided her home address and her place of business, a health club in Robinson Township.

She dialed the number and introduced herself. "I'm investigating the disappearance of a man charged with a string of robberies at the airport," she said. "We found your number among his effects. Do you know a Brad Walker?"

"I don't recall the name," the woman responded. "You say you had this number? It's my cell phone. I don't give it out to many people. Never to men I don't know."

"He's twenty-nine, well-built, dark brown hair and light brown eyes, with a cleft chin. From his mug shot, he appears to be quite handsome."

"That sounds like—" The woman paused, and Lydia waited her out. "Carl was his name. Let me look through my records."

Lydia gave her time, raising her water bottle to her mouth and taking a deep swallow.

"Carl Ferris," Moira said, "not Brad ... What did you say his name is?"

Barnwell repeated Walker's name and was about to thank the woman when something told her to take a chance. "I'm going to send you his photo. See if you recognize him." She tapped on her computer, sending Walker's mugshot to her cell phone. She heard an electronic whoop as the message arrived at the other end. As she waited, she raised the water bottle again, then put it down. One more gulp, and she'd have to pee. This conversation shouldn't take long.

"That's him," the voice responded, "but like I said, his name isn't Brad. It's Carl."

"Why did he have your phone number?" Barnwell asked.

"I'm a personal trainer. I ran into him somewhere. Oh, I was sitting at a bar at a Mexican restaurant out here. This guy started talking to me. I tried to ignore him. I take care of myself, and guys are always coming on to me." Moira said Walker had represented himself as an investment adviser and said he was new to the area. He'd asked what she did, and she told him she was a personal trainer.

"He said he was looking for a health club," she said. "We had a promotion going on. If we signed someone up rather than going through the club, we got a bonus. It was in late summer when people stayed outside and business was slow. That's why I gave him my number, rather than the club's. I rarely do that, but if he'd signed up, I would have made enough to pay down my credit cards."

"You say 'if he'd signed up.' I take it he didn't."

The woman issued a snort. "We offer a free introductory lesson. He signed up for that, gave me his personal information, but never followed up. I tried calling him once, but got a message saying the number was no longer in use. I must have taken it down wrong."

"You said he provided his own information. If you got a non-working number, it was one he provided."

"You're right. I haven't given it a lot of thought until you called. It's not the first time someone's taken the free lesson and ghosted me. I can't afford to dwell on it. I just move on." She paused. "You say he was arrested?"

"Yes, he was part of that theft ring at the airport," Barnwell said. "You may have read about it."

"I don't recall seeing it," she said. "Maybe that's why he gave me a wrong number."

"I suspect so," Barnwell answered.

"And maybe I dodged a bullet," Moira said.

"I'd say so." Barnwell thanked the woman, took down her information, and ended the call. On a hunch, she searched for the name Carl Ferris. It didn't take long to get a hit. Ferris was one of those who'd reported his wallet missing after going through the TSA line at the airport. Walker hadn't just taken travelers' money. He'd stolen their identities.

***

As BARNWELL DONNED her jacket to end this long day, Detective Jeffrey poked his head in the door. "You're getting your wish," he said. She replied with raised eyebrows. "A member of the theft ring is doing more talking, trying to cut a deal. They've agreed to let us interview him."

"Now?" she said. She needed to get home to feed Howie.

"You'd rather wait for them to change their minds?"

She ignored the barb and followed him to his cruiser.

The county jail is on 2nd Street in Pittsburgh, near the point where the Liberty Bridge crosses the Monongahela River. While the entrance looks like a downtown office building, sheathed in aluminum and glass, the buildings flanking it are in cold brick with small windows that resemble embrasures in a medieval battlement. Jeffrey checked them in, and Detective Mark Sanford came out to lead them the rest of the way.

"His name's Jason Crawley," Sanford said. "He was caught on a DUI last night, so the court revoked his release. We began questioning him this morning, not expecting to get any more out of him than we did after his attorney told him to stop talking. He began spilling and hasn't stopped. The team had been operating for months before federal security caught on, he says. At first it was small stuff, one or two robberies a week, but as they became more successful, they got bolder. That made them careless." As he opened the door to the interrogation room, he turned toward the two of them and sneered. "He claims it was all Walker's idea. He was just a poor guy along for the ride. I'm sure he'll tell you all this."

It took ten minutes before the prisoner shuffled in, dressed in his orange jump suit. He had a thin face and fine, sandy hair that hugged both sides of his face in search of a comb. The left side of his mouth sagged as though he'd had a stroke, but it took only a few minutes before Barnwell decided his woeful look went with his personality. From the moment he said, "What's this? Haven't I already told the other folks everything I know?" to the last glance over his shoulder as the guard escorted him back to his cell, Crawley took responsibility for nothing. Walker was the mastermind. He'd planned the operation and talked the two others into it. "Shep and I," he said, referring to the other partner, "we didn't want no part of it, but Walker insisted. I'm sorry I ever set eyes on the guy."

"I'm curious where you got the idea," Barnwell said.

"Three guys at Miami International Airport pulled the same job," Crawley replied. "Walker read about it and thought we could do better."

"Weren't those three caught?" she asked.

"Yeah, but Walker said it was because they were Hispanic. They'd never expect three white guys to do the same thing, he said. We'd be more careful and were a lot smarter than they were. That's what he figured."

Barnwell hid her contempt behind a stone face. "Didn't it occur to you that Miami's experience might have taught the TSA to tighten things up at other airports?"

Crawley ran a hand through his hair. "I see that now, but Walker, he convinced us it would work."

*Not just racist, but stupid*, she thought.

They'd picked their marks with care. "Families with kids, specially if one brat is in a stroller. The kids distract them, so they're not paying much attention to what we're doing. And business people, men and women, who keep looking at their watches like they're going to be late. They're the best. They always carry cash on them, sometimes have a nice watch they have to take off, and all they want is to get through the line and get out of there."

Crawley said all this as though he were instructing the detectives how they might pull off a similar heist. "People with time on their hands, you don't want to touch them. They're going to stop in the food court and pull out their wallets to pay. We was looking for folks who wouldn't notice anything missing till they got to wherever they was going. Then," he said with a canny smile, "they wouldn't know where they'd lost the money. Before they got on the plane? While they went to the head during the flight? Somewhere after they landed? Walker said there was no way they could trace it to us."

He gave a derisive snort, because, of course, "they" had done exactly that.

"Walker, he was the money man. We had to turn everything we got into him. He'd count it and split it with us." Crawley seemed to think about it. "I don't know about that. I always suspected he was shorting us. But I made a few thousand off it."

Barnwell had heard enough, because she didn't much care how they'd operated. She was out to learn two things. "Did you ever suspect the supervisor, Ben Thorson, was in on it?"

"He didn't pay us much attention," Crawley said. "I don't think he and Walker got alone too well, even though they was related."

"You knew they were half brothers?"

"Oh, yeah," he said. "Walker told us once. Said he was a goody-two-shoes. I hadn't heard that one in a while. That's why it stuck with me."

"But did he know what the three of you were doing?" she persisted.

"I dunno," he said, giving them an elaborate shrug. "He never mentioned it. Once, he said his brother would never turn him in. If that meant he knew what we was doing, I can't say."

"Have you had any dealings with Thorson outside of work?" she asked, homing in on the second thing she wanted to know.

"I dunno what you mean."

"Did Thorson ever ask you to do something for him?"

"No."

"Ask you to help him move something?"

"Like what?" he said. "I hardly know the guy. He's a supervisor. Why would he hang around me?"

Neither detective wanted to ask the direct question: Had Crawley helped Thorson transport his brother's body from wherever he was holding him to the bridge at Old Mill? Jeffrey had been specific during their drive here. "Don't tell him Walker's dead. It will make it too easy to pin every aspect of this operation on him." Not that Crawley needed any encouragement to do so.

Instead, they danced around the subject, trying to get the prisoner to admit Walker had dealt with his brother, anything as insignificant as his asking Thorson to fetch him a cup of coffee. The man didn't budge.

"If Thorson was in on it, why wouldn't he say so?" Barnwell asked as they returned to headquarters. "He's negotiating with the DA. Why hide his get-out-of-jail card?"

"The fact he doesn't know if Thorson was in on the operation doesn't mean he wasn't," Jeffrey cautioned. "Walker wouldn't have wanted someone that ignorant to know every detail."

MOIRA GLANCED AT THE CLOCK. Fifteen minutes until her last appointment of the day. She clicked a number on her cell phone. "Hello?" Annette Henley's voice carried a lilt of uncertainty, as though she expected her phone was a Tazer.

"A police detective just called me," Moira said. "She found my telephone number in his clothes and wants to know how he knew me."

She heard Annette wheeze as she drew in her breath. "What did you tell them?"

"The truth," Moira said. "At least the part where he started chatting with me while I was having lunch. I gave her the pitch he'd given me and how I gave him a free lesson. Then I told her he'd never returned, and the number he gave me was bogus."

Again, the heavy breathing. "Did she buy it?" Annette asked.

"Of course." Moira snickered as she replied. "And if she checks the club's records, it will confirm what I told her. Carl Ferris is booked for one session in September, and there's nothing more on him."

"I hope you're right."

"But I got more out of her than she did out of me," she said. "His name was Brad Walker. He was one of those security guards who scan your stuff at the airport. Right after the first of the year, they arrested him for stealing money from people's bags. He was released pending his trial or something, but he skipped out. The cops have been looking for him ever since."

"So he had more than one scam going?" Annette said.

"Yeah, the world won't miss him." She punctuated the judgment with another chortle.

"I wonder..." Annette said and paused as she gathered her thoughts. "She didn't mention he's dead. Does that mean they still haven't identified him?"

"Either that or she knows and is hiding it."

Annette wheezed again as she considered the information. "What happens now?" she asked.

"Nothing. We go about our business. I've covered my tracks, and there's nothing to connect him to you."

"It's Sharon I'm worried about," Annette said. "She called again last night. Told me she's lost her job. She was hysterical. They've sent her to a shrink."

"Jesus!" Moira said.

A coworker poked her head through the door and said, "Your six o'clock is here."

"I gotta go," she said. not responding to what Annette had just told her. But as she ended the call, she feared one of them would have to deal with Sharon. If she saw the psychiatrist, she'd start babbling. Did head doctors have to keep what patients told them in confidence, the way real doctors did? Moira wasn't sure. And what had she done or said at work that led to her dismissal?

Sharon was like a water bottle perched on the edge of a sink. God knew what she'd spill when she toppled over. Yes, they'd have to put a stopper in it.

It was dark when Lydia returned home. She found Tommy Molnar bent over Howie's dish. He straightened up as she entered the kitchen, his face contorted in alarm. "I was just — He's hungry," he said.

"And you're feeding him," Lydia replied. "Thank you."

"I didn't know if I'm allowed to—"

"You did fine. Just no people food. And no chocolate."

"I know," he said. "My dog Ginger got into a chocolate cake one day. We had to take her to the vet."

Howie had not turned to greet her, his muzzle buried in

the chunks of dry food. Now he finished, turned, and lay at her feet as she faced the boy. "I need to pay you," she said, reaching for her billfold. "Three evening walks. That's nine bucks."

Tommy shook his head. "You don't have to do that. I like Howie. I take him out when I walk Ginger, so he's no trouble."

"No," she said. "A deal's a deal." She rummaged through the wallet and pulled out a ten-dollar bill. "Keep the change."

He shuffled his feet, holding the bill in his hand and looking at it. "No, you're paying me in advance. You'll only owe me two dollars tomorrow."

"You know, Tommy, if everyone were as honest as you, I wouldn't have a job." She smiled at him, but he lowered his head and shuffled his feet. *Okay*, she thought, *uncomfortable with the attention.* "I appreciate what you're doing for me. Given my schedule, I have no business caring for a pet." But David's father, Wayne Kimrey, had given her no choice after her son's death, almost forcing the dog into her arms.

She thanked him and watched as he backed out her door. "Oh," he said, "I had to clean up some scraps of paper around his bed. It looked like newspaper."

"Yes," she said, "he's been getting into things even since we moved in. It's like he's building a nest back there."

As the boy retreated into the lengthening darkness, Lydia told herself to get together with his mother. Too many police officers had no friends other than cops. She didn't care to be one of them.

She almost collapsed onto her sofa, rubbing the dog's ears as he nestled onto her lap. It had been a trying day with hours of action and no results. Much police work was like this. Long periods of boredom punctuated by moments of intense action. Fishing in her back pocket for her cell phone, she stared at the screen, debating what to do. After weighing the pros and cons, she dialed Calvin's cell. When he answered, she could hear a flurry of activity behind him. "Busy?" she said.

"Yeah," came the answer. "We have a domestic. I'm going to be tied up for a while."

"Tomorrow, then." About to hang up, she called, "Please be careful."

"Promise," he said and ended the call.

She sat for a moment, conflicted as she weighed her concern for his safety with her relief at being spared the conversation she needed to have with him.

Lydia poured herself a glass of wine and returned to the sofa. Howie hadn't moved, expecting her to return and keep him company. She thought about the busy day, from North Fayette to headquarters to county jail and back. She didn't know that she'd made progress and was vaguely dissatisfied.

Was she giving in to self-doubt? No sooner had she identified Ben Thorson as a potential suspect than she'd begun undermining the case against him. Was this a product of insecurity? All those years enduring her father's disapproval had left scars. She recalled the first time she'd met Chief Novak after he'd been hired to clean up Boyleston's demoralized police force. What had she asked him? *Will I be okay?* What had made her think she would bear the blame for the former chief's misdeeds?

Even after solving the case of Thomas Walsh, falsely convicted and jailed for the murder of his wife, even after Novak had promoted her to detective, she'd felt like a fraud, convinced she didn't quite measure up. Solving the staged abduction of little Rose Fallon hadn't assuaged her fears. Indeed, she brooded about the fact the child's mother had taken her in for so long. In her mind, even this victory was tainted.

Yet, for all her uncertainty, she found herself pushing Jeffrey at a faster pace than he wanted to move. Despite his repeated advice to take things step by step, to wait until the ME identified the body, not haul Ben Thorson in until they'd determined the cause of his brother's death, Lydia was impatient.

*This isn't over*, she told herself. *Something's about to happen. Someone is going to be hurt. I know it.* Howie stirred beside her as though sharing her concern.

If Calvin were here, she would ask him what made her so certain. But he was not. And wasn't the fact she couldn't determine this for herself another testament to her lack of confidence?

Lydia grabbed her notebook and sketched out a timeline.

> *1/18, Walker arrested*
> *1/19, Preliminary arraigned; released*
> *2/2, Formal arraignment, Walker noshow*
> *2/6, Walker's body left beneath bridge*
> *3/20, Cindy Thorson discovers body*

She left space between each item, confident she'd have more entries.

She turned on the TV to catch up on the evening news. The meteorologist told her the weather was changing. "I guess it's just the two of us tonight," she told Howie. He looked up at her and emitted what sounded like a contented sigh.

OVERNIGHT, a front moved in. The temperature dropped, and southwestern Pennsylvania was covered in another snowstorm. In the Laurel Highlands, winds churned the snow into whiteout conditions. East of Somerset, a tractor-trailer emerged from the Allegheny Mountain Tunnel and jackknifed as it headed down the 3 percent grade toward the US 220 exit. Traffic backed up behind it for miles, even into the tunnel. First responders fought their way up the eastbound lanes to reach those trapped, but at dawn, hundreds of trucks and passenger vehicles remained on the highway, engines running to keep their occupants warm.

Around Pittsburgh, the storm was less intense, but schools closed for the day and many businesses did as will. For Barnwell, the wintry blast brought a welcome benefit. "We won't find many empty homes today," she told her crew.

"Are you sure we should do this?" ACPD Officer Mullins said. "It's treacherous out there."

Barnwell fought the urge to engage with the man, but

Nadine Foster spared her the trouble. "We're all in four-wheel-drive vehicles," she said. "The weather's a blessing."

They worked out from the center, working the same roads they'd covered the day before. Barnwell directed Mullins to the house across the road at which he'd received no answer the week before. "What are we looking for?" he said as he inched the Ford PI Utility vehicle up the unplowed driveway.

"The same as yesterday. Anyone who noticed unusual activity six to seven weeks ago," she said. "We ask questions and listen to answers."

She climbed out of the vehicle, her boots sinking into the snow, pushed her way to the front door, and rang the doorbell. A man about her own age answered, a youngster of about three peering around his legs. "Detective Lydia Barnwell, Allegheny County PD," she said. "This is Officer Mullins."

"Yes?" the man said, shaking his head in apparent disbelief that the two officers would be out on a day like this.

"Do you mind if we step inside?"

"Well..."

"Who is it?" a woman's voice cried out.

"Cops," the man shouted over his shoulder.

"Don't just stand there with the door open," she said. "Bring them in."

The man backed up, nearly tripping over his son, who regarded the pair wide-eyed. Barnwell stepped inside, perching on a rubber mat to avoid getting the floor wet while Mullins pushed in behind her, uncomfortably close.

"Have you come about the body?" the man said. "We know nothing about it."

"Did you or your wife see—"

"We're not married," he said.

*An unnecessary detail*, Barnwell thought. "Did either of you notice any unusual activity in early February?"

"Across the road, you mean?"

"Yes, or at a neighboring house. Any strange comings and goings?"

The man shook his head. His companion emerged from the kitchen, rubbing her palms against her jeans as though she'd just finished making something. "Did you see anything?" Barnwell asked.

"No," she said. "It stays pretty quiet around here. Except for trucks gunning their engines after they pass the police station, but we don't hear them so much in winter with the windows closed."

Barnwell asked a few more questions, but got nowhere. She presented her card and asked them to contact her if they recalled anything or heard something from a neighbor. "We don't see too much of them," he said. "We both work."

"Is the entire morning going to be like this?" Mullins asked as he turned southwest on North Branch Road and advanced up the next driveway.

"Possibly," she said. "Then again, maybe not." Never one to suffer fools, Lydia had placed Mullins in the category.

She asked the same series of questions at the next house and the one after that. As they gathered for lunch, the two other teams reported the same results, but Foster, at least, had had a breakthrough. "We had a rash of porch thieves following a UPS truck around Christmas," she said. "As we questioned this middle-aged couple, the husband wouldn't let us in, but I saw a stack of Fedex and UPS packages in the next room. The guy kept blocking the view by stepping in my way like a slow dance every time I tried to peer around him. I returned to our patrol car, radioed one of our detectives, and they're getting a warrant now."

"At least something got done today," Mullins said.

Barnwell stared at him, but Mullins looked away. She'd had enough. "Officer Foster," she said. "Let's switch places this afternoon. I'd like you to join me, and Mullins here can go with your partner."

The North Fayette officer's grin could have cracked her face open. "Love to," she said.

The snow had stopped by the time they left, and the temperature was rising. Soon, snowmelt would creep down the hills and turn the gentle stream where Walker's body had lain until the previous week into a raging torrent.

The pair finished their sweep of Whittengale Road when Barnwell decided they'd run too far afield. They returned to North Branch and called at the next two homes along the road. Near the orchard Barnwell had visited the day before, they crept up an unpaved driveway toward what looked like an old farmhouse. There were no tire tracks along the unpaved lane, but melting snow revealed a narrow ridge in the center. The house was white, but as the cruiser curved around the southwest side, Barnwell noticed paint peeling where the sun had baked it. They parked before a detached garage whose roof missed several shingles.

Foster, who'd recited a running inventory of most of the homes they'd visited, said, "A single woman lives here. I hear her husband died a while back. She keeps to herself. I know little about her."

She rang the doorbell, and hearing nothing, knocked. No one answered. "I know she's here," Foster said. "There were no tire tracks when we came up the drive.."

"Perhaps she stayed somewhere else last night," Barnwell said.

"I spotted the roof of a car through the garage window as we pulled up."

Barnwell hummed in appreciation, pleased to work with someone who used her head. The thought no sooner left her mind than she realized assigning Mullins to the other team left it short-handed. She hoped that team didn't miss anything.

Foster knocked again, her pounding taking on a demanding tone. Footsteps approached the door. "Who is it?" a voice said.

"Police officers," Foster said. "We're visiting every house in the neighborhood. We need to ask you a few questions."

"What sort of questions?"

"Please open up," Barnwell said. "This will only take a minute. It's important."

The door cracked open, and a tired face looked out at them, a middle-aged woman with medium cut hair a dark shade of blond. Her blue-gray eyes held no life, and her mouth drooped. She wore a look of perpetual disappointment. Foster had said she was a widow. Was she still grieving over her husband's death?

"We're trying to find anyone who might have seen strange activity at one of these houses several weeks ago," Foster said.

"I didn't notice anything," the woman said in a quavering voice.

"No people coming or going? No strange activity at night? Nothing odd being carried from a house?"

To each question, the woman shook her head, never loosening her grip on the doorknob. She looked from one of them to the other, like a small child watching adults argue. "I live alone here. I — I was taking a nap. I've just lost my job and..." She glanced upward as though searching for the right words. "I have a doctor's appointment. I'm being treated for depression. I can't talk right now."

"We're sorry to hear that," Barnwell said, thrusting a business card at the woman. "I hope things look up for you. If anything comes to mind, if you see or hear anything we should know about, please call us."

The woman glanced at the outthrust hand, staring at it as though the officer had pointed a weapon. Finally, she released her grip on the door, snatching the piece of paper and crushing it in her hand.

The officers returned to the car, Foster making a U-turn to return to the highway. "That poor woman is about to explode," she said.

Lydia sat lost in thought for a moment. "Would you do a wellness check on her in a day or two? Maybe if she senses someone is concerned for her, it will lighten her load."

As they approached the next house, her phone chimed. "Hello, sir," she said after glancing at the ID.

Detective Jeffrey didn't return the greeting. "Where are you now?" She described their location, but he interrupted. "How quickly can you return to headquarters? There's been a development, and I need to share it with you in person."

Lydia placed a hand on Foster's arm as she was about to open the driver's door. "Give me half an hour," she replied. As she had Foster return to the North Fayette police station, she offered no explanation, for Jeffrey had given her none.

---

"They were just here," Sharon's shrill voice tumbled out of the phone like shattered glass. "They know."

Annette Henley held the phone away from her ear as the voice at the other end screamed. The project estimator at the next desk looked up and stared at her over his half frame reading glasses. "Hold on," she said. She left her desk, the sound of Sharon's bawling trailing her as she made her way to the women's restroom and locked the door.

"Calm down," she said. "Who are they, and what do they know?"

"The police. They came to my door."

Annette felt the pinpricks of fear. "Why? What did they want?"

She waited as the voice collapsed in sobs, gasping for breath. "Sharon," she said. "What are they after? Are they searching your place?"

"No," she cried. "It's — They want to know if I've seen anything."

"Like what?" Annette said.

"Anything suspicious."

"And what did you tell them?" She chewed her wad of gum in time to some imagined music.

Sharon squealed like a child having a tantrum. "I told them I haven't. I said I don't know a thing."

Annette tried to imagine this woman, trembling, denying things she hadn't been asked. She shuddered. "Did you let them in?"

"No, I told them they'd awakened me, that I'd just lost my job, that I'm under a doctor's care."

Annette wondered if she'd given them her life history, her husband's death and how she'd struggled all these years. Everything she'd showered on the two of them the first time they met her. Why had they ever gotten involved with this woman? "What else did you tell them?" she asked.

"Nothing. I swear. I just answered their questions, and they went away."

"Let me get this straight. They came to your door, asked

a few questions, and left. They didn't accuse you of anything."

"No," Sharon blubbered. "They claimed they were knocking on every door near the—"

"They mention the body?"

Sharon stopped sniveling, taking in air like an accordion. "No, come to think of it. They just asked if I'd seen anything strange. 'Comings and goings.' That's how the detective put it."

Someone knocked on the bathroom door. "You coming out any time today?"

"Yeah," Annette called back. "I'm just finishing up here."

"Make it snappy."

"That's Lois," she explained. "She has to go every hour, so I gotta go, too." She forced a small laugh. "Listen, they didn't mention the body, didn't accuse you of anything, and said they're checking every house along the road. It's routine."

She flushed the toilet and ran water in the sink. "So you need to chill. They don't know what they're looking for, and if you keep your mouth shut and act innocent, they won't suspect a thing."

Lois pounded on the door. "Gotta go," Annette said and ended the call.

"Jesus Christ!" she snapped as she left the room. "Can't you hold your bladder for two minutes?"

She returned to her desk and continued where she'd left off, entering due and completion dates into project management software. "Who was that?" the estimator asked.

"A sick relative," she said. "Now, mind your goddamn business."

After a few minutes, however, she donned her coat and

carried her phone out the front door. Standing in the cold, with slush from melting snow encircling her boots, she called Moira. Her call went to voicemail. She hung up without leaving a message.

Should she text? If Sharon blabbed, and the cops went for her cell phone, could they tell who she'd called and what she'd said? But she had to alert the woman with whom she'd formed this unpropitious partnership. She called again and listened as it went to voicemail. "Our sparrow's spotted a hawk and is turning chicken," she said.

---

Lydia shrugged herself out of her parka, refilled her water bottle, and knocked at Jeffrey's open door. "C'mon in," he said.

She parked herself in one of his chairs and waited. What was it that had come up he didn't want to discuss over the phone? Jeffrey stacked a few sheets of paper, laid them in an open file folder, and turned it around to face her. She glanced at the first page and saw a cover sheet from the crime lab.

"The toxicology report," she said. Jeffrey didn't answer, but waited. She scanned the pages, then returned to the second and studied it.

"Why didn't they catch this at the autopsy?" she asked, when she'd read two more.

"Keep going. They address it after the tox findings." She spent a few more minutes wading through the report while Jeffrey sat with his arms folded, not saying a word.

At last, she looked up. "So they found a high level of insulin in his tissues, but no evidence of diabetes. Given that, they reexamined the body and found a discoloration in the chest tissue that skin slippage had concealed."

"That's it," he said.

Lydia turned the report to face him again. "Someone injected him with a high dosage of insulin. This caused a—" She stumbled over the word.

"Hypoglycemic episode, creating a fatal air embolism that led to a heart attack," he said.

"And since his hands were tied," she said, "this is something he couldn't have administered himself. Not that he would have, since he didn't need it. He was murdered."

Barnwell closed her eyes and leaned back in the chair. Someone had kidnapped Brad Walker, poisoned him, stripped his body to conceal his identification, and deposited it in a stream along a state road. All that from a call she'd received to investigate a drunk who'd fallen into a ditch. Despite the gravity of the situation, she couldn't suppress a trace of satisfaction.

"I've asked the Technical Service Unit to expedite getting his call records. While we haven't found his phone, they'll show where it last pinged."

Barnwell had suggested the same thing forty-eight hours before, but let it pass. "I think it's time to bring Ben Thorson in for a formal interview. I'll get the paperwork started," she said.

"I already have," he said.

"Oh," she said. This was hers to do as the investigating officer, but she hid her resentment. "Thanks. When do we pick him up?"

Jeffrey folded his hands, cocked his head to one side, and looked directly at her. "These findings have escalated the situation. This morning, we were dealing with a case of false imprisonment, death from natural causes, and tampering with the corpse. This is homicide. Given the evidence of false imprisonment, my guess is the DA will try for Murder 1. On that basis, Inspector Morris feels it best if I take the lead going forward."

Barnwell let her mouth sag. "What have I done wrong?"

Jeffrey held up his hands as though stopping oncoming traffic. "Nothing. Not a thing. This has nothing to do with the fine job you've done. And are doing. He simply feels that, given this new information, someone with commensurate experience should lead the investigation. Lead," he repeated. "You'll remain on the case, but under my supervision."

An inner voice told her to hold her temper, but a louder voice screamed foul. "Because I'm not trusted."

"No," he barked. "Because you're green. You're new here and have never handled a case this complex."

"The Rosie Fallon case was complex," she snapped. "The Thomas Walsh case was no picnic."

"Those were when you were with Boyleston PD. In both cases, you were working under Chief Novak and with us. This is Allegheny County PD. It's your first homicide investigation."

"But it's no longer mine," she said.

Jeffrey shook his head, closed the file, and placed it aside, signaling that the meeting was over. "I'm truly sorry, but the decision's made," he said. "It's out of my hands."

* * *

CALVIN MAYFIELD HALTED his cruiser in front of Lydia's home and bounded up the front steps. He knocked at the door, remembering he'd promised to fix the doorbell, and cracked the door open. He found her sprawled on her sofa, an empty beer bottle on an end table, and Howie resting his head on her lap. The dog looked up with a woeful expression but didn't move.

"Tell me," he said.

"They've taken the case from me." Her voice was hoarse, as though she'd been crying, and her outraged tone was an angry sunset.

He sat across from her, laid his hat on the coffee table, and leaned toward her. "Why?"

"Walker was murdered," she said. "The inspector says I'm too inexperienced to handle it."

Mayfield snorted, his upper body convulsing at the thought. "Don't they recall the cases you solved when you were with us? It's why they recruited you."

"That was then, and this is now."

She recounted what the forensics team had uncovered. "Now that we know he was poisoned, they're taking the steps I asked for days ago. They're actually going to check his phone records. Imagine that."

"They've removed you from the case?"

"No," she said, stretching and rising from the sofa. "You want a beer?"

"Yes, thanks," Mayfield said, following her into the kitchen. "Are you having another?"

"One's enough," she replied. She reached in the refrigerator, removed a can of IPA, and popped the top with one hand. "I'm still on the team, just no longer in charge."

"What will you do?" he asked as she poured the beer down the side of a glass.

She handed him the drink and wiped her hands on her slacks to dry the condensation. "I wish I could walk away and join another unit," she said.

"You don't mean that," he said, following her into the

dining room. "You're not the kind to take your marbles and go home."

"Of course not," she said. "But I'm that angry. I'm downright pissed."

"It doesn't help," Mayfield said. He sat before the jigsaw puzzle and pushed pieces around. "You're making progress."

Lydia was not to be distracted. "If I were a man, they wouldn't pull this on me."

"You don't know that," he said.

She peered up at him as though she were looking over reading glasses. "Trust me. I do."

"All right," he said. "But the way to win is to solve the case. Let him run it. You've no other choice. But maintain that independent outlook you always carry with you."

She scrunched up her eyes and leaned toward him. "Me? Independent?"

Mayfield reared back, his torso convulsed in a paroxysm of laughter. "Yes, you. You're always off on your own somewhere, thinking your own thoughts, doing things your way. Don't tell me you don't know that."

In a small voice, she said, "I just try to use my judgment. Isn't that what the brain is for?"

Dropping a puzzle piece back where he'd found it, he reached out for her hand. "It is, and you use it well. None better."

She leaned toward him and melted into his embrace. "Thanks. I need the vote of confidence." She broke away and headed into the kitchen. "Are you hungry?" she said as she pushed containers around in the refrigerator. "I can pull something together. There's leftover chicken from the other night."

"Let me take you out," he said.

She considered it for a moment. "No, I'm not ready to face my public." She tried to chuckle, but choked instead.

"Then let's order something and let DoorDash deliver it."

"What's with you and chicken all of a sudden? Anyway," she said, backing into the living room as she pulled him along and tugging him alongside her on the sofa, "I want to ask you something."

Mayfield made a small sound meant to sound like "okay."

Still holding one of his hands, her blue eyes bore into him. "Would you like to move in?"

His mouth hung open, and he gawped at her. "I — You mean...?"

She dropped his hand and threw both of hers into the air. "Okay, you don't. No need to explain. It was a whim. Just something that came to me in the moment."

"So you're not serious?" he said.

She placed her hands in her lap and looked down. "After I kicked David out, I promised myself I'd never fall for another cop. I've also been telling myself I'm not ready for anything serious. But here I am, proposing," she said with a tiny laugh. She looked up again. "Yeah, I'm serious. I don't want to go on with what feels like a series of one-night stands. It's not who I am. I either want a relationship, or I need to move on."

Mayfield smiled and reached out a hand to her shoulder. "You leave me no choice, then," he said. "When do you want this to happen?"

Ben Thorson arrived at nine the following morning wearing chinos, a blue cashmere sweater, and a puzzled look. An officer led him into the interview room, where Barnwell and Jeffrey awaited him. Jeffrey introduced himself. "You've met Detective Barnwell."

Thorson nodded, pushed his dark hair off his forehead, and said, "Why am *I* here?" He emphasized the pronoun, his baritone voice, which Barnwell found incongruous given his soft, almost feminine features, conveying an aggrieved tone.

Jeffrey began the recording, giving the location, date and time, and identifying the two of them. He asked Thorson to state his name for the record, which he did. "We have a few questions," he began.

"I told Ms. Barnwell everything we know," Thorson said. "Despite my objections, she subjected our daughter to aggressive questions. We filled in the blanks. I have nothing more to tell you."

"Where is your brother?" Jeffrey asked.

Thorson sighed and shook his head at the unexpected change in subject. "I've also answered that question a dozen times. I don't know."

"When did you last hear from him?"

He closed his eyes and shook his head, telegraphing his annoyance. "In mid-January, the day of his arrest."

"That would be January 18th?" Barnwell asked.

"If you say so. I haven't seen or spoken with him since."

"You're sure?" Jeffrey asked.

"Of course, I'm sure." His voice turned from annoyance to anger. "How many times do I have to answer this question? Brad did what he did, but I'm paying the penalty. You arrested and charged him. Then you released him—why, I don't know. He skipped out. You're asking me where he is? You should look for him."

Jeffrey cast a sidelong look at Barnwell, who, taking his cue, said, "We've found him."

"You have?" A note of incredulity this time.

"Rather, your daughter did," she said.

Thorson either didn't get it or pretended not to. He rested his chin on his fist, stared at her, then shifted his gaze to Jeffrey. "What is that supposed to mean?"

"The body she found beneath the bridge. It was your brother."

He leaned back in his chair, again shifting his attention from one detective to the other. "What is this? Some kind of joke?"

Jeffrey retook the lead. "On the night of February 6th, as the snowstorm moved in, a vehicle turned off North Fork onto Old Mill and parked alongside the bridge. At least two people emerged from the car and pulled out your brother's body. They dragged it down the bank and beneath the bridge, covered it with some rotting fence slats, and left. Snow and ice concealed the body, which wasn't discovered until Cindy's dog got off his leash."

Thorson's mouth dropped open. His eyes fixed on the microphone resting between him and the two detectives. "I had no idea," he said. "Who left him there? Why?"

"That's what we'd like to know," Jeffrey said. "It's why I'm asking."

His head jerked up. His shoulders twitched. "Why ask me? I had nothing to do with this."

"Your brother led a small gang of thieves who stole money, credit cards, and IDs from travelers at the airport security line. They got caught. Walker's accomplices fingered him as the mastermind. You were the supervisor on duty through much of this."

Thorson spoke with defiance, enunciating each word as though speaking to a child. "It went on beneath my nose. I'm aware of how that looks, but I knew nothing about it."

Jeffrey continued as though he hadn't spoken. "When he didn't show for the formal arraignment, everyone thought he'd gone into hiding. But that's not what happened, is it? You found him, held him captive for a few days to get information from him. What did you need to know?"

"Nothing." He leaned forward in his chair, raising his voice until it filled the room. "I didn't — What are you saying? Someone kidnapped him?"

"Did you get what you wanted from him, or did he refuse to talk?" Thorson shook his head. "Why did you kill him?"

Thorson became an ice sculpture. Not even his chest moved. "He was killed?"

"Murdered," Barnwell said. "He was poisoned."

Thorson closed his eyes and turned his head from side-to-side. "Brad, Brad, Brad. Why did it come to this? Who did this to you?"

He wiped tears from both eyes. Barnwell saw they were genuine. But was it all an act? If so, she thought, it's a damn good one.

"Where did you hold him?" Jeffrey asked. "Did you grab him after the preliminary hearing, or did he run off on his own and reach out to you for help?"

"As God is my witness, I took no part in this. I didn't know what had become of him until this moment. I don't know who did this to him or why."

"We're getting his phone records today. Our team

upstairs will trace his last location. We'll find where you kept him."

Thorson glared at him, his soft mouth set in a perfect line. "Do I have to talk to you? Don't you have to read me my rights?"

When Jeffrey paused, Barnwell took over. "We haven't formally charged you. But once we've found answers to our last few questions, we will. We'll give you the Miranda warning then, but you can look it up on your own. You don't have to talk to us now, or ever. It's your choice. And you may want to find yourself an attorney."

"Don't you have to give me a lawyer? I can't afford one. I'm going through all this TSA bullshit on my own."

"If you convince the court you can't afford your own counsel, they'll assign a public defender. But that's only if we file charges."

He took a deep breath and planted his hands on the edge of the table.. "That's it for now? I'm free to go?"

"You are," Jeffrey said. He ended the recording.

Thorson rose, carrying his jacket in one hand. "You guys have this all wrong," he said. "I didn't kill my brother. The last time I saw him was the day he was arrested. And I was suspended, in case you've forgotten."

Barnwell escorted him out the door and returned to Jeffrey's office as he stacked papers and slid them into the file. Looking up, he gave her the slightest of smiles. "What do you think?"

She took a deep breath before plunging ahead, recalling all the objections she'd made to her own conclusions. "He's pretty convincing," she said. "Maybe we've got this wrong. Perhaps he's telling the truth."

Jeffrey shook his head. "No way," he said. "Have you looked at his background?"

She shook her head. She'd been so focused on where Walker had been held and, then, consumed by anger over being sidelined, she had neglected this most elementary step.

"He's a Point Park grad." He slapped the file folder closed with a thump and flashed her a sarcastic smile. "Drama major."

THREE ROWS of cardio machines looked out on the indoor swimming pool — one with cycling equipment, another with treadmills, and the third with elliptical trainers. A bank of overhead TV monitors faced them. Most were tuned to sports channels, but one was reserved for news. It was usually tuned to a cable service, but on this day, it carried KDKA's early afternoon news.

Moira Buller had just finished a training session with an overweight man who confused chatter with exercise. He'd spent most of his hour telling tales about his grandchildren and talking with friends who he seemed to have known since grade school. How anyone in his sixties could cling to memories of third grade was beyond her, but it seemed to be a fixture of life in Pittsburgh. Grabbing the towels her client had dropped on the floor, she left the office where she weighed guests before and after training. She passed behind the row of ellipticals, giving the monitors a fleeting glimpse.

She stopped in her tracks. The screen showed a reporter standing in waning light before the Old Mill Bridge. The image of the man who'd called himself Carl Ferris appeared, a man now identified as Brad Walker. Below his photo was his name and the years of his birth and death.

So they'd not only identified him, but released his name

to the public. Moira couldn't hear the audio. You need to wear headphones to do so. But something about the story—its length, perhaps—told her this was more than just another progress report.

As she stared at the screen forty feet away, she saw the banner at the bottom. That couldn't be right.

Her breath caught in her throat. Her lips trembled as she stood in the narrow aisle between the offices and machines, holding the towels at her side like a Roman statue.

"Moira?" said a voice behind her. "Moira? Move. I gotta get through." The trainer put a hand on her shoulder and moved her aside. "You all right?"

"Yeah. I thought I saw something."

"You sure? Your skin's gone all pasty looking."

"I'm fine, I told you."

"Okay, okay. I was just checking. Jesus Christ!" the trainer hissed as she moved past her.

Moira looked down, her breath coming in quick gasps. Aware she was hyperventilating, she tottered toward the front desk, dropped the towels in the hamper, and entered the employee changing room. She sat on a bench, her head in her hands, controlling her breathing until the moment passed. Opened her locker. Took out her phone. Clicked on the web browser with shaking hands. Typed KDKA. Scrolled until she found the story.

She left the phone on the bench, stumbled into a stall, and vomited.

———

Annette Henley didn't watch the news. She didn't listen to newscasts. Didn't read the paper. Wars raged, elections came and went, the high and mighty fell from their pedestals with no awareness on her part. Except for the "Stillers," of course. Anything having to do with Pittsburgh's NFL team arrested her attention. The Penguins, not so much. The Pirates not at all, unless she scored a free ticket from someone at work. Otherwise, the world spun on its axis without her aid or hindrance. Keep Pandora playing through her earbuds and Netflix streaming on her TV, and Annette camped happily.

She pulled her pickup into Freddy's Beer Stop along the highway and rolled the bed cover open a crack. It wouldn't do to have a half case of beer alongside her if a cop pulled over her for some imagined violation. They loved to ticket people along this stretch. Women driving alone, Blacks or Hispanics, any easy prey.

She wandered up the aisle of the store until she found a twelve-pack of Iron City, carried it to the cash register, and stood as an old geezer stood fishing in his pockets for bills. "And two scratch-offs," he told the owner, whose name was not Freddy or even Fred. The old man scratched the two cards with a coin.

Her eyes drifted to the small TV set on the shelf behind the register. WPXI's evening news was on. Nothing that interested her. She cleared her throat, but the owner looked up and gave the slightest of shrugs. "Crap!" the customer said. "Gimme a Pick-3: 2-5-6."

The owner took the man's dollar, ran the number through his machine, and handed him the ticket. The man fumbled at the pocket of his flannel shirt. Annette was tempted to ask if he needed help. She emitted a long sigh, hoping he'd take the hint, but the man stood there, taking up space. The line of cigarette packs behind the counter tempted her, but she stuck another piece of gum in her mouth to combat a relapse.

Her eyes returned to the screen. Some fool reporter was standing in front of the Old Mill Bridge, yapping about something or other. She couldn't make out what he was saying, but as traffic passed behind him, she wondered why they'd sent him out to stand in the cold. Was it just about being there? Wasn't that the name of an old movie? Who was the actor? Peter Sellers. He played a character named Chauncey Gardiner. Despite her annoyance at the customer, she smiled, recalling how her mother had watched the film over and over until the cassette got tangled in the machine. That was the end of the film. And of the VCR, come to think of it.

The old man stopped talking and tucked his six-pack under one arm while tapping his cane with the other. In the silence, she caught a snatch of the reporter's banter: "... searching for the killer..."

*Killer?* she thought. *What the hell are they talking about?*

---

Sharon Easterling had spent the day in bed, alternately weeping and sleeping. She'd had nothing to eat except a piece of toast with butter and strawberry jelly for breakfast. She'd had little coffee. It made her too nervous. She'd drunk tea, instead, and didn't understand why she still felt jittery.

The visit from the two detectives had sent her over the edge. It made no difference what Annette had told her. Those cops knew something. Or suspected it. And they wouldn't leave her alone until they found out what she was hiding.

Which wasn't much. Annette and Moira had cleaned the place up, removing any trace of Jerry's presence. Not that Jerry Pratt was his name. They hadn't been able to tell who he really was. He'd sat there, his hands and ankles tied to the chair, refusing to say anything. Even when he had to go and she couldn't get there fast enough and would have been too scared to free him on her own and he'd peed all over himself. That had been disgusting to her and humiliating to him, but still he hadn't talked.

When the two women helped her strip him and tied him to the toilet seat, he'd still been unwilling to answer the simple questions: Who are you, and where's our money?

The Hallmark movie ended. Another one began, but she'd already seen it. She rose from the couch, smoothing the blanket over the cushion he'd ripped when he fought back as they confronted him. God, that Moira woman was strong. She padded out to the kitchen in her slippers, found a can of chicken noodle soup, poured half the contents into a bowl, and stuck it in the microwave.

The bowl was so hot when she tried lifting it off the turntable, she slopped it all over the nuker. Balancing it between a pair of cloth potholders, she lowered it onto a plate, stuck a spoon in it, and carried it back to the living room. She'd clean up the mess later.

Sharon picked up the remote and clicked up and down the channels. She found nothing to watch at this hour. For days, she'd avoided watching the local news, but in the absence of anything else on, she turned to WTAE. She slurped at her soup as the sports reporter recounted the latest from spring training camp. A last look at the weather, two minutes of a commercial for a bath remodeling store that promised no payments and no interest for twenty-four months. *But then what?* she wondered. She had no job, no prospect of one, and Jerry had stolen her life savings.

With that thought, tears cascaded down her cheeks. Perhaps she should just end it. It would be easier on her and on everyone else. Not that there was anyone left to care. This realization only deepened her despair. She lowered her head and bawled, rocking back and forth, hugging herself, the sound of her suffering echoing through the old house but unheard by anyone else.

The next half-hour of news began. There was only thirty minutes' worth, repeated three times. Same stories. Same commercials. Victim identified. Cause of death...

Had she heard that right? Her hand shot out for the remote, and she boosted the audio as she stifled her sobs. "The medical examiner has ruled Walker's death a homicide after it was determined he'd been poisoned..."

She stared at the screen in disbelief as the reporter continued. "County police ask anyone with information about his murder..."

*Murder?* she thought. Her hand opened, and the remote tumbled into what remained of the soup. *Who said anything about murder?*

---

Cathy Thorson emptied the last of the wine bottle into her husband's glass. Their daughter had gone to bed. She'd showered and donned her pajamas, but wasn't ready to turn in. Instead, she sat across from Ben and leaned on the hands she'd folded as though in prayer. "What's wrong?" she said.

Thorson looked up from his phone and stopped scrolling through messages for a moment. "Nothing," he said in a solicitous voice. "What makes you say that?"

"You're acting nervous lately. You toss in your sleep. Today, you left earlier than usual, but you didn't come home until late."

"I had to cover another shift," he said. He looked down at his phone again.

"I don't see your badge. You used to put it on the dresser at night. You haven't worn it in weeks."

He sighed, turned his phone over, and stared at her before answering. "I'm not working for TSA at the moment. Now that the holiday's over, they've cut back on shifts. I'm filling in at a shipping company, and my hours are all over the place."

"Why haven't you mentioned this?" she demanded.

"I didn't want to upset you," he said. "It's not a big deal. I'm still working at the airport. When summer vacation comes, TSA will recall me."

"It's spring break," she said. "All those families flying down to Florida. Don't they need you now?"

Ben Thorson sighed and picked up his phone. "Don't walk away from me," she said. But he did so anyway. Cathy rose from the table and transferred cups and plates to the dishwasher. She turned on the TV, caught the start of a newscast, and was about to change channels when a breaking news story made her stop. "Ben," she shouted.

"What?" he called from the bedroom.

"They say your brother is dead. Come see this. They say he was murdered."

He returned to the living room, leaning against the bedroom door. "I know."

"You know? When did you find out?" When he hung his head without responding, she repeated the words with which she'd confronted him minutes before. "What's wrong, Ben? I need to know."

"The police told me this afternoon. That's why I'm preoccupied."

"Why didn't you tell me?"

For a moment, he said nothing, covering his mouth with his hand and looking down at her feet. "Look, there's some stuff going on I haven't wanted to mention. I know how nervous and upset you get."

"Don't put this on me," she said. "You're hiding something. Tell me what it is."

It took several seconds before he responded. When he did so, his voice had a slight tremor, and he spoke so softly she could barely make out his words. "This thing with Brad, it's pretty serious." He returned to the table, motioned her to sit across from him, and said, "They think I killed him."

Her mouth fell open. She jerked as though struck, and a wave of nausea swept over her. "How can they say that?"

"That scam he was running on the security line?"

"Scam? He was stealing from people."

Ben shrugged, as though the distinction was irrelevant. "They have it in their heads that I knew about it and let it happen. They've suspended me while they investigate. It's taking forever."

She shook her head and buried it in her hands. "I warned you to stay clear of him. When he came back into your life, I knew something like this would happen."

He continued as though she hadn't spoken, his voice cracking. "So now they think I did away with him to keep him from implicating me. I did no such thing."

"I know you didn't," she said, reaching out and grasping his hand. "That little bastard has caused you trouble since you were kids. I'm glad he's gone. But you? You're always making excuses for him, always giving him a second and third and fourth chance. You'd never hurt him. You wouldn't hurt anyone."

CHAPTER EIGHT

LYDIA APPROACHED a small brick house sporting a pair of curved dormer second-floor windows. Squirrel Hill was one of the most fashionable Pittsburgh neighborhoods, the home to many members of the Jewish community whose Tree of Life Synagogue had suffered the worst antisemitic attack in US history a few years before.

A short, wiry man with a mane of unkempt salt and pepper hair answered the door. "You're the detective?" he asked. He stuck out his hand and said, "David Faber. Faber, as in the college."

When Barnwell looked confused, he added, "Animal House?"

She smiled, but shook her head. "Sorry, professor."

"My generation gap is showing," he said, returning the smile. He retreated into the house and ushered her in. The front of the living room was cloaked in dark draperies, but dozens of signed photographs adorned the long wall facing it. She studied the faces, a few of which she recognized. "All students of mine," he said. "Some have done very well."

A woman appeared from what Lydia took to be the

kitchen carrying a tea service. The professor introduced her as his wife. While she poured both of them cups, Professor Faber said, "Some never leave, but they build successful careers. A few work on Broadway, others in TV or films. They travel to New York to audition. When they get a part, they stay there for the length of the production, then return until they land their next role. They keep their base of operations here because of the low cost of living."

The longer she stayed in Pittsburgh, the more curious things she discovered about the city. "But you didn't come here for that. What's this about Ben Thorson? I hope he's not in some sort of trouble."

"We've just identified a body as that of his half brother," she explained. "He was murdered, so we're running checks on everyone who knew him."

The professor gasped and shook his head. "Just a matter of routine, I hope?"

"Exactly."

"I don't recall meeting any of Ben's relatives. I don't think I knew what his family situation was. That's not unusual. If parents live in the area, they attend our productions. Otherwise..." He let the rest of the sentence dangle.

Lydia had spent the evening learning what she could about the brothers. They'd been raised in Louisville, and as Thorson had told her, had different fathers. Ben had left after high school and come to Pittsburgh to attend Point Park University. He'd never been in trouble. Nor had his half brother until his arrest at the airport four months before. Brad, three years younger, graduated from the same high school, but hadn't been a good student. Instead of attending a university, he enrolled in a community college, earned an associate degree, and held a succession of small white-collar jobs, none of which lasted for long.

"What kind of student was he?" she asked.

"Attentive. Hard working. He was quick to learn his lines, took direction well, showed up on time. You'd be surprised how many don't." She refrained from injecting that she wasn't at all surprised. "Pretty agreeable, as I recall. Didn't bring a lot of ego to the roles he played. That's also rare."

"A model student?" she said.

"In most ways." He used his middle finger to steer his cup around in a circle. "He had one fault, and it sometimes got in the way. I said he had no ego. He didn't consider himself a star. But he demanded a lot of others. He wanted things done a certain way, and when they weren't, he become somewhat—" He searched for the right word.

"Controlling?" she suggested.

"That may be too strong. He expected a lot of himself and assumed others did the same. When they didn't, he lost patience with them."

"Did this lead to any altercations?"

"None that I'm aware of," he said. Faber looked about the room, hunting for the right word. "He just cut them off, as though they weren't worthy of his time. I think others mistook him for a snob, but he wasn't."

Despite her questioning, the professor couldn't come up with an example, so she moved on. "With all the education and stage experience Point Park gave him, why isn't he acting?"

Faber leaned toward her and removed his glasses. "Success in this business isn't just a matter of talent. Some is sheer luck. If you don't find roles that get you noticed, you're always consigned to bit parts. That's not enough to live on. While many of my students enjoy successful careers, the majority go on to something else. The skills they learn here can be useful in other endeavors."

"Sales, for instance," she said.

"Great example. Also, the hospitality industry. Managing a restaurant, for instance. It takes a good actor to put on a reassuring front when things are falling apart in the kitchen."

"So Thorson tried, but failed," she said.

"There was another thing, but it's nothing he could do much about. Have you met him? Then you've seen how attractive he is in a feminine sort of way. I'm not suggesting he's gay, though he might have been. Many actors are. They learn to play roles long before they come to me, so acting comes naturally to them. But Thorson's appearance was too delicate to make him a leading man. Action films, war stories, detective roles—I couldn't see him in any of these."

"But a good actor?" she said.

"That he was, but he was tough to cast."

***

Barnwell left the professor's home with a more complete picture of Ben Thorson's life. He'd studied to become an actor, put in long hours, and probably worked to raise his own tuition, given his family situation. Perhaps he'd taken out student loans. All the effort had gone for naught. He'd taken other jobs. Most actors did something else while they waited for a break, but his had never come. He'd found himself trapped in a job that, while it paid well, didn't take advantage of his acting skills.

Then his brother had ruined even that. Did Thorson have a piece of the illicit action? She'd seen no sign of it at his apartment. Had he turned his back on Walker's activities out of filial loyalty? He hadn't sounded supportive. While her visit hadn't produced any revelation, she'd learned that if he was lying to them, he'd studied how to do so convincingly.

She'd also learned he was controlling, though Faber had rejected the term. Was exacting the word he'd been searching for? What she suspected from Cathy's body language was that he channeled it into his life at home. Had he displayed it at work? If so, how had he missed what Brad Walker was up to? A man who went by the book supervising a sibling who tore it to shreds.

Is that what had made him crack? Had he learned about Walker's activities, tried to put an end to it, and when the operation blew up, put an end to him?

As she crawled through the morning traffic on the Fort Pitt bridge—Why was there always a traffic jam here?—her cell made the distinctive ring that proclaimed Jeffrey's call. He didn't use her direct line unless he had something he didn't want on the police scanner.

"Barnwell," she said.

"The digital forensics team has his cell phone records. They've pinged his last location."

"Yes?" she said when he went no further.

"When I looked it up, I recalled seeing it in the report you wrote about your search yesterday. You've already visited this place."

Barnwell didn't have to ask for the location, but she did so anyway. "I'm heading out there now," he said. "You want to meet me?"

Calvin was supposed to move in this afternoon. She'd promised to help. But he, above all people, would understand. "Wait up," she said. "I'm in the Fort Pitt tunnel, headed your way."

BARNWELL EMERGED FROM THE TUNNEL, climbed Greentree Hill, and exited at Parkway Center. Jeffrey stood at the ACPD entrance and climbed in. She was back on the interstate in two minutes. "What tipped you off?" he asked. "You knew the location before I even mentioned it."

"She was incredibly nervous when we spoke to her. She explained a doctor was treating her for depression. Officer Foster thought she was about to explode. Her words. I asked her to do a wellness check in a few days."

"We're doing one now," he said.

As she drove, she recounted her conversation with the drama professor and speculated about why Thorson might have abducted his brother. Nothing she suggested made sense to them. "And why dump his body where he did?" she said, repeating the question that dogged her for the nth time. "It's like leaving breadcrumbs to follow."

"Hmm," Jeffrey said, though whether in agreement or to acknowledge he was listening, she couldn't tell. "We may soon know."

She drove past Old Mill Bridge and the police station, turning off North Branch onto the gravel driveway to the house. With most of the snow melted, the deep ruts were even more obvious. The cruiser bottomed out in one spot. She followed the drive to the side of the house, parking behind a Chevy Camaro over two decades old. "She has company," Jeffrey said.

"No, I think that's her car. She may have just returned and plans to go out again."

She tried ringing the doorbell, remembered it didn't work, and knocked at the front door. Getting no response, she knocked louder. She learned to the right of the porch to peek through the front window, but saw nothing. "Let's check around back," she said.

They walked around the house, peering through each window, and stepped onto the back stoop. She knocked again, cupping her eyes to block the sun as she looked into the kitchen. "Maybe she's upstairs, sleeping. Do we need a warrant?"

"We have evidence a murder victim was held here. If she's inside, she may try to destroy physical evidence. Don't you agree?"

"That and the need to check on her condition." She turned the door handle, which offered no resistance. She stepped inside. "Ms. Easterling?" she called. "Sharon?"

Empty soup cans littered the kitchen counter. The remains of one had congealed in a saucepan on the stove. An unwrapped loaf of white bread lay on the counter, the exposed slices hard to the touch. Barnwell made a cursory search of the dining room, which looked like it hadn't been used in weeks. Its table was marred by scratches and fossilized stains. In the living room, she found a tattered sofa with a blanket at one end and throw pillows cast to one side, an armchair, and an old television set. A half-eaten bowl of soup rested on the coffee table alongside an open bag of saltines and a stack of paperback romance novels.

Barnwell called again and crept up the narrow stairway, walking to one side to make as little noise as possible. *As though a sleeping woman wouldn't have heard my calls*, she thought. At the top of the stairs, facing doors led to two rooms. The one to the left was dark. Its shades were pulled. Jeffrey, who'd followed her, not bothering to match her light tread, reached behind her to flip the switch. The room remained in darkness, but the thin blade of sunlight from the hallway window showed a single bed. When she ran a hand across the comforter, dust flew off.

She turned the handle of the other door and found a room in chaos. The bed was unmade. Piles of clothing littered the floor. The venetian blinds on the single window were closed, but two slats were missing. The bathroom was in similar disarray: open jars of face cream, an uncapped tube of toothpaste, towels scattered on the floor. There was no sign of life here.

They returned to the ground floor. "Let's check the basement," Jeffrey said. He turned the switch and a single light came on from a bare bulb over the stairway. Navigating the stairs demanded caution, as the wooden steps gave a bit with each footfall. "Watch it," he warned, spotting a plank cracked in the middle. "No one's been down here for a while."

"I'm not so sure about that," she said as she scanned the room with a flashlight. A furnace dominated the back wall, but alongside it a toilet was anchored to the floor and a shower head protruded from the wall above a drain. Called a Pittsburgh potty, it had been used by coal workers returning home after a day in the mines. They entered by the basement door, went to the bathroom and showered, and only then joined their family upstairs. A washer and dryer, both decades old, stood to the right of the commode. "She could put these to some use," she said, recalling the clothing piled on the bedroom floor.

"But look how the floor's been swept." Her light illuminated tracks through the dirt on the concrete floor, as though someone had passed a broom over it. Following the path, she focused the beam on an ancient corn broom whose red handle rested against a corner.

"And look here." An upholstered chair sat against a

wall, nestled between two metal shelving units filled with paint and brushes, weed killer, detergent, and other cleaning products. "Notice the scuff marks in the dust where someone's dragged it?"

"Umm," Jeffrey said. He opened his cell phone and turned on the flashlight app. "It stinks to high heaven. Someone's urinated in it." He stared at her for a moment, asked her to train her light on the marks on the concrete, and knelt next to the chair. He uttered another guttural sound. "A line of paint's been stripped from the back legs, and it appears to be recent. See how fresh the wood beneath it looks?"

She leaned over him and studied the spot. "Tape," she said.

"My guess, too, but the crime lab will tell us for sure. Still," he said, rising to his feet so fast she had to spring out of the way, "no sign of the owner."

Barnwell bowed her head. "Oh, no," she groaned. Without a word, she turned and crept up the rickety stairs and out the front door, with Jeffrey in pursuit. She approached the old Chevy, gave a quick look inside, then advanced on the garage and stood on tip-toes to look through the windows.

"Oh, God!" she said. She pulled at the handle, and the door creaked back on its hinges, revealing a body dangling from a rope tied across the rafters.

---

IN THE HANDS of a skilled executioner, hanging is an efficient and purportedly painless way to end a human life. The hangman measures and weighs his victim, calculates the drop needed to kill him, and measures the length of rope that will accomplish the task. He then mounts the neck of the noose to the left side of the prisoner's neck and opens a trapdoor. The subject drops, gaining speed as he falls. If the hangman has calculated the drop accurately, the victim suffers a jolt that breaks the neck bone, severing his spinal cord. While the body may twitch for a few seconds and bodily functions continue unabated for several minutes, the victim feels no pain because the impulses never reach his brain.

That is the theory. No one thus dispatched has confirmed it.

When performed by an amateur, however, death is neither instantaneous nor painless. Whether dropped from a small height or partially suspended from a ligature attached to a brace of some sort, the body's weight tightens the noose around the neck, compressing the arteries that provide oxygen to the brain. It swells, blocking the top of the spinal column and pinching the vagal nerve, bringing on a heart attack. Death can take from ten to twenty minutes, during which the victim is aware for a time as he suffocates. It is an excruciating death, second only to being burned alive.

Sharon's neck was suspended from a length of blue, braided rope, but her feet touched the concrete surface of the garage. This was a partial suspension, a method of hanging Barnwell knew was agonizingly slow. Sharon's eyes bulged, broken veins painted her face like red pick up sticks, and her tongue hung from her mouth. Worse than the sight was the smell for, as is common in all deaths, her bladder and sphincter had released their contents.

Jeffrey donned a pair of plastic gloves and felt for a pulse, a superfluous act that nonetheless had to be performed. "Cold," he said. "The forensics team will tell us for sure, but she did this overnight or sometime yesterday."

"You're assuming it's suicide?" Barnwell asked.

He shrugged. "You told me she was nervous and depressed."

Barnwell looked around the garage, trying to picture how she'd managed the grisly task. A ladder lay behind her, its legs locked in place. She imagined Sharon backing her car out and closing the door, fashioning a noose on one end of the rope, standing on the ladder to loop the free end around the rafter—she counted six turns around the beam—and knotting it. Finally, standing on the ladder, placing the loop around her neck, and kicking the support away.

Had she known the loops would tighten and the rope would stretch, leaving her feet dangling on the floor? Had she ever paused as she executed these steps to consider other options? Barnwell was struck by how purposeful she had been, how painstaking her preparations.

"Should we cut her down?" she asked.

"No. I've alerted the ME. They're on their way." In her shock, Barnwell hadn't noticed him leave the garage. "They'll want to see this the way we found it."

*Her*, Barnwell thought. *Not it. Her.* But she kept the rebuke to herself. She closed the garage door and, while she waited for the medical examiner's team, stood guard.

She radioed the North Fayette police department to alert them to what they'd found. Minutes later, Nadine Foster pulled up the driveway. Barnwell motioned her to park alongside the county cruiser, hidden from the street. "If neighbors see all this activity, we'll attract a crowd," she explained as the officer stepped out of her vehicle.

Lydia introduced her to Detective Jeffrey, who'd been sitting in their cruiser on the radio. He extended his hand

and said, "Barnwell's told me what a fine job you're doing," he said. "Thanks for all your help."

Barnwell was grateful for his acknowledgment. The county detective didn't always show such deference to a local cop, as she well knew. For her part, Foster rewarded him with a grin and said, "All part of the job."

Turning to Lydia, she said, "Suicide?" Her face was contorted in pain.

"That's what it looks like," Barnwell replied.

"I did as you asked, came by yesterday morning to check up on her. She didn't seem as nervous as the day before, said her physician had prescribed an antidepressant. She told me she felt better, but that it was making her woozy. I didn't question her, but she blocked the door and seemed relieved when I left."

Taking the information in, Barnwell looked north toward the ridge line on the opposite side of the road. Had Easterling forgotten to take her medication, or had it not worked as well as she thought? Had the prescription had the opposite of its intended effect, deepening her depression? "It's damn tragic," Foster said, bringing her back to the present.

Before she could think of a suitable response, the medical examiner's van inched up the gravel drive. Brandy Timmons stepped out from the passenger's side, cocked her head toward Barnwell and said, "We have to stop meeting like this."

She'd never known members of the team to show a sense of humor as they went about their gruesome tasks. Not knowing how else to respond, Barnwell said, "Yes."

Timmons asked what they'd found, and Jeffrey took over. As he pulled up the garage door, its arms creaked, protesting the weight and begging for oil. Her crew followed him, photographing the body and the scene. Soon, they'd cut Sharon's body down. Barnwell didn't care to witness it.

"What do we do now?" she asked as Jeffrey emerged from the garage.

"We wait." There it was again: she, prepared to lunge forward despite any obstacle, while Jeffrey expected events to come to him. As she tried to control her impatience, she said, "Where's his car?"

He raised his eyebrows, trying to follow her thoughts. "Either someone brought Brad Walker to this house, or he came here on his own," she explained. "In either case, what's become of his vehicle?"

"We've been looking for it ever since he failed to appear in court. Until now, we've assumed he left the state. It appears he didn't get far." He rubbed his hands together against the chill. "You've asked a damn good question."

Still, he seemed content to stand guard before the garage, waiting for the crime scene investigators to finish their work. She needed something to do. "Do you mind if I take a look in the house?"

"You know the routine. Keep gloves on and bag anything you take with you." *Yes*, she thought, *I do know the routine*. But she acknowledged the warning and took the North Fayette officer with her as she reentered the house.

"What are we looking for?" Foster asked.

"A note. Her medications. Anything that can shed light on what she did and why."

While Nadine worked the first floor, Barnwell returned to the basement. Aiming a flashlight around the room, she spotted a single bulb dangling from a cord above the washer. Why hadn't Sharon replaced it? She reached up, intending to unscrew it, but as she touched the bulb, it flickered. She twisted it in the opposite direction, and the room was painted in weak light. It was evidently connected to the same circuit as the overhead fixture on the stairway. Why had someone unscrewed it?

She inspected the chair, paying attention to the back legs where the paint had been stripped. There was a pronounced urine odor too strong to have been made years or even months before. The exposed surface of the wooden legs, which had been stripped of black paint, was about two inches wide. With considerable effort, since it was heavier than it looked, she flipped the chair over and saw paint had also peeled off the rungs linking the front and back legs. She took photos and returned the chair to its original position.

In the light of the forty-watt bulb, the attempt to clean the cellar became more apparent. Piles of dust lay beneath the shelving where the broom couldn't reach. Near the center of the room, a clean patch, a yard square, interrupted the sweeping pattern. Barnwell studied it, got down on her knees, and sniffed at it. A chemical smell assaulted her. Backing toward the edge of the cleared area, she detected an equally recognizable odor, identical to the stench emanating from the chair.

She took another photo, although she knew the forensics team would treat the area to illuminate it. Rising to her feet, she examined the potty, noticing as she did so that this area too had been scrubbed. She got down on her knees again and flashed her torch around the back of the bowl. Although she knew what she'd spotted, she couldn't see it clearly and knew not to remove it. Angling her phone behind the base, she took three photos, rose to her feet again, and studied them. She'd caught only an edge of the object in the first frame, and the third was out of focus. But the second image displayed a torn strip of duct tape someone had left when they'd torn it from the commode.

A single door led outside, standard issue in a house once occupied by a miner. It was locked. Turning her attention to the metal shelving, she searched through the bottles of cleaning supplies and chemicals. Behind a gallon bottle of Pine-Sol, she found a roll of duct tape. She'd leave it to the forensic experts to make certain, but it resembled the strip she'd found behind the toilet.

Barnwell had learned what she needed to know. Brad Walker had been held here, tied first to a chair and, when he soiled himself, confined to the toilet seat. She returned to the main floor, where Nadine had finished searching. "Found anything?" she asked.

"The keys to her car were on the kitchen counter, along with a pay stub from a warehouse store in Robinson Township. There's no sign of her meds."

The pair went upstairs. The heaps of clothing on the floor made searching difficult. Despite forty-five minutes of work, they found no trace of the antidepressants Sharon Easterling was supposed to have had. Nor of another object Barnwell hoped to find.

They left the house, but she took the long way around it as she returned to the garage, pausing at the side door that led to the basement. Someone had rolled a large rock down the three concrete steps, wedging it against the door. Even had Walker untied himself and forced the lock, he couldn't have opened it.

At the garage, the medical team was loading a body bag into the forensics van. "Before you leave," she said, "you need to go through the house." With Jeffrey listening, she told them what she'd found in the basement. "Someone was held captive there. Your crew should go through every floor, gathering prints and DNA samples."

"The man we found beneath the bridge," Brandy said. She didn't pose it as a question, and Barnwell didn't take it as such.

"She'd been prescribed a medication for anxiety, but it isn't in the house. Did you find it in the garage?"

"No," Brandy said.

"How about her phone?"

"No sign of that either."

Barnwell held up a hand as though to keep everyone in place. "Have you determined the cause of death?"

The crime scene investigator narrowed her eyes as she spoke. "That's up to the pathologist."

Barnwell gave her the blue-eyed, x-ray stare that sometimes melted witnesses. It didn't work on Brandy. For some reason, she was unwilling to speculate on what the autopsy might find.

LYDIA DROPPED Jeffrey off at ACPD headquarters and retraced her route to the warehouse Nadine had found on the paystub in the kitchen. She stepped to the member services desk, showed her ID, and asked to speak to the manager. "He's pretty busy right now," the woman behind the counter said.

"So am I," she responded. Five minutes later, a man dressed in a white shirt and blue slacks and a matching badge appeared from somewhere in the store. He introduced himself as Jack Caulfield, flashed two rows of teeth, and said, "You've caught them?"

"I'm sorry," Barnwell said. "Caught who?"

His smile faded. "We had a bunch of thefts out in the parking lot. A gang of young people swiped electronics after dark, took them right off people's carts while they stood helpless. It happened two nights in a row during the Christmas rush, stopped for a while, but resumed last month. I hoped you'd caught them."

"I'll look into it and see if we've made progress," she said, "but that's not why I'm here. It's about one of your former employees, Sharon Easterling."

At mention of the name, the last vestiges of his smile disappeared. Caulfield glanced behind him at the row of customers at the services desk. "I don't think we should discuss this here," he said. He led her into a small office off the break room, sat at the edge of his chair, folded his hands, and said, "I'm not sure I'm free to discuss the situation. What's she done?"

"What sort of situation?" Barnwell prodded.

"I'd better call my regional," he said. "We're protective of our employees, and the courts, you know…"

"Go ahead if it helps, but I need to know why you terminated her employment."

"We didn't," he said.

"She told me she'd lost her job. Perhaps she was moon-lighting somewhere."

"I'm sure she was referring to something that happened here, but we didn't let her go. We suspended her until she gets well." His face brightened. "We're covering her medical bills."

"What seems to be the problem?" Barnwell said.

Caulfield twisted in his seat, picked up a pencil, and played with it. "I'm not at liberty to say."

"She told us she was being treated for depression."

"Then, you know," he said.

Barnwell had grown tired of fencing. "Another officer and I spoke with her two days ago while we were searching for a missing person. She was upset, told us she was under a doctor's care and had lost her job. We had reason to return this morning and found her dead. I want to know what happened here."

The manager gasped. "She killed herself?" It came out as a high-pitched whine.

Lydia noted his assumption, but didn't pursue it. "We're trying to determine that. Why did she leave here?"

Choking back tears, Caulfield reached for the phone, dialed a number, and waited until his regional manager came on the line. He explained the situation and asked if he was allowed to speak to the officer. Barnwell made out the regional's shrill response. "Of course you can," she said. "We've done nothing wrong. Give them your full cooperation."

Caulfield hung up, his hands shaking. "I'm going to bring in the shift supervisor."

It took five minutes before the woman arrived, a delay caused, Barnwell thought, by the fact the manager had washed his face and regained his composure. The supervisor was a youngish woman, just past thirty, dressed in jeans and a tight fitting white shirt. The color combination seemed to constitute a uniform. "Sharon is dead?" she said. "What happened?" Her voice was flat and unemotional.

"You don't seem surprised," Barnwell said.

The woman scratched the back of her neck and stared at the linoleum tile floor. "She was quite a mess. She took her own life, didn't she?"

"The medical examiner will determine that." Barnwell repeated what little the dead woman had revealed about her condition. "She didn't explain what happened here. That's why I'm asking you." Lydia turned her intimidating gaze on each of them.

The woman scratched at her scalp, wrinkled her face, and looked away. "She'd been a pretty good worker until a few months ago. Around Christmas, maybe, she began turning up late. I had to talk to her about it on two occasions. She was missing items on the bottom of the carts. The cashiers had to prompt her to fetch electronic items when a member turned in a card to purchase it. Things were already bad, but then she began taking unscheduled breaks. She'd get upset, wander off for a phone conversation, then come back shaking."

The shift manager turned her attention to Caulfield as though explaining her actions to him. "I knew I was going to have to deal with it. I shouldn't have let it go on so long. It affected everyone's performance. When she freaked out last week, things came to a head."

"We had to suspend her," Caulfield said, "but we sent her to a counselor and told her if she improved, she could return."

"That was not going to happen," the supervisor said.

"One never knows," Caulfield replied.

Barnwell spread her hands. The two could debate this some other time. "You say she 'freaked out.' What does that mean, precisely?"

"She locked herself in a stall and began hallucinating, screaming that someone was out to kill her."

Barnwell forced herself to conceal her reaction. "Who did she say wanted to do this?"

"She didn't. 'They' was all she said. 'They're going to kill me.'"

"And who did you think that meant?" Barnwell asked.

"I figured it was just crazy talk."

"Did she mention anyone specifically?" The shift supervisor shook her head. "Give any clues?" She continued to answer with her head, not saying a word.

Barnwell sighed, twirled her pen in her fingers, and looked past the pair. "Were there any other incidents you can think of? Anything out of the ordinary?"

"No," the supervisor said, but Caulfield raised a finger as though asking for permission.

"What about that thing with her sister?"

"Oh, yeah. That was a couple of weeks ago. This woman comes in—nice-looking girl—and demands to talk to Sharon right away, insists she take a break. She was damn pushy about it. We were busy that day and had to scramble to get coverage."

"Did she tell you what was so urgent?" Barnwell asked.

"Sharon said there was a problem in the family." She grimaced again. "But I remember Marcia, the cashier on duty, saying the sister hadn't mentioned why she needed to interrupt her. She just said they needed to talk. Marcia thought Sharon just assumed that's what her sister needed to discuss with her. But if Sharon knew someone in the family was sick, she didn't need it spelled out, did she?"

"No," Barnwell said, "I suppose not."

<hr>

"I'M sorry I wasn't here to help," Lydia said as she placed her backpack on the counter. Howie ran up to her and attached himself to her ankle.

"I managed," Calvin said. "I'm a big boy."

"You certainly are," she said.

"And I knew you were busy."

"That's an understatement." She opened the refrigerator door and pulled out two cans of amber ale. "I see you've stocked it."

"Moved it, to be precise," he said. He sat at the counter, raised his bottle, and clinked it to hers. "You're certain this is what you want?"

"I am," she said. "Are you?"

"Very." He reached out for her hand. "But my lease doesn't run out until the end of April, so if it doesn't work out..."

"Why wouldn't it?"

"There's the pizza issue," he said.

"I can put up with a bit of pepperoni on occasion. Just not all the time."

They continued bantering for another few minutes. He carried his drink to the dining room table where, she noticed, he'd added more pieces to the puzzle. "Your dog-walker came by," he said. "I told him I had it under control and took Howie out myself."

"You should have let him do it," she said. "We can't be here all the time, and I like to make it part of Tommy's routine."

He took a swig and regarded her over the end of the bottle. "You trust the kid?"

"Absolutely. He even refused to take my money. I had to force it on him."

"Hmm," Mayfield said. "All right, I'll let him do his job. By the way, as I was unpacking, Howie got into some wrapping paper, carried it back to his bed, and tore it into pieces."

"He's building a nest," she said. "I try to keep anything important out of his reach."

"Is he pregnant?" Mayfield asked.

They shared a laugh. Calvin had picked up a small tray

of lasagna for dinner. He returned to the kitchen, leaving the puzzle behind, dialed the temperature into the toaster oven, and removed the aluminum tray from the freezer.

"How are you getting along with Jeffrey?" he asked.

"I was just thinking about it as I parked the car," she said. She told him they'd discovered where Brad Walker had been held before he was killed and had found Sharon Easterling hanging in her garage. "Jeffrey let me search her home with a local officer. He didn't direct me, other than cautioning me to protect evidence. He didn't follow me around, didn't even enter the house. If he's running the investigation now, he's doing it with a light hand."

Mayfield massaged his lower lip. "He must trust you. He recruited you, remember? It's the inspector you have to win over." He turned to find her staring off at a point in space as if she hadn't heard a word he said. "Something wrong?"

Lydia placed both hands on her knees and leaned forward. "Follow this. A woman decides to hang herself in her garage. She pulls her car out, finds some cord, loops it over a rafter, ties it off, and fashions a makeshift noose at one end. Very methodical."

"Okay," Calvin said. The toaster oven dinged, and he slid the meal onto the tray as she continued talking.

"At some point, she locks the car. Why would she do that?"

"It's a normal reaction. You get out of the car, press the fob, and walk away."

"True," she said, "but this is an older car. She had to turn the key in the lock. Or depress the lock on the inside and close the car door. Either way, it was a deliberate act."

"Maybe," he replied, "but she could still have acted out of habit."

"She returns to the kitchen," she continued, as though he hadn't spoken, "and places her car keys on the counter. She returns to the garage, closes the door, and finishes what she started."

"It's the keys that bother you," Calvin said.

"That and a lot of other little things." Should she tell Mayfield she'd expected something like this to happen? She kept the premonition to herself.

"Picture this. Her bedroom is a disaster area. Bed unmade. Clothes all over the floor. I couldn't tell those that were clean from the dirty ones. The bathroom's a mess. I wouldn't pee in there unless I had no other choice. Yet, she takes great care to clean up her basement, where we know she'd held a man captive for at least a day or two."

"Like there were two different people involved, a slob and a neatnik."

The toaster oven chimed. He removed the dish and shoveled it onto two plates. Rather than taking them to the table, they stood at the kitchen counter as she continued speaking. "Then there's her mental condition. She told us she was depressed. Her employer says she suffered a breakdown at work, said people were trying to kill her. They suspended her, but sent her to a counselor who prescribed some sort of medication. Yesterday, she told the local officer it was working, though it made her 'woozy.'"

"Maybe she reacted to the medication," Calvin said between mouthfuls. "Some of this stuff can backfire on you."

"You're right," she conceded, "but compare that to the careful preparations she made in the garage, locking her car, placing her keys on the counter..." Something more tugged at her memory, but she couldn't put a finger on it. "Could she have done all that on her own if the medication made her dizzy?"

She thought for a moment, making a mental inventory of all that bothered her. Her dinner was getting cold, but she paid no attention. "We haven't found her bottle of pills or her phone, but in that hellhole of a bedroom, they could be buried in the debris."

Mayfield finished his beer and fished out two more. He opened them and stared at her, drumming his fingers on the counter. "You don't think it was suicide, do you?"

Lydia closed her eyes, picturing the scene. "The ladder," she said. "It was lying open behind her. Try to imagine you want to hang yourself. You're standing on a ladder. Do you step off it or kick it out from under you? And if you kick it away, in which direction do you push it? Do you have the strength to push it over ... behind you?"

Mayfield gave a rueful smile and nodded his head in time to some imagined melody. "No," he said. "Not while you're dangling. It couldn't have happened that way."

CHAPTER NINE

DETECTIVE SERGEANT LYLE JEFFREY stood as Barnwell entered the office. He pulled a chair from the front of his desk to alongside it and slid his own chair closer. "Let's review what we know," he said. "The crime lab found Walker's prints on the back of the commode in Sharon's basement, so we can confirm that's where he was held. We suspect Thorson had reason to silence him."

He paused, and Barnwell took it as an invitation to argue the point. "The motive hinges on Thorson being aware of his brother's larceny operation, but when we spoke to Jason Crawley, he couldn't implicate. Since he's trying to cut a deal with the DA, you'd think he'd do so."

He made a note to himself. Lydia couldn't decipher his handwriting. "We also can't tie Thorson to Sharon's house or show they even knew each other," she said.

"We're getting her phone records. If they called or texted each other, we'll find out." He made another note, and Barnwell could see he was building a decision tree.

This led them to whoever had taken Walker's body from Sharon's house to within sight of Thorson's apartment on the night of the storm. "The location argues against Thorson playing a role in it," she said. She pushed a curl off her forehead as another thought occurred to her. "What if whoever got rid of his body wasn't the same person who killed him?"

"It's possible." He screwed up his features, his pen poised in mid-air. "This might explain why they left it so near his apartment. If they knew Thorson killed his brother, they used this way to incriminate him."

They sat looking at each other, allowing the unanswered questions to hang between them like a cloud. "By the way, you're right about Walker's vehicle," Jeffrey said. "It's a 2021 Toyota RAV4. Every law enforcement agency east of the Mississippi is on the lookout for it." He shook his head. "When we couldn't locate him or his car in the first few days, we may have assumed he'd left the state and stopped looking close to home. I've issued an alert to every agency in the county to find that car. "

That resurfaced the question she'd asked the day before when they found Sharon's body. "How did Walker get to Sharon's house? Did they abduct him and bring him there, or did they lure him?"

"In either case," he said, finishing the thought, "where's his vehicle? It's not at Sharon's, and we haven't found it anywhere else."

They considered the problem for a moment. "Suppose he drove to Sharon's," Barnwell said. "Wouldn't whoever murdered him place his corpse in the hatch of his own car and abandon it alongside a road or in a parking lot?"

Jeffrey made another note, then struck out in another direction. "We got a warrant for Walker's banking records when he was arrested. I've asked to see them. They may not tell us much. I doubt he would have been stupid enough to deposit cash he took from traveler's wallets into his checking account."

"The gang also took credit cards," she said. "Let's find out if they ran up charges on them before the passengers discovered them stolen."

"Already underway," he said.

"Something else bothers me." He raised his eyebrows and nodded at her to continue. "What if Sharon's death wasn't suicide?" She ran through the litany of questions she'd raised with Mayfield the night before. "The CSI team hasn't recovered her cell phone. They found a lot of pill bottles, but none were antidepressants. We have only her word she was taking them, of course."

"Contact the psychiatrist who was treating her to learn whether he'd prescribed anything."

"It's she." Not wanting to sound confrontational, Barnwell explained. "The store manager provided her name. They've referred employees to her in the past. Do we need a warrant to get at her health records?"

"Given that she's dead, perhaps she'll give us a yes or no on that matter."

"If it wasn't suicide, someone killed her."

Jeffrey twirled the pen in his hand and used it as a pointer while suggesting a chain of events. "Thorson abducts his brother and holds him at Sharon's. When he can't get whatever he wants, he kills him. Sharon helps dispose of the body, then falls apart. To silence her, Thorson hangs her, staging it to look like suicide." He twirled the pen like a conductor ending the last note of a concerto.

Despite the objections she'd raised, Jeffrey couldn't let go of Thorson as a killer. Barnwell wished she'd never suggested it. "Let's not forget what Sharon told her coworker when she had her anxiety attack, that 'they' were trying to kill her. They, meaning more than one."

Jeffrey drew a circle around the chart he'd created, placed arrows at all four points of the compass to make an endless loop, and turned the notepad to face her. "Here's where we are," he said, spinning his pen in the air.

"Let's have another conversation with Thorson."

"First, I want his phone records," he said. "That requires a warrant. Do we have enough evidence to convince a magistrate to issue one?"

"Not yet," Barnwell admitted.

"Okay," he said, leaning back in his chair, "here's the plan. One, you speak to the psychiatrist, see if she'll confirm Sharon was on meds. Two, we await her autopsy to determine whether we're dealing with a suicide or something more. Then, we bring Thorson in, confront him with what we know, and see if we learn enough to justify an arrest. Sound like a plan?"

"And meanwhile?" she said.

Jeffrey exhaled loud enough for a person in the next office to hear. He rubbed his hand across his chin as though in need of a shave. "We wait."

---

Barnwell was prepared to fight her way past Dr. Joy Danoff's palace guard, but the man who answered said the counselor was with a patient and would return her call as soon as the session ended.

With nothing to do, she went over the back-and-forth with Jeffrey. Their next step, he said, was to wait. She was unprepared to do so. Every hour that passed made solving the case more difficult. Witness's memories faded and were replaced by cobwebs. Perpetrators swept their trails clean and shoveled clues into the trash.

Lydia needed to know more about Ben Thorson. She knew where she might find it without a warrant and wouldn't seek Jeffrey's permission. Before she could act, the psychiatrist's assistant called and said he was putting Dr. Danoff on the line.

Barnwell identified herself and thanked her for returning the call. Knowing what she was about to ask might be privileged, she donned her most agreeable tone. "I regret to tell you one of your patients had died. Sharon Easterling."

"Hmm," was all she heard.

"We found her hanging in her garage yesterday. She appeared to have taken her own life, but a few things are making us dig a little deeper."

When the psychiatrist still didn't respond, Barnwell suppressed a laugh. Dr. Danoff was treating her like one of her patients. She needed to turn the tables. "When I spoke to Ms. Easterling earlier in the week, she informed me you'd prescribed medication for her. I know HIPAA protects a patient's personal information. I can get a warrant if I need to. But if she didn't commit suicide—if someone killed her, in other words—I can't afford to waste time. So I have a simple question: was she taking an antide-pressant?"

Barnwell had expected a runaround, but Dr. Danoff gave her a one-word response: "Amitriptyline."

"Thank you, I know this is—"

"It's a common treatment for depression," the psychia-trist added. "While it can help relieve anxiety, it's not fast-acting. It also causes drowsiness, so I'd instructed her to ease into it, taking one in the morning unless she was planning to get behind the wheel and one before bedtime. You can count the remaining pills to see if she was overdosing."

"We haven't found the bottle," Barnwell said.

"I see no reason anyone would have taken it. It's not a narcotic. It's sometimes prescribed for migraines."

She paused as though expecting a response, but she'd spoken so quickly Barnwell was still scribbling when she finished. "Does that answer your question?"

"It does, and I thank you. One more thing if I may? When was her next appointment?"

"Today. She's due here now. It's why I have time to speak with you."

"Oh," Barnwell said. The woman's abrupt, matter-of-fact nature had left her speechless.

"I'm sorry to learn of her death," Dr. Danoff continued. "She was a new patient, and I'd seen her only twice. I was made to understand it was urgent, so I made time in my schedule for her. I sincerely hope she didn't take her own life, but if so, I'm confident I did what I could for her in the short time we had together."

Barnwell suppressed another smile. The woman was rehearsing her response to the plaintiff's attorney. "I'm sure you did," she said.

---

"Am I too early?" Moira Buller turned to find her noon appointment standing behind her, bulging out of her tracksuit, holding a towel in one hand.

"No, you're fine," she said. "I'll be with you in a sec." She stood with her arms akimbo, staring at one of the TV monitors facing the treadmills. The midday news had just started. Though she couldn't hear what was being said, she studied the graphics behind the anchorwoman. A morning accident on Parkway East. A robbery of a jewelry store in Shadyside. An overnight shooting in Wilkinsburg.

The woman behind her cleared her throat. "I'll just be another minute," Moira said over her shoulder. She slid between the ellipticals to study the crawl at the bottom of the screen. It finished with the weather and a promo for the station's news app, then resumed the same list of stories she'd already seen.

"Look," the client said, "I have to get back to work at one. If you're too busy…"

"No, we're fine. I apologize. I was just…" She stopped, unwilling to say what had drawn her attention to the screen. She led the woman to a mat behind the press and curl machines and began a series of stretching exercises.

Had they found the body? There was nothing on the news. Perhaps they didn't report on suicides. She'd heard something to that effect. That must be it. And wouldn't they have reported the death if they'd made the connection to the man she now knew to be Bradley Walker?

Moira felt the tension leave her body. Perhaps she was in the clear.

---

BARNWELL TOOK the elevator to the third floor and started at the end of the hall. No one answered at the first door, nor at the second. When she rang at the next apartment, a young woman opened the door a crack and peered at her. "Baby's asleep," she whispered.

In a low voice, Barnwell identified herself, flashed her badge, and said, "Do you happen to know the Thorson family in 317?"

The woman shook her head. "We're new here. I haven't met many of the neighbors. Except for the old fart next door. I only see him when he bitches about Daphne crying. What am I supposed to do?"

Barnwell thanked her, apologized, and turned to the door across the hall. When she introduced herself, the older woman who answered invited her in. Lydia was about to refuse, but thought it might be a good idea to get out of the hallway, so she agreed. The woman asked if she cared for coffee, and Barnwell refused. "But a glass of water would be nice."

The woman left and returned with a glass filled with ice and a round of lemon perched on the rim. She sat across from the officer, folded her hands in her lap, and leaned forward with a smile on her face. "So what's going on?" she said.

"Nothing that I know of," Barnwell said. "I'm trying to see if anyone knows the Thorson family."

"What's he done?" the woman said, her eyes widening as she awaited information she would surely turn into gossip at the earliest opportunity.

"Do you know him?" the detective repeated.

"I've only seen him leaving for work. He never speaks to me, and I wouldn't try talking to him."

"What about his wife?" Barnwell asked.

"She seems nice enough, but a bit mousy, if you know what I mean."

"I don't," Barnwell said. "What's she like?"

"You really should talk with Greta Norlund. She lives two doors down. She sort of looks after her."

"In what way?"

"Oh, you know," the woman said. And when Barnwell cocked her head to one side, inviting her to dish, she lowered her voice and leaned toward her. "I shouldn't say this, but … I hear her husband can be difficult."

"Controlling?" Barnwell prompted.

"I'm getting this second-hand. You didn't hear it from me. Talk to Greta."

"I will," Barnwell said. She finished her water and stood to leave. "What do you know about the man in 305?"

"Oh, that sourpuss. Always moaning about something. Have you met that nice girl across the hall? Linda? The one with the baby? She has the cutest little girl. Adorable. But whenever she gets hungry, she cries to let mommy know. And Cranmer—that's his name, Frank Cranmer. The name fits. Frank the crank—"

"I take it he doesn't like to hear the baby."

"Doesn't like it?" she said. "He pounds on the wall, comes storming into the hall, and hammers on her door."

"Have you reported his behavior to management?"

"Huh!" the woman said. Barnwell refrained from wiping the spit off her jacket. "You might as well tell Congress. We all have. Many times. They do nothing about it."

Barnwell thanked her and moved down the hall to 311, Greta Norland's apartment. It took a moment before she answered the door, and when she did so, she held a cordless phone in her hand. "You're the police officer Bernice told me about."

*How in God's name had the old gossip been so quick on the draw?* She introduced herself and showed her ID. "You've come about Cathy."

"May I come in?" Barnwell said. "We shouldn't discuss this out here."

"Of course, of course," Norland said, backing into her apartment. She offered Lydia a seat at her dining room table and sat across from her. "What can I tell you? She's a prisoner in that apartment."

"Prisoner?" the detective said, her suspicions about Thorson's role in his brother's abduction sending smoke signals.

"Perhaps that's a bit strong, but she and her daughter are isolated there. She has no car. Her husband goes off to work and doesn't come home until all hours. When he needs groceries, she has to call him to pick them up. When she gets out, he goes with her. I get the impression she has to get his approval for anything she buys, even her own clothes. He's a—" She reached beneath the table, apparently smoothing her skirt. "I'd better not say what I think of him."

"Is he physically abusive?"

"I've asked her, but she doesn't say. Women can be such fools, can't they? She doesn't complain about him. Just says she can't do this and can't do that."

"How did you become so close?" Barnwell asked.

"One day, she needed a prescription of some sort. I don't know if it was for her or Cindy—that's her daughter. We'd talked while we were doing laundry downstairs, and she asked if there was any way I could take her. I was happy to do so. We began having coffee together. Only when he's not there, you understand."

She looked away, resting her index finger on her cheek. "Something's going on there. I'm sure that's why you're asking."

"What sort of thing?"

"He's in some sort of trouble, isn't he? I knocked on her door yesterday, and I could tell she'd been crying. I asked her what was wrong, and she said she couldn't talk about it. 'They say he's done something awful, but he hasn't.' That's what she said. She told me she doesn't know what to do. I tried to get more from her, but she wouldn't tell me."

Her face became a mask of concern. "You folks are questioning him, aren't you?"

"We've asked him to help us with an investigation."

"Is it about the body they discovered at the foot of the hill? It is, isn't it? Did he have something to do with it?"

"I'm not at liberty to discuss our investigation, but we haven't charged him with anything."

"But you're talking to him, aren't you?" She reached out a hand toward the detective, who did not take it. "Please keep me out of it. I live alone. He's right across the hall. I'll tell you the truth. He frightens me."

"I have no reason to mention you at all."

"Good, because if he found out what I do for her..."

"Listening to her? Taking her places?"

"More than that. I sometimes let her take my car when she needs to run errands. I trust her. I've sat alongside her and let her drive. He has her in a cage. If he knew I let her fly free once in a while, he'd be furious."

"I promise," she said. She thanked the woman and left, her suspicions about Thorson reignited. Before leaving the building, however, she returned to 305 and knocked at the door. "What d'you want?" He was an elfin man wearing a two-day stubble and a look of high dudgeon.

Without a smile, she withdrew her badge and allowed him to examine it. "What's wrong?" he snapped.

"We've had reports you're causing a disturbance in the building. We've tried to let management deal with it, but your behavior only escalates. This is just a warning, but the next time you disturb other residents by pounding on some-one's door, we'll be forced to bring charges."

The man stared at her, slack jawed. "Who's complaining?" he demanded.

"We've had more than one report," she said. "Your tantrums disturb many on this floor." She raised a finger. "This is a warning. You don't want to make me come back. Got it?"

"I just want a little peace and quiet."

She leaned toward him. "You're not listening. Perhaps a warning is insufficient."

"Okay, okay," he said. "I didn't know I was disturbing anyone."

She out-stared him until he closed the door. Barnwell left via the stairway, hoping she'd accomplished some good.

---

THE PROJECT ESTIMATOR looked up as Annette Henley returned from the restroom to her desk, her third trip in an hour. "You all right?" he asked.

"I'm fine."

"Because you look kinda—"

"I told you I'm fine," she snapped.

"Oh, sure," he said. "I get it." Donning a cunning expression, he buried his nose in the open file on his desk and tapped figures into his computer.

*So he thinks I'm having my period*, she thought. *If only he knew.* For most of the day, she'd fought nausea, often losing the battle and the contents of her stomach. She had nothing left to give. What came up now was mustard-colored bile, leaving a burning taste in her mouth and throat and a chemical odor so revolting it induced more vomit.

Her reflection in the mirror had startled her. Her skin sagged beneath her eyes and at the corners of her mouth and had the color of albumin. She had no business staying at work, but she'd never taken a sick day and couldn't image breaking her streak. Besides, work gave her something else to think about. She wished she had a cigarette, but knew that the cost of calming her nerves was another round of vomiting.

Annette didn't mourn Sharon. She'd scarcely known the woman and wouldn't have given her a minute of her time if they'd met under different circumstances. She had brought this on herself. Annette didn't know how she had caused the death of that prick, not that she was wasting any tears on him. Perhaps it had been an accident, but why had she given him anything? They'd told her not to harm him. She'd endangered them all by leaving the house when no one was there to take her place.

Sharon had created the mess, then gone haywire, leaving the two of them to clean it up. Had they thought of everything? They couldn't do much about the car. The storm had left them with that detail, too.

They couldn't leave her phone lying around. She'd bombarded both of them with her emotional eruptions. She wondered if they should have left her pill bottle where they'd found it. Ah, well. Too late now.

They'd first had to deal first with him and then with her. If they'd done things right, the cops would tie Sharon to Mike's death—why did she continue to call him that?—and figure she'd killed herself when she thought they were on to her. That would be the end of it.

But could she be sure? She and that fucking phone! Annette launched herself from her chair as another wave of nausea hit her.

"You GOT YOUR WISH." Detective Jeffrey sounded triumphant as his voice barked through her cell phone.

"What wish?" she asked.

"They've found Walker's car. Care to guess where?"

Barnwell was driving through a rainstorm that had kicked up while she was questioning Thorson's neighbors. She needed to concentrate on the winding road. "Tell me," she said.

"The airport parking lot."

It took just a moment to register the implication. "Of course," she said.

Had Thorson been so careless he'd left his brother's body yards from his front door, then abandoned his car in a public parking lot near his work? Of course not. If someone wanted to point the finger at him, however, they would do both. Before she could share the thought with Jeffrey, however, he said, "It's in the long-term lot beneath the 12B sign. I'm headed there now."

"I'll beat you," she said. She doubled back on US 30, took State Road 576 across the interstate, and entered the lot twelve minutes later. As she drove, she tried to square Greta Norland's description of Cathy Thorson's virtual imprisonment with a growing conviction someone was setting Ben up. Couldn't both things be true? She'd talk this through with Mayfield tonight. He was such a great sounding board, if she could tear him away from the jigsaw puzzle.

Despite the pelting rain, she had no trouble finding Walker's Toyota. The flashing lights from the parking security and ACPD cruisers made it easy to spot. She pulled up behind them, fished her rain jacket out of the trunk, and joined the crowd.

"I'm glad you found it," she told an officer, "but why did it take so long?"

"I didn't find it," the officer said. "Officer Rodman from airport security did." He nodded toward an overweight man with water drooling down his face who stood nearby, leaning on the car. "The reason it didn't turn up on the plate scan is because it's obscured."

She glanced at the license plate and saw it had been partially painted over. The middle numeral, eight, had been subtracted to a three. The Turnpike Authority had recently closed its toll booths. Unless a driver had an EZ-Pass mounted on the windshield, the car was identified by its plate number and billed by mail. With tolls at a record high and increasing each year, many had made their plates unreadable by the cameras towering over the highway at each entrance and exit.

"How did you notice it?" she asked the security officer.

"I've always wanted one," he said.

"Please don't lean against the vehicle," Barnwell said. The security officer shrugged and stood up straight, which Barnwell thought would do him good.

"He likes this model," the ACPD patrol officer repeated as though the man hadn't spoken, "so when he sees one, he pays attention."

"The light blue color makes it stand out," the security officer said.

*Though not in this rain*, Barnwell thought to herself. "How long's it been here, do you think?"

"Two, three weeks," he said. Barnwell asked how he was so sure. "We towed a car out of this spot a few weeks back. After it's been here forty-five days, we mark a car abandoned and impound it. No one keeps them here that long, though. It's too expensive."

"You're certain it's this exact spot?" He assured her it was. "And no more than three weeks?"

"Maybe less. I can pull up the date. We take time-stamped photos. We're required to document the whole thing. But you can check it yourself. The ticket's in the visor."

She approached the driver's side window and peered up above the windshield. As he'd said, one-half of the ticket protruded from a clip.

Jeffrey pulled in behind them. She walked to his door and briefed him through his half-open window. He showed no sign of getting out. *Let the new kid drown,* she thought. She told him what steps she was about to take, and he offered to issue the order. From his closed vehicle, of course.

She returned to the group of officers. "No one's to touch this car. We've called for the crime scene investigators. Preserve the scene. This is evidence in a homicide investigation."

THE RAIN HAD ENDED when she arrived home, having clocked out for the day. Lydia parked behind Mayfield's cruiser, surprised to see him home that early. "Hi," she called as she burst through the door. "I thought we'd go out—"

Something in the way he looked up as she glimpsed him at the dining room table made her stop mid-sentence. She entered the room and found him sitting across from Tommy Molnar, who was fitting pieces in the jigsaw puzzle. Half of it was complete, and they were slowly filling in what remained. "You've been busy," she said.

Tommy looked up and grinned. "Never done one of these before," he said.

"I've done too many," she replied, recalling the hours she'd spent putting them together when her father was off doing his bit for the country and ignoring her. "How's your mom?"

"Good," he said. "She said thanks for the cookies. She's not supposed to eat them, but she does anyway."

"I'm sorry," she said. "Is she on a diet or something?"

"Diabetes," he said.

"I had no idea," Lydia replied, her shoulders drooping as she realized her attempt to thank Anna Molnar for providing dinner the week before had backfired. "I'll keep that in mind."

"It's cool," he said, as he snapped another piece into the puzzle. "She gives most of them to me." He rose from the table, gave Calvin a high-five, and shrugged himself into his jacket. She pushed some bills into his hand. As he had before, he looked down at them as though they'd catch fire. Why was he so reluctant to take her money? He'd worked for it.

"He's a good kid," she said once he'd closed the door behind him.

"Yeah," Mayfield responded. "Listen, I—"

Before he could finish, her cell phone rang. "Barnwell," she said.

"I know you just went off duty," Jeffrey said, "but you'd better come in. The ME is emailing the autopsy report on Sharon Easterling. You'll want to see this."

"Ten minutes," she said. And to Mayfield, she added, "Later."

Traffic was still heavy on the parkway. The Penguins were to face off in an hour, and it appeared half those south of the Mon had tickets. It took her a quarter hour to make it to the second exit. As she entered ACPD headquarters, the sun, hanging low on the horizon, peaked out from behind the trailing end of the front. How many times, she wondered, did they get their first glimpse of sunshine thirty minutes before it disappeared?

As she headed toward her office, Jeffrey waylaid her, standing at his door with a sheaf of papers. "Have a seat." He thrust a pdf of the autopsy report into her hands. She scanned it, then returned to the second page and read a few sections in detail.

"Heels of both shoes dragged across the floor," she said. "Ligature on neck inconsistent with having been dropped." She flipped to the end. "Ruled a homicide."

"You were right," Jeffrey said.

"Small comfort."

"Did you catch the toxicology section?"

"Sort of." She flipped to a separate report. "How did they come up with this so quickly?"

"Once they determined this was no suicide, they rushed to test for the amitriptyline the shrink prescribed. As you can see, she'd ingested a significant quantity."

Barnwell closed the file and her eyes, sitting immobile as she thought. "She takes enough pills to pass out ... or someone forces them down her throat," she said. "Once she's out of it, this person drags her out to the garage. Had they already moved her car and looped the rope over the rafter? Maybe they did it after she'd passed out."

Jeffrey watched as she tried to piece together the sequence of events. "Either there was more than one person involved, or the killer had to be quite strong."

"You keep saying 'someone,'" Jeffrey said. "We have a strong suspicion who that person might be."

She opened her eyes and stared at him without conveying her doubts.

"It's time we hauled Thorson in for a formal interview," he said.

---

"WHAT'S HAPPENED?" Mayfield asked when she returned home.

"Just a minute," she said. "I need to do something before I forget."

She opened her notebook and turned to the page on which she'd sketched an outline.

> *1/18, Walker arrested*
> *1/19, Preliminary arraigned; released*
> *2/2, Formal arraignment, Walker noshow*
> *2/6, Walker's body left beneath bridge*
> *3/20, Cindy Thorson discovers body*

She added a new line to the list, while still leaving room for more:

> *3/25, Sharon is murdered.*

Turning to Calvin, she said, "We were right."

CHAPTER TEN

ELEVEN DAYS HAD PASSED since Cindy Thorson's dog Rudy had uncovered the body concealed beneath the bridge connecting Oak Hill Road to North Branch. As Lydia arrived at ACPD headquarters this morning, she felt they were making progress. The tea leaves floating to the surface, however, told not one story, but several, none of which came together.

She hoped this day would bring clarity. Opening her computer, she found a message from Detective Jeffrey. A defense attorney, Ceil Adams, had called to say she would bring Thorson in for questioning at ten. Barnwell knew Adams. She was a brash woman with flaming red hair and a vocabulary to match. She had once heard the woman use the word fuck three times in one sentence, as a subject, verb, and modifier.

Last year, Adams had represented Thomas Walsh when he was a suspect in the murder of a man whose silence had sent him to prison two decades before. Barnwell was proud of the roles she'd played in that investigation and in the previous one that had led to Walsh's exoneration. Chief Novak, she'd heard, was now doing investigative work for Adams. She hoped he wouldn't show up today. She had no interest in being on opposite sides of her old boss.

She opened another message, sent both to her and to Jeffrey, a report from the crime scene investigators on the results of the search of Brad Walker's automobile. The team had found several sets of fingerprints on the door, the dashboard, and three sets on the steering wheel. One they'd identified as those taken from Walker at the time of his booking. The other two were unidentified.

The parking ticket found clipped to the visor was time-stamped at 7:13 a.m. on March 3.

Inside the storage compartments of the center console, they'd recovered six cell phones. One was registered to Walker himself. The other five were burner phones, wiped clean of data, and their SIM cards removed.

The investigators' most important finding was in the trunk. They had recovered a blue polyethylene tarpaulin. While someone had tried to remove evidence by hosing it off, the team recovered plant debris of the type found on the bank of the North Fork stream. Further tests found skin samples from a deceased human body. They couldn't yet prove it came from Walker's corpse, but DNA results would resolve that question.

Barnwell leaned back and took a long drink from her water bottle. Someone (or some ones) had placed Walker's body in the trunk of his car, driven it to Old Mill Road, removed the body, and returned it to—where? Probably Sharon's. But why? Weeks later, someone had driven it to the airport and abandoned it in the long-term lot.

She reread the report. Something didn't compute. Barnwell called crime scene investigator Brandy Timmons. "The car at the airport," she said. "The report says three sets of latents were found on the steering wheel. One belonged to Walker, but the other two didn't match anyone on file."

"That's right," the investigator said.

"Did you compare them to the dead woman we found two days ago, Sharon Easterling?"

"Of course," she said.

"And no match?"

"Nope."

Barnwell thanked her and hung up. The man who'd spotted someone removing an object from the trunk of a vehicle on the evening of February 6th had seen two or three people emerge. If Sharon Easterling was one of them —and she had no proof of that—the evidence suggested two others were involved.

As she rose to meet with Jeffrey to plot their strategy for questioning Thorson, she had a hunch he was not one of them.

BARNWELL COULD NOT IMAGINE A GREATER contrast between two people as they entered the interview room. Ceil Adams had a face like a bulldog. Her jaw jutted out as though spoiling for a fight. Her eyes stared around the room with contempt, suggesting it needed to be fumigated. Her bright green eyeglass frames clashed with her red hair like a holly wreath overcome by its berries.

Ben Thorson looked like he'd spent the night in the gutter. His slacks and shirt were rumpled, and he hadn't shaved. To his attorney's bulldog, he was the basset, with deep circles beneath his eyes and a woeful countenance like one suffering from a terminal illness. Which, in a way, he might be.

"What's this about?" Adams demanded. "You've already questioned my client twice. He tells me you didn't give him the Miranda."

"Have a seat," Jeffrey said. Was he suppressing a smile? Barnwell glanced at him and decided he'd played chess with the attorney before, and this was an unvarying opening gambit.

"Miranda," she repeated.

Ignoring her hostile demeanor, Jeffrey remained emotionless. "We haven't charged him." His tone was perfunctory.

"Then, we'll leave," she said, raising her raincoat as though to don it.

"If so, we will file charges," he said. "I suggest you sit down while I ask Mr. Thorson a few questions."

She glared at both detectives and sighed to signal her exasperation. "All right, but make it snappy. Unlike the two of you, he doesn't have a steady income or an overly generous retirement plan."

Barnwell wondered where Thorson had come up with her retainer. Ceil Adams, as she'd once heard her proclaim, was not a charity.

Jeffrey began the recording and set the scene as though she hadn't spoken. "Mr. Thorson, where were you between four and six p.m. two days ago, on Wednesday the 8th?" This was the date and time the medical examiner had determined Sharon was hanged.

"At home," he said. "I spent the morning with you two and reported late for work. When they told me I wasn't needed, I returned to the apartment. You cost me a day's wages."

"Can anyone vouch for you?"

"My wife, of course. And I picked up my daughter at the bus stop. That's usually something Cathy does, but since I was home—"

"How about earlier that afternoon, between one and three?"

"I was driving around. I left here and went to work at the warehouse. Or tried to. I hadn't told Cathy I'd left the TSA, so I couldn't just go home—"

"Your wife didn't know you've been suspended?" Barnwell didn't hide her incredulity.

"She knows now. I told her that evening." She studied his face for any sign of remorse. Apart from the hangdog expression he'd carried into the room, she saw no reaction.

"What's the point of this?" Ceil Adams asked.

Jeffrey again ignored her. "Do you know a woman named Sharon Easterling?"

Thorson looked from one detective to the other, as though wondering why the conversation had taken a turn. "No."

"Lives in a big, white, two-story a mile down North Branch from you."

He buried his head in his hands. "I've never heard of this woman and never been to any house along that road."

Jeffrey found three different ways of asking the same question, but Thorson insisted he didn't know the dead woman and had never visited her. "Why?" he said.

Barnwell looked to Jeffrey for guidance. He nodded his head. "Your brother was held in the basement of that house for days, perhaps weeks. It's where he died," she said.

"Who? Why?" He didn't finish either question, but gave them a baffled look.

"That's what we want to know," she said. "The

woman who owns that house, Sharon Easterling, was murdered on Tuesday afternoon. It was made to look like suicide, but it wasn't. So, again, where were you between the time you left the shipping warehouse and when you got home?"

He emitted a long sigh and tore at his hair. "I can't account for every minute of the time. I stopped somewhere for lunch. Had a burger. Wendy's, maybe. Five Guys? No, I would have remembered that. Anyway, I went to the library and spent an hour or so on a computer looking for work." He snapped his fingers. "They'll remember me. You have to sign in to use the terminal."

"Which branch?" Barnwell asked, her pen poised above her notepad.

"South Fayette, right off Route 50."

"That's a long way from the airport," she said.

"It's near where I grabbed lunch. It was McDonald's. I remember now."

"It's out of the way. Robinson Township has a good library."

"You folks had questioned me all morning. accusing me of murder. Do you know what that does to a person? I drove around, trying to decide what to do." He returned her stare, imploring her to believe him.

"This would have taken you right by the Easterling house on your way home," Jeffrey said.

"Look," he said, leaning toward them, his voice hoarse, "there are only two ways to get to our apartment—from the northeast on North Branch or from the southwest. I just happened to be coming from that direction."

The attorney, who'd let the conversation drift along without interrupting, did so now. "This has gone on long enough. My client is here voluntarily. You've not charged him with anything. He's answered all your questions. Your time is up."

Jeffrey ignored her. "Did your brother ever mention knowing a woman in your neighborhood?"

"No." He looked from one to the other. "Look, we were on the outs. I'd helped him get the TSA job and regretted it from day one. He was nothing but trouble. Late to work. Always cutting corners. I'd stopped speaking to him. Maybe that was the problem. I turned my back on him, and he set up this scheme of his. If I'd paid attention..."

"Why weren't you speaking?" Jeffrey asked. "What came between you two?"

"I'd rather not say."

"You'd better."

He gave a long, drawn-out sigh, whispered to his attorney, then moaned as she gave him her advice. "All right. I told you before I'd loaned him some money. It was quite a lot, and he wouldn't pay it back. Kept putting me off. If Cathy had found out..."

It was Barnwell's turn. "How much was this?"

Thorson sighed, shook his head, and folded his hands against his mouth as though in prayer. "He said he needed ten thousand. We didn't have that much. I loaned him $6,480. It was all we had."

When he'd mentioned giving his brother money before, he'd make the amounts seem trivial. This was substantial. Did it give him another motive for murder? "When was this?" she asked.

"Almost two years ago now. I kept asking him for it. He'd promise to get it next week or next month, but he never came through. The bastard."

"You haven't told Cathy about this? Your wife?"

"She hates him. He's done so much to us over the years.

She was pissed when I helped get him on at TSA. If I'd told her I'd given him our savings ..." He shook his head, and his eyes sparkled as he fought tears Or appeared to. "It's the last I would have seen of her or my daughter."

She lowered her head and turned toward Jeffrey, uncertain what to ask next. He returned her gaze, raised his eyebrows, and said, "Let's take a break."

---

"WHAT DO YOU THINK?" he asked as they slipped into his office.

"He's a louse," she said, "but he may be telling the truth."

"I agree. I'll check out his alibi with the library. You ask his wife when he arrived home. We'll let him stew for a few minutes, ask a few more questions, then turn him loose."

"I may offer a few words about how he treats his wife."

"Be my guest." He chuckled as he scrolled through messages on his computer. "Well, hello," he said.

"What is it?" she asked. He didn't respond, examining a document with a puzzled expression on his face. "Grab this off the printer," he said as he tapped a key.

Barnwell pulled sheets out of the tray as the machine disgorged them, reading as she went. "Six thousand," she said. "That must be from Thorson. "Then there are all these smaller amounts. What am I seeing here?"

"This is his checking account. Keep looking. There's more."

As the printer spit out sheets, she skimmed months' worth of deposit and withdrawals until she realized she was looking at a different account. "BJW Investments," she muttered to herself. "What the hell? Eight thousand, eleven thousand ... Look at these deposits, and then..." She laid the two files on the desk and lined them up. "It looks like this company transferred money into Walker's checking account every so often."

Jeffrey grabbed the phone, dialed a number, and put Detective Ross Sutton from the digital evidence department on his speaker. He introduced Barnwell and said, "We're looking over those bank records you sent. Five—no, six big deposits into what looks like a corporation of some sort and money flowing from there to Walker. What can you tell about this?"

"The second account is a limited liability corporation called BJW Investments," the detective said. "We discovered it when we got into Walker's records. It was established two years ago in Delaware, which doesn't require an LLC to list its owners. While we can't prove it belonged to Walker, his initials are BJW."

"I caught that," Jeffrey said. "What's the nature of its business?"

"Use of the word 'investments' suggests it represented itself as a financial management firm, but it's not listed with the SEC," he said, referring to the Securities and Exchange Commission. "It wasn't that active, however. Since its inception, it's taken in only $79,000, all from only five sources. After the LLC received a deposit, a series of smaller amounts was transferred to Walker's checking account. There's no pattern to the deposits to BJW or the transfers to Walker."

"What was going on? Drugs?"

"Dealers don't use banks," Sutton said with a chuckle. "Our boy was feeding a habit of some sort, but we don't think he was a user or a dealer. My guess is a scam of some sort."

Lydia, already been on the edge of her seat, tried to interrupt, but Sutton forged on. "Each time the LLC's balance got low, another deposit would replenish it. Walker would then move money into his account, a few hundred at a time, sometimes two or three times a week. It was inconsistent. Last fall, for instance, no money moved out of the LLC for nearly six weeks. Walker continued his regular spending habits at grocery stores, the state liquor store, that sort of thing. We suspect he was dealing in cash during that time, but we can't prove it."

"What was he doing?" Jeffrey asked. "If he wasn't into drugs, where was he spending all this money?"

"We're still working on that," Sutton said, "but at the end, he ran out of runway. On January 20th, he transferred more than $4,000 from the LLC, leaving it with less than $200. It went into Walker's account and came out again to pay the attorney who got him released. From that day on, he was essentially broke."

"What makes you think he was running a scam?" Jeffrey asked.

Sutton chuckled to himself. "Five separate women have written checks to the investment company over the two years since it was formed. One paid out $26,000 over twenty months. Another, three checks totaling $19,000. The others made single deposits, all at least five figures. He received nearly $79,000 from them."

"He was living off women," Barnwell said. "A gigolo, maybe? Do you know who they are?"

"We've identified all five of them. I'll send over the list."

"Is a Sharon Easterling among them?" she asked,

"How'd you know? She was the most recent one."

"You won't be able to reach her," Jeffrey said. "She's dead."

He ended the call, looked at Barnwell for a moment as though expecting her to solve the mystery, and said, "Let's learn what Thorson has to say about this."

---

"You've taken long enough," Ceil Adams snapped.

"Something new turned up," Jeffrey said. "Ben, why did your brother borrow money from you?"

"He had a debt to pay off," Thorson replied

"What was the nature of this debt?"

"He didn't say."

Jeffrey leaned toward him, striking a conversational tone. "But you know, don't you? Or suspect?"

"Yeah," Thorson said, nodding and wearing a pained expression. "He had a gambling problem. It began years ago. My mother bailed him out a few times, but when her husband put an end to it, he turned to me. Twice I helped him out. Both times, he promised to stop. He didn't. A couple of years ago, he got into some sort of trouble. A private bet of some sort. He came running to me. He was scared shitless. So ... I saved his useless skin one more time."

"That was—" Barnwell searched through her notes. "The $6,480."

"Yeah. All we had." He gave an involuntary shudder. "This time, I really let him have it. I said if he came near me again, I'd—" He didn't finish the thought. Had he done so, Barnwell figured, it would have incriminated him.

"And he hasn't come to you since," she said.

"No," Thorson said. "I thought he'd learned his lesson."

"But then he was arrested. He'd stolen money from passengers, fenced their phones and items he'd bought using stolen credit cards, all to feed his gambling habit."

"That's how I figure it," Thorson said. A spark came into his eyes as a thought occurred to him. "Maybe that's who killed him. Do you think he made another bad bet?"

Neither detective answered him. "He's come by a great deal of money over the past two years," Barnwell said. "Do you know where he got it?"

"No," Thorson said, then repeated the word in a high-pitched voice. "How much?"

"Have you even seen him with a woman?"

"A woman?" Thorson snorted. "He's gay."

Neither detective shared their surprise. "Did you know several women have given him large amounts of cash over the past two years?"

"No. Why would they do that?"

"An excellent question, Ben," Jeffrey said. "We intend to answer it. Meanwhile, I'd advise you not to leave the state. If you do, we'll issue a warrant for your arrest. We're also seeking a search warrant for your cell phone records."

"Why?" he asked.

"To be sure you're telling us the truth, that you had no contact with him from the time of his arrest."

"You won't need a warrant," he said, sliding his phone across the table.

"No," the attorney said. "Make them work for it."

Thorson turned on her. "I've done nothing illegal. I'm not afraid to share anything with them. If my phone helps end this nightmare, let them have it."

Ceil Adams harrumphed. She wasn't used to anyone ignoring her advice. "All right, but you're making a mistake."

As they rose to leave, Barnwell escorted Thorson, leaving Adams trailing. "I want a word with your client in private," she said.

"Forget it," the attorney said. "Anything you have to say to him, you can say to me."

Barnwell shrugged. "I won't tell your wife about your loan," she said.

"Thank you."

"I want you to."

"She'll — You have no idea how angry she gets. She may leave me."

"And she may not. You two need a fresh start. I can tell she's afraid of you."

Thorson's laugh degenerated into a coughing fit. "She is not."

"Cathy's a virtual prisoner in your apartment. She doesn't have a car. There's nowhere to walk—"

"Why would she need a car?" he said. "She can't drive."

Barnwell shook her head. What he didn't know wouldn't kill him, but it might do her a great deal of harm.

"If I ever catch you abusing her, it's not just the courts you'll be dealing with. It's me."

She glared at the attorney, daring her to warn her for making a threat, but Ceil Adams said nothing.

***

WHEN THEY RETURNED to Jeffrey's office, they discovered another message from Detective Sutton. It contained the names of the five women who had written checks to BJW Investments, along with the amounts they'd paid. "Sharon Easterling," Jeffrey said. "paid him $10,500."

It was the first name on the list, however, that captured Barnwell's attention. "This Moira Buller," she said. "That's the woman whose number I found in his pants pocket. She's a personal trainer. She told me they'd met somewhere, that he signed up for a free lesson but never returned. Look up my report."

Jeffrey turned to his keyboard and tapped his way into their records on the case, scrolling down her account with one hand while resting his chin on the other. "She told you he started a conversation with her at a Mexican restaurant, said he was new to town, and was an investment adviser."

"But he didn't use his own name," she said. "He called himself Carl Ferris, whom we subsequently learned was one of his TSA victims. Walker took his money and a phone, but he also stole his ID."

"Who are the other names on this list? Ruth Eckman," Jeffrey said, pawing at the printout Sutton had sent. "She's the one who paid out nearly $26,000 over a year and a half. Rachel Zimmerman, three checks for $19,000. Annette Henley, one payment of $13,300. Then this Buller woman and Sharon Eastlerling."

"Sutton is right," Barnwell said. "Walker defrauded these women. We need to find out how he did it."

"Starting with the one who lied to you."

"Remember why you delayed bringing Thorson in at first? You wanted to have all the facts, so you'd be one step ahead if he lied. Let's do the same with Buller. She has to have a reason for hiding the fact he'd stolen from her. Let's talk to the others first, then confront her."

"Starting with?" he asked.

"He took more from Ruth Eckman than any of the others, and he seems to have strung her along for a while. Let's begin with her."

Ruth Eckman lived in a well-kept two-story brick house in Scott Township, eight minutes from ACPD headquarters. Somehow, between the time Jeffrey called her and the two of them arrived, she had time to brew a pot of coffee and put out a tray of cookies. *Ah, Pittsburgh*, Barnwell thought. *Always with the cookies.*

She was a short, wiry woman who appeared to be in her early sixties. Her reedy face was framed with tight black curls and punctuated with a toothy smile that never wavered. "You asked about my investments," she said after Jeffrey made the introductions.

"Yes, and we don't mean to pry. Your name came up in an investigation into a larger case. There's nothing you've done wrong."

"I'm happy to help," she said. "Would you like some cookies?"

"Sure," Jeffrey said. He loaded two on one of the small plates she'd placed next to the silver tray. Barnwell did the same. Anything to break the ice.

"Oh," she said, "these are good."

"Of course," the woman said, as though it was unthinkable she'd share anything ordinary.

"You made out several checks to a firm called BJW Investments," he said.

"Mr. Martin's firm. Poor fellow. He got wiped out when the company in which we invested went bankrupt. Me, it was just one of those things."

"What was the name of this company?" Jeffrey asked.

"I have it in my papers somewhere." she said as she thumbed through a series of files in an expandable folder. "Oh, yes. ForwardDrive Technologies. They combined two words into one. I don't know why everyone seems to do that. The English language is fine as is."

Through a series of questions, Jeffrey teased out the story. "Ted Martin," as he called himself, had found her sitting alone in a coffee shop. Every other table was filled, so he asked if he might join her. She was only too happy. "Such a nice young man," she said, as Barnwell suppressed an eye roll. "We got to talking." She made it sound as though she had led the conversation, but Barnwell suspected it was the other way around, that Walker had drawn her out.

Over several weeks, she came to trust him. When he mentioned he was on the ground floor of one of the experimental self-driving vehicle companies springing up around Pittsburgh, she became intrigued. "I put a little money toward it," she said, "but he was all in. It worked well for a while. I kept getting statements from him, showing how well they were doing. It wasn't publicly traded yet. These start-ups never are, but things seemed to roll long." She giggled at her pun.

"You said he provided the statements," Jeffrey said.

"That's right. Through his firm."

"And then?" Barnwell interjected, knowing that there had to be a "then" then.

"They lost their government contract. The whole thing fell apart. It was all politics. He was so apologetic. He'd gotten me into it, he said, and felt personally responsible. But I'm a big girl. I can take care of myself."

"And Martin?" she said. "What's become of him?"

"He's gone back to Iowa where he came from. He'd invested every penny he owned and had to start over."

"You hear from him?" Barnwell said.

"He calls me every so often, just to see how I'm doing." For the first time, the smile left her face. "I haven't heard from him for several weeks."

"Is this Mr. Martin?" Jeffrey said, sliding a photograph toward her.

"Oh, yes. Such a good-looking young fellow. And so thoughtful. I hope he's doing all right."

The detectives looked at each other. Jeffrey nodded, granting permission for Lydia to break the news. "I'm sorry to tell you, Ms. Eckman, but he's passed away."

"Oh, no!" She covered her mouth with her hands and looked about to burst into tears. "What's happened?"

"Do you have someone who helps look over your finances?" she asked.

"No. I inherited quite a bit from my father and have stuck with most of his investments. Why?"

And Lydia told her.

"I can't believe she never figured him out," Barnwell said as they returned to headquarters.

"Still hasn't," Jeffrey said. The woman had fought against the allegations. This couldn't be right. His name wasn't Walker, she insisted. He'd graduated from the University of Iowa with a degree in finance. He'd been engaged to be married, but his fiancé had died in an automobile accident. On and on it went, Ruth Eckman regurgitating the story Brad Walker had fed her during his months of financial courtship.

In the end, however, she'd allowed them to take the file BJW Investments had sent her, documenting her stock purchases. "A cut-and-paste job if I've ever seen one," Barnwell said.

Rachel Zimmerman turned out not to be as gullible. Brad had introduced himself as Norm Cassidy from

Phoenix, an identity that was not on the list of those who'd reported a theft at the airport. Had Cassidy not realized where he'd lost his wallet? She identified Walker from his photo and said, "He's a slick one. I've tried to reach him for weeks, but he's disappeared."

Walker had pitched her on bitcoins, telling her the difference between this fund and others floating around on the internet was that it was insured. He'd even shown her a policy. When she produced it, Barnwell marveled at the care he'd taken. The front page was printed against a light blue, mottled background, bordered by an intricate filigree, and carried an impressive seal. "Some sort of layout software," she muttered to Jeffrey.

She'd initially "invested,"—she created quotation marks using two fingers of both hands—$10,000, then another $5,000, and finally $4,000 just before Thanksgiving. "By then, I was pretty cautious. All the documents were coming through this investment firm, and I wanted them sent to me. That's when he ghosted me. I tried to reach him for two months. At first, he didn't return the call, and then his line went dead. I wrote the insurance company, but my letter was returned.. No such address." She brandished the letter, but didn't hand it over.

"Have you reported this?"

"I've tried to reach authorities in Delaware, but hit a brick wall. I reported him to the Maricopa County Police. They first said it wasn't their jurisdiction, that I'd have to report it to you folks. Then they said they'd spoken to a Norman Cassidy, who told them we'd never met and that his ID had been stolen months before."

And when she called the ACPD, Barnwell thought, we'd gone looking not for Brad Walker, but for a man named Norman Cassidy, which was why Zimmerman's report hadn't come to her attention.

"So have you found him?" she asked.

"We have." This time, Jeffrey issued the news bulletin. "He's dead. Murdered."

"You don't mean that guy they found under the bridge out west of here?"

"The same."

"Good," she said. "Whoever did it should get a reward, but first I want my goddamn money back."

---

THE NEXT NAME on the list was Annette Henley, who had been bilked out of $10,000. As they drove toward the construction company for which she worked, however, the cyber detective, Ross Sutton, messaged Jeffrey to call him. He pulled into the parking lot of a fast-food restaurant and put the detective on his speaker.

"I have Sharon Easterling's phone records from her wireless provider," he said. "First off, she neither called nor received a call from Ben Thorson's number."

Jeffrey took the news with a resigned sigh. Barnwell nodded as though it confirmed what she was thinking. By almost throwing his phone in their faces, Thorson had convinced her he had nothing to hide. "But you will check his phone?" Jeffrey asked the detective.

"Yes, but it won't change anything. She didn't call him, and he didn't phone her. She placed several calls to a number we haven't yet identified. We're trying to determine whether it's to one of the burner phones he used."

"I suspect he used one for every woman he bilked," Jeffrey said. "He kept in touch with at least two of them, perhaps hoping he could dip his hook into the same ponds twice."

"Easterling made frequent calls to two numbers over the past two months," Sutton continued. "Their frequency multiplied in recent days. They belong to two other victims on your list, Moira Buller and Annette Henley."

"Christ!" Jeffrey swore under his breath. Barnwell leaned back in the passenger seat and let the implications sweep over her.

Sutton said he'd have a full report in Jeffrey's inbox by the time he returned to headquarters. The detective thanked him and ended the call. "Let's find somewhere to discuss this," he said. "You want a burger?" Barnwell did not, but she accompanied Jeffrey into the restaurant, took a booth in a far corner while he ordered, and reached for his fries when he joined her.

"We know of five women Walker defrauded," he said. "Three found each other somehow and were chatting on the phone for weeks. One owned the house where Walker was held. First he was murdered, then she was. So one of these two may be our killer."

"Or both," Barnwell said.

He repeated her words, leaving his hamburger untouched. "I wonder how they got together."

"Facebook?" she said. "It's not the right message for TikTok."

"And how would they have found each other on Facebook, unless they already knew each other?" He grabbed his phone from his jacket pocket and redialed the last number in its history. "Russ, can you get into Easterling's social media accounts?"

"I'm ahead of you," he said. "Working on it now."

He disconnected and massaged both cheeks as he

scowled. "If you're not going to eat that..." she said. Jeffrey shoved the uneaten burger across the table. "Who's next?" she said. "Buller or Henley?"

"Your original instinct is the correct one," he replied. "Buller lied to you, so let's speak first with the other woman. But before we do—"

"We wait." Barnwell said it before he could.

"Yeah, let's see what Russ comes up with. How did these three women connect?"

---

"What's the occasion?" Calvin said as he entered the kitchen, spotting a bottle of Cabernet Sauvignon and two filet mignon steaks on the counter.

"It's premature, but I'm celebrating," Lydia replied. "I sense we're in the closing stages of this investigation."

Before leaving headquarters, she'd opened her notebook and made two additional entries in the timeline. It now read:

> *1/18, Walker arrested*
> *1/19, Preliminary arraignment; released;*
>     *transfers funds for attorney; now broke*
> *1/25, Three women begin texting and call-*
>     *ing; continues through 3/25*
> *2/2, Formal arraignment, Walker noshow*
> *2/6, Walker's body left beneath bridge*
> *3/3, Walker's car left at airport*
> *3/20, Cindy Thorson discovers body*
> *3/25, Sharon is murdered*

A pattern had emerged. All Lydia had to do was fill in

what blanks remained and prove it. As she seared the steaks, she related what they'd uncovered during the day. "So one or more of these women kidnapped Walker, one of them poisoned him and got rid of the body—"

"Perhaps both of them," she said.

"And then murdered Sharon Easterling. Why?"

"I haven't figured that out, but on the day she fell apart, she told a coworker 'they' were out to kill her. That must mean Annette and Moira."

"When are you bringing them in?" he asked.

"We need one more piece of evidence to tie them together. We hope to have it by morning." Donning a heat-proof glove, she lifted the pan containing the steaks from the burner and slid it into the oven.

"Good luck," he said, as he poured them each a glass of wine. He looked across the counter, sliding his hand beneath a folder she'd placed aside as though fishing for something. "Have you seen a report I left here this morning?"

"No, I left before you did."

Calvin rose from the barstool and combed the living room. "I know I left it on the counter," he said, more to himself than to her.

Lydia turned as she stuck a fork into the potatoes baking in the oven. "Have you checked the nest?"

"Oh, no. I hope he hasn't..." He left the room, and she heard him muttering near the rear entrance. "C'mon, Howie. Can't you leave stuff that doesn't belong to you alone?"

He returned carrying scraps of paper he deposited in the garbage. "I hope it wasn't important," she said.

"It was, and it wasn't. I shouldn't have left it out."

"What was it?" she said.

He opened his mouth to speak, but stopped. "Nothing that won't hold."

"You're sure," she said as she removed their dinner from the oven and threw sliced mushrooms into the sizzling fat in the pan.

"Yeah," he said. "Now's not the time."

Something was on his mind, but she wasn't about to pressure him. If he wanted her to know, he'd tell her.

CHAPTER ELEVEN

BARNWELL ARRIVED at headquarters the following morning to find Detective Sutton lurking outside Jeffrey's office. She introduced herself to the digital forensics investigator, who was nothing like she had pictured him. Instead of a small, bookish man, she found a behemoth, easily six feet four and with a statement of net girth that strained his belt. "You found something?" she said.

"Yeah, but let me wait for Lyle. I only want to go through this once."

She walked the three doors to her office and fidgeted while she waited. Ten minutes later, Jeffrey showed up. "Sorry I'm late."

"We were both early," she replied. They crowded around Jeffrey's desk as Sutton pulled documents out of a folder, panting with the effort. "I rarely make the rounds in person," he said, chuckling at his impending joke, "but this patient requires surgery. Have you heard of a website called Neighborhood?"

Both shook their heads. "It's a social media site for communities. People post notices about missing dogs and cats, traffic hazards, and the like. Sometimes it gets more personal. On January 25th, a woman with the handle of 'SharonE' wrote this message." He handed Jeffrey a printed copy, which Barnwell read over his shoulder.

> Does anyone have experience with a company called BJW Investments? I bought into a real estate program they offer. Now they're saying I have to send more money to pay taxes on the properties they've purchased. I'm new to this and grateful for any advice.

"That's a new one," Barnwell said. "Walker kept changing the offer. First it was self-driving vehicles, then bitcoins, then real estate."

"The woman gets a bunch of responses warning her it sounds like a scam, but sprinkled among them are two messages," Sutton said. "The first is from someone named Annette H. The site requires you to post under your real name, but a lot of women just use the initial of their surname."

He handed over a sheet of paper containing several responses, one of which he'd highlighted in yellow.

> I know this company and the person behind it. Send me a private message.

"On the next page, you'll notice a third party, Moira Buller, marked it with a heart," Sutton continued. "The three women exchanged private messages over the following twenty-four hours, culminating in this from Annette."

We need to meet in person. Let's get together for breakfast tomorrow at First Watch in Settler's Ridge. How does
7:30 sound?

"Great work," Jeffrey said. "Anything on Thorson's
phone yet?"

"We're going through it now, but so far, we haven't
found a thing."

Jeffrey and Barnwell exchanged glances. This was what
both now expected. He thanked Sutton, who lumbered off.
"So now we have them together," he said.

"Is it time to question Annette?" Barnwell asked.

"It is, but here's our strategy."

<hr>

THEY ENTERED B&M Construction Company on the
Washington Pike at ten and asked for Annette Henley. The
man at the front desk swiveled in his chair and said to the
woman behind him, "It's for you."

"Yeah?" she said as she approached them. Barnwell put
the woman somewhere in her forties with green eyes in a
long oval face and shoulder-length chestnut hair that fell in
curls around her neck. She was husky, with stocky hips and
big-chested. Lydia couldn't help noticing she walked with
her feet splayed and her fists clenched, as though she were
ready for a fight.

The detectives flashed their IDs. She showed no reaction. "We're investigating a series of frauds," Barnwell said.
"Your name has come up as a likely victim. We'd like to ask
you a few questions."

"Okay," she said, drawing the word out.

Barnwell asked for some place they could speak in private. "Or we can do this at headquarters. "

"We have a conference room," she said. "Charts all over the place, but I can clean it up. How long will this take?"

"An hour, maybe," Jeffrey said. "The sooner we begin, the sooner we'll finish."

She clamped her thin lips shut and puffed out her breath. "Okay," she repeated, seeming to accept the inevitable. "Nick, tell Mort I'm using the conference room. I need to help these people."

The man at the desk said, "Sure."

His eyes follow them as Annette led them into the conference room. She picked up piles of what appeared to be building plans and stacked them at one end of the table, then took a seat at the head. Barnwell and Jeffrey sat across from each other. As agreed, Barnwell initiated the interview. "Last fall, you issued a check for $10,000 to a firm called BJW Investments."

Annette nodded vigorously, her lips drawn tight as though clamped in a vise. She stuck a stick of gum in her mouth and began chewing like a recovering nicotine addict, which Barnwell decided she probably was. "What was it for?" she asked.

The woman smirked as though she was a fool. "Investment," she said.

"In?"

"Have you ever heard of a REIT?"

"Real Estate Investment Trust," Barnwell said. "It's like a mutual fund that owns commercial properties."

"Well, that's what it was."

"Was?" Barnwell said.

Henley rested her right elbow on the arm of the chair and rested her weight on it, but kept her hands wrapped around her. "If you're talking to me, you know it went bust. Or disappeared. Whatever."

"You're saying it was a scam?"

"Like I said, you already know that or you wouldn't be here."

"Who sold it to you?" Barnwell asked.

"Man named Fitzhugh. Mike Fitzhugh."

"How did you come to know him?"

"I met him in a bar. Stupid me, right?" Neither detective replied, both staring at her in a practiced maneuver. In the ensuing silence, Annette said. "Young guy, but slick. He gave me a line about being new in town and starting his own firm. We got to chatting. He was quite a talker, that one. He was buying the drinks, and my tongue started wobbling. I told him too much, and he spotted an easy mark."

"So he talked you into investing in this deal. Then what?" she said.

"Then nothing. He sent me some paperwork. It looked official. I didn't hear from him for a while. I got suspicious and started asking questions. He didn't respond. I kept calling, and his phone went to voicemail. Then the number was disconnected. That's the last I heard from him. I haven't seen him since. I hope you get the son of a bitch."

Jeffrey, who'd been silent during this conversation, slid a photograph toward her. "Do you recognize this man?"

She glanced at it, not touching it. "Could be," she said. "Looks a bit like him, but I can't be sure."

"He goes by several names," he said, "but his real name was Brad Walker." He emphasized the past tense, but Henley didn't bite.

"Would you like to know what's happened to him?" he asked.

"Sure. You got him?"

"He's dead," Jeffrey said. "Murdered."

"Oh," she said, shaking her head and drawing it out. "I can't say I'm surprised. If he's done this to others, I mean."

She looked from one to the other. "That it? Are we through here?"

"Do you know a woman named Sharon Easterling?" he asked.

She blinked twice, her brash confidence taking a break. "No," she said, looking off to one side. "Can't say I have."

"That's odd," he said, "because the two of you were spotted having breakfast in Settler's Ridge back on January 27th. You and another woman. You remember that?"

"No. You've confused me with someone else," she said. "I don't go out for breakfast."

"How about Moira Buller? Know anyone by that name?"

She seemed to search her memory, then shook her head. "Sorry," she said.

"Annette," Barnwell said, giving her the x-ray eye treatment, "We have you on the Neighborhood site responding to a question Sharon posted about BJW Investments. You suggested taking the conversation private. Moira Buller joined it. The three of you decided to meet at First Watch. Now do you remember?"

She stared back at Barnwell, allowed herself a slight smile, and cocked her head. "So what if I did? He asked her for more money. For taxes, he said." She snorted. "We tried to keep her from digging in deeper. There's nothing wrong with that."

"Then why deny meeting her?"

She gave the slightest of shrugs, but still kept her arms braced around her breasts. "I didn't want to involve anyone else."

"Who?" Barnwell said. "Moira? She'd identified herself as another victim. You say she was also trying to help. Why protect her?" When Annette didn't respond, she said, "Or was it Sharon? She was still being swindled. You lied to us to protect her? From what? This makes no sense."

"If she wants to talk to you, she will. It's not my business to involve other people."

"Only, she can't speak with us," she said. "She's also been murdered."

Annette twisted her face in pain and pretended to dab her eyes. "I am truly sorry to hear that. She seemed like a nice person. A little nervous, but who wouldn't be if some creep had taken your life savings?"

"The two of you spoke eight times by phone. She called you six times, you called her twice."

"Uh-huh. She kept asking me questions. What should she do? I told her to talk to the police and not take his calls. I tried to be nice, but if I couldn't help myself, how could I help her?"

"Have you ever been to her house?"

"I don't even know where she lives. Lived." Her cockiness having returned, she said, "I've told you all I know. I need to get back to work now."

The detectives kept questioning her, but she evaded them. She claimed she'd had no further involvement with the man she knew as Mike Fitzhugh and had met Sharon Easterling only once.

"She's smarter than she looks," Jeffrey said as they returned to their cruiser.

"How is a smart person supposed to look?" she shot back. Then she conceded the point. "Yeah, she kept her hands to herself and didn't touch Walker's photo. She gave us nothing, particularly not her fingerprints."

Moira Buller sat in an interview room fuming. Two uniformed officers had barged into the health club, asked for her, and in full view of the clients and her fellow staff members, ordered her to come with them. Sitting alone in the windowless room, she glanced at her phone, wondering why she couldn't get a signal. She knew only that they'd brought her here. They hadn't given her a reason, though she thought she knew. She couldn't know how much they'd discovered. As the officers drove her to headquarters, Moira was also unaware Annette Henley had just been questioned at her work.

As two detectives entered the room, she laid her phone on the table, then slid it into her hip pocket. Her face was devoid of expression as the male detective passed his eyes over her. She was accustomed to that look. She wasn't beautiful, but with wavy brown hair and blue eyes, she wasn't bad to look at. Despite being thirty-six, she had a youthful figure, with firm breasts, a toned butt, and attractive legs. She often wore tight-fitting tights and tops to show off her shape. When selecting a personal trainer, old guys always went for her.

"This is Detective Sergeant Lyle Jeffrey," the woman said as she slid into the seat opposite her. "I'm Detective Lydia Barnwell. We spoke by phone last week. You told me how you met a man you knew as Carl Ferris. Do you remember that conversation?"

"Is that why I'm here? About Carl?" she said.

"Just answer the question. Do you recall speaking to me?"

"Yeah, vaguely."

"You told me this man Carl came in for a free training

session, but that you never saw him again. Do you remember saying that?"

Moira nodded, and Barnwell asked her to repeat it aloud for the recording. "That wasn't true, was it?"

"I don't recall ever ..." She broke off. Her shoulders tensed. Whatever lie she was about to tell lay frozen on her tongue.

"On October 17th last year, you wrote his firm, BJW Investments, a check for $10,000."

Some of the tension left her shoulders. "Okay. I didn't mention that because it's embarrassing. He was a flimflam artist, and I got taken. You don't like to admit that sort of thing."

"Not even to the police? You think we haven't heard stories like this before? You must have had a better reason for concealing it from me."

"No, I was just ashamed." She ran her tongue over her lips and swallowed.

"Are you thirsty?" Barnwell asked. "We can get you a glass of water or a cup of coffee."

Moira smiled. "Yes. Tea if you have it." Jeffrey rose to leave the room. Barnwell stated for the recording device she was suspending the interview for a moment. but she continued to look at the suspect, who glanced back and forth at her surroundings like a caged animal looking for a way out. Barnwell knew she welcomed the interruption. It was a chance to collect her thoughts and come up with a plausible story.

Jeffrey returned with a white mug, which he held by the handle, wrapped in a napkin. "It may be hot," he said, laying the mug before her.

She slid the napkin aside, lifted the mug to her lips,

sipped at it, and wrapped her hands around it. "I like it hot," she said.

"Detective Jeffrey has returned to the room, and we're resuming the interview," Barnwell said. "Does the name Sharon Easterling mean anything to you?"

If she was shaken by the turn in the conversation, she concealed it. "Not that I recall."

"Annette Henley?"

Once again, her body tensed. "I may have heard the name. You meet so many people at the health club."

"We've just spoken to her," Barnwell said. "It's why we had you wait a few minutes."

"All right. I've met her."

"In a restaurant at Settler's Ridge on January 27th. The two of you had breakfast with Sharon Easterling, who was a victim of the same scam that ensnared you, run by a man you later came to know as Bradley James Walker. BJW."

"All right. We did. She'd posted online she'd invested money with what was supposed to be an investment firm. The man behind it demanded more, claiming she owed property tax. Annette said to take the conversation private, and I joined in."

"What happened at that meeting?"

"We told her this real estate thing was a fraud, that she shouldn't give him any more money, and should go to the cops."

"Then what?" Barnwell said.

"And then she went away. That's the last I've seen of her. I can't speak for Annette."

"Remember," Jeffrey said, leaning toward her, "we now have her side of the story."

Moira backed away from him, pushing at the table with both hands. "Whatever she told you is a lie."

"What part of it?" he said. "What did she lie about?"

She was frightened now, her eyes wide with panic as she turned her head back and forth.

"How do you even know what she told us?" Barnwell said.

An officer knocked at the door. Barnwell rose to answer it. "There's a man here says he's an attorney for your witness. Name's John Gimble."

"John?" Moira exclaimed. "He's one of my clients."

"That's odd," Jeffrey says. "He claims you're his client."

"He is. I mean, I am. He's come here to represent me. You have to let him in."

An older man with a fringe of white hair ringing his scalp and what seemed like pounds of flesh hanging from his face barged into the room. "Gerrie called me and said they'd arrested you."

"We're questioning her," Jeffrey said. "We haven't filed charges."

He glared at Jeffrey, then at Barnwell. "I want to speak to my client in private," he said. "Now."

Jeffrey ended the interview and left the room with Barnwell in tow, but not before he'd scooped up the mug, shielding it with what was now a tea-stained napkin. He carried it into the break room, emptied what remained of the liquid into a sink, and placed the mug into an evidence bag. Then they waited.

Five minutes passed until Gimble emerged from the interview room. "Are you holding her? I've told her not to answer any more questions. Unless you're filing charges, she's coming with me."

"She's not under arrest," Jeffrey said, adding a pointed, "yet."

"Then we're leaving." He returned to the room, said

something to her, and the two of them emerged, heading toward the entrance.

---

"Should we have let her go?" Barnwell asked.

"We had no choice. We have no physical evidence linking either of them to the house or to Walker's vehicle. But this may change things." He hoisted the evidence bag and called for a police cruiser to transport it to the crime lab.

"I hoped we could break her," he said as he filled in the form that would accompany the bag, "but someone at her work was smart enough to call a lawyer. By this afternoon, we may have enough evidence to seek warrants for both of them."

"And meanwhile, they get to compare stories."

"Yes," he agreed. "It can't be helped." The officer appeared. Jeffrey printed and signed the form, sending him on his way.

They settled in to discuss how they would question the pair when Ross Sutton appeared in the doorway. "Sorry to disturb you two, but you'll want to hear this. We now have records for all the cell phones found in Walker's car. He used a different one for each victim and made no other calls with them. That way, when a phone rang, he knew who was calling."

Sutton snorted as he said, "He even wrote their initials on the back with a Sharpie. Thorough bastard, that one. He also had an old iPhone that he used for everything else. That struck me as odd, since we seized his phone at the time of his arrest. Where did he get this one?"

"Where, indeed?" Jeffrey said.

Turning to Barnwell, he said. "Every phone has a

unique identifier, an IMEI. It stands for International Mobile Equipment Identity."

Barnwell knew this, but wasn't about to slow Sutton down. She was willing to endure his mansplaining as long as it led somewhere.

"Someone had used a sharp tool to scratch out the identifier on the back of the phone. He didn't seem to realize you can get it by putting in a six-digit series. We did." He paused, and Barnwell sensed he was about to drop a bombshell. "This phone is registered to Benjamin Thorson."

"What?" Jeffrey shouted. His mouth hung open as he turned to Barnwell.

"It doesn't have a SIM card. It ran only on Wi-Fi. Walker set up a Google voice number for it, just as he did for his burner phones."

"So he didn't have to register it through a cellular service," she finished for him.

"Oh," Sutton said, recognizing Barnwell was familiar with the process. "To anticipate your next question, we found no record Walker called his brother on this phone, nor did he receive one."

"What about Thorson's phone records?" Jeffrey asked.

"I'm getting to that. He made most of his calls to his wife, the TSA, the distribution center where he now works, and a pizza place. He and his brother were in regular communication until more than a year ago, but then nothing."

This tallied with what Thorson had told him about breaking contact after Walker refused to repay the loan. "How about the three women, Easterling, Henley, and Buller?" Jeffrey asked.

"Nothing. If he contacted them, he didn't use his phone. We also checked the websites he visited. Most were for job-hunting purposes and ordering pizza and Chinese food. He had a language app and was trying to pick up some Spanish."

"Maybe so he could communicate with people going through the security line," Barnwell suggested.

"There's nothing suspicious about his search activity. Nothing like where do I dispose of a body?" He allowed himself a small laugh, which shook his entire body. "And no sign he was trying to trace anyone's location."

They thanked him, faced each other, but said nothing for several seconds. Barnwell broke the silence, placing both hands on her hips as she rocked in the chair, staring at the ceiling as though reading from its tiles. "Ben told us he had no further contact with his brother after his arrest. He implied they hadn't spoken in some time. So, how did Walker get the phone?"

"The simplest explanation is he lied to us."

"We need to ask," she said, "because if he did, we should take a step back."

THEY DECIDED to question Thorson at work rather than bringing him in. Returning his phone gave them a pretext that might avoid involving his attorney. As Barnwell drove, heading west on I-376 and taking the business loop behind the airport, Jeffrey said, "The library confirms his story. He signed in to use a computer at 1:15, stayed for nearly an hour and a half, and checked out at 2:40. The trip to Old Mill takes twenty minutes at that hour."

"So he's in the clear," she said.

"As far as Sharon's death is concerned."

Was he still holding out the possibility Ben had killed his brother? Lydia didn't ask.

Carnegie Distribution Center was a sprawling, three-story structure that looked like a huge white brick left in an open field. Trucks lumbered into the facility, making their way around the back of the building to the loading docks. Barnwell parked in front. They entered through a pair of glass doors that seemed shoved into place as an afterthought.

A uniformed guard sat behind a glass pane thick enough to be bulletproof, reminding Barnwell that this center transported cargo to and from aircraft. She asked him to summon Thorson. "What's the nature of your business?" he demanded.

"Police business," she said and flashed her badge. Jeffrey did the same.

He frowned, reached for a phone, then suspended his hand in the air. "Is he in some sort of trouble?"

"No," she said. "He's helping us with an investigation."

That seemed to satisfy him. He let his hand fall to the phone, picked it up, and spoke into it. "Thorson to the front. You have visitors."

Jeffrey peered around the room, which was devoid of chairs, tables, lamps, and printed material. "As sterile as an operating room," he said.

They waited four minutes before Thorson appeared. He pushed open a windowless door and stood staring at them. "What now?" he said. "Why are you disturbing me at work?"

Jeffrey fished a plastic bag out of his pocket. "We're returning your phone."

His stance relaxed, and he displayed what passed as a smile. "Thanks," he said, holding out his hand.

"If you have a moment, we have a few last questions."

"Last?" he said.

"We hope so. Is there somewhere we can go for a few minutes?"

Thorson glanced around the room as though seeing it for the first time, which perhaps was the case. He glanced toward the guard, who seemed to listening. "Okay if we talk outside?" he asked.

Barnwell nodded, and Jeffrey said, "Sure." It was a rare cloudless day, with the temperature having soared into the low fifties, so Thorson didn't don a jacket.

"You found nothing on my phone," he said. It was a statement, not a question. "It's as I said. I've had no contact with my brother in at least a year, other than to see him when we were both working. He always gave me a hello like nothing was wrong. I tried to ignore him."

Barnwell took a step forward and stared up, her blue eyes boring into him. "Then how did he get hold of your old cell phone?"

"What?" He stepped back as though she'd taken a swing at him.

"When we arrested your brother, we seized his cell phone. But when we found his car, conveniently parked on the airport grounds, we found an iPhone 8 registered to you. Did you give it to him?"

"No," he said. "It was Cathy's. When I upgraded her last year, it wasn't worth anything, so we threw it in a drawer. The idea was to give it to Cindy when she turns ten. By then—" He stopped, lost in thought.

"How did he get his hands on it?" she asked.

"I have no idea," he said. "None, zero."

"Could your wife have given it to him?"

"Cathy?" He snickered, his face wreathed in disbelief. "She wouldn't give him the time of day. No way."

"What's your guess then?"

He spread his legs and rested his knuckles on his hips. His voice rose to a shout. "Have I told you my brother is a fucking thief? He must have broken into our apartment when we were out. I'll ask Cathy if anything else is missing, like money. That piece of shit."

They spoke for another two minutes, but Thorson could think of no better explanation. "That it?" he said.

Jeffrey was about to answer, but Barnwell put a hand on his arm. "Have you told Cathy about the 'loan?'"

"Yeah," he said. He rubbed his hands together and shivered, though whether from the cold or from reliving the conversation, she couldn't tell. "She was furious. Beside herself. I've never seen her so ... 'How could you?' She kept repeating that."

"Well..." she began.

"But I'm glad you made me do it," he continued. "This thing has been hanging over me for nearly two years. We're going through a rough time right now, but you made me come clean. We'll work things out."

They watched him retreat into the building. "Do you believe him?" Barnwell said as she got behind the wheel.

"I don't know. He seemed genuinely surprised. You?"

"Either he's telling the truth or all that acting experience serves him well."

They were silent as they headed back toward Pittsburgh. As they approached the Greentree exit, Jeffrey received a call. He listened for a moment, responding in monosyllables. As he disconnected, he turned toward her and said, "We've got a match."

ANNETTE ARRIVED at headquarters at 2:55 looking defiant, her jaw set and her bearing rigid. She shook off the touch of an officer who guided her down the hallway toward the interview room. By contrast, Moira, accompanied by her attorney, appeared deflated, her shoulders slumped and wearing the look of someone who's lost a child. The same officer escorted her to the adjoining interview room, but Jeffrey had ordered Annette's door left ajar, allowing her to spot Moira as she passed.

The warrant that had brought them in on a charge of tampering with a corpse allowed the ACPD to collect their fingerprints and DNA. While the women waited in their respective rooms, the crime lab ran a quick check on Annette's prints and reconfirmed those Jeffrey had taken from the mug Moira had cradled earlier in the day. They placed both women at Sharon Easterling's house, in her garage, and in Brad Walker's car.

They had not found Sharon's prints inside Walker's vehicle. At first, this had surprised Lydia, but she now imagined a sequence of events, which she tucked away to use when the opportunity arose.

They turned first to Moira, allowing Annette and her attorney to hold their collective breath, worrying about the story the detectives were hearing down the hall. "Ms. Buller," Jeffrey said, "you've been charged with tampering with a corpse. We found your prints in the vehicle used to carry Brad Walker's body to the bridge over the North Fork. It's a misdemeanor under Pennsylvania law, but it carries jail time. Do you want to tell us what happened?"

"My client will make no statement at this time," the attorney, John Gimble, said.

"But that's not your worst problem," Jeffrey continued. "We'll be charging you with false imprisonment, because we also found your prints in the house where you held Walker. That too is a misdemeanor, but it's more serious."

"No comment," Gimble said.

"The most serious issue you face is your role in two murders, that of Brad Walker and later the staged suicide of Sharon Easterling. We have ample evidence both deaths were planned. Mr. Gimble, would you explain to your client the penalty for premeditated murder in the commonwealth?"

"We have no comment."

"That's fine. I expect your cohort, Ms. Henley, will be more forthcoming."

"My client knows no such person."

"She admitted to us this morning they met with Sharon Easterling." Jeffrey rose to his feet and leaned past the attorney, addressing Moira. "We have your phone records. You two chatted back and forth throughout this activity. That argument won't wash."

They left the room and spent a moment watching the monitor in an adjoining room as the two conversed, Moira waving her arms as she spoke and tearing tissues out of her pocket to wipe tears from her face. Gimble patted her arm, trying to calm her. "She'll cave first," Jeffrey said.

Lydia didn't argue. He had more experience with interrogations, but Moira, in her opinion, had the sharper of the two lawyers and could hold out the longest.

They entered the second interrogation room, meeting Annette's scowl with bland faces. Barnwell introduced them to Rita St. Germaine, a general practitioner with limited criminal experience.

Whereas Jeffrey had started with the least serious

charge and built up, she began at the top. "We're investigating the murders of Brad Walker and Sharon Easterling. You were present in the house where Walker was held. We can place you in his car, which the three of you used to carry his corpse to the Old Mill Bridge. So far, we've only charged you with that crime, but we'll soon add more."

She stopped and waited for Annette to react. When she merely returned her gaze, she said, "How did the three of you capture Walker? Did you bring him to Sharon's or lure him there?"

"I don't know what you're talking about."

"Annette, we have you at the scene. Your prints are all over Sharon's house, in her garage, on the trunk of Walker's car. You wiped your prints down the chair and toilet in the basement, but it's harder to destroy DNA. We can put you at the scene of both murders."

Barnwell paused and stared at her for a moment. "So I'm not asking you to confess. We can prove you did it, so how you play this is up to you. I'm interested in how it happened. He showed up on his own, didn't he? He'd been after Sharon for more money. You told her to call and tell him to come collect it. When he did so, what happened? How did you go about it?"

"I'm not telling you nothing." She reached for a stick of gum, unwrapped it, but reconsidered with it halfway to her mouth.

"All right, fine," she said. "We'll stick with Moira's version." With that, she ended the recording, closed her notebook, and rose from the table, Jeffrey following her. They watched the interaction between the two women on the monitor for a moment. The attorney seemed to plead with her, but Annette sat with her arms folded, looking straight ahead.

"She's a tough nut," Jeffrey said.

"Maybe, but when she cracks, she'll leave shells all over the floor."

The other monitor showed a calmer Moira. She and Gimble stared straight ahead, neither speaking to the other. "Time to shake things up," Jeffrey said.

They returned to the room wearing masks of triumph. "Your friend Annette's been a bit more forthcoming," Barnwell said.

Gimble smiled. "I've been telling Ms. Buller how the game is played. How you go from one room to the other, suggesting one is accusing the other of such-and-so, so that this one will tell you something to make the other talk."

"You drove Walker's car the night of February 6th," Barnwell continued. "You'd never intended to leave his body beneath the bridge. It was too close to Sharon's house." Now Lydia was flying by dead reckoning, but she'd pieced together enough of what *must* have happened to be certain of her destination. "You hadn't intended to pull his body from the car. You were going to abandon it with him in it. But the snowstorm hit, and you, at the wheel, were afraid to go on."

She saw a small flicker of reaction as she spoke the last few words and realized it was not Moira who'd insisted they change plans. She could use that against Annette, but to Moira, she said, "At least, that's how she tells it. Do you want to correct me?"

"My client has nothing to say," Gimble said. His sneer told her he was enjoying himself, seeing through everything she was trying to do. But Moira might not be convinced, so Lydia changed subjects, posing questions only she would know, such as when Walker had first spoken to her about investing with him.

"No comment," the attorney said.

"She can tell us that," Barnwell said. "She's already admitted he swindled her. We have his bank records. I just want to know how he operated."

"We don't stipulate that. She might have loaned him the money."

"She didn't," Barnwell said. "We'll let you sit for a while and think about it."

"What now?" Jeffrey said as they switched their attention from one monitor to the other.

"She reacted when I suggested she'd chickened out during the storm."

"So it was Annette," he said.

"Yes. Annette and Moira drove Walker's car. Sharon was following them in hers, because—" She broke off for a moment. "Where are the reports on their calls to each other?"

They went into Jeffrey's office and compared the records from the three phones. Then they returned to the room where Annette waited, now openly fidgeting. "Sorry it's taking so long," Jeffrey said. "We can only interview one of you at a time."

Annette didn't move her head, but her eyes darted from one detective to the other. She'd ended her debate over whether to put the gum in her mouth, and her chomping was, for a moment, the only sound in the room. "We hadn't been able to discover why you left Walker's body so close to Sharon's house, but Moira enlightened us. You never intended to ditch the body. You were going to leave the car at the airport and cover the corpse with the blue tarp."

Annette's eyes shifted again. She clasped her hands and massaged her fingers as Barnwell took up the narrative, her mouth punishing the chewing gum. "Moira's driving. You're in the passenger seat. Sharon's following you in her car because she's going to bring you back after you ditch Walker's vehicle. And ..."

"And it starts to snow," Jeffrey chimed in.

"Boy, did it ever," Barnwell said with a laugh. "You remember I had to dig my car out the morning of February 7th? I finally gave up. You had to send a four-wheel for me."

The detectives hammed it up for a moment. "No wonder Sharon got scared," Jeffrey said. "She couldn't drive in the snow."

"So she called you," Barnwell said, as though remembering Annette was in the room. "She was too frightened to continue, but neither did she want the body back at her house."

"You argued with her, but in the end," Jeffrey said, "you pulled across the road and debated what to do with the body."

Annette said nothing for a moment, and Barnwell feared their gambit had failed. "That was a mistake," she said, looking at the woman. "If you'd just continued on, we might never have tied you to these murders."

"It was Moira," she said. "I told them to go on. I pleaded with her to take the wheel of Sharon's car, but she wouldn't. Meanwhile, the snow kept getting worse. I was worried we'd all be trapped there."

"So you dumped the body," Barnwell said.

"Yeah." She doubled over, her head nearly hitting the table. "But I didn't kill him. Moira did."

"How did she do it?"

"I don't know. Sharon left him alone. She was supposed to call one of us whenever she had to leave. I couldn't come out there that day, and she couldn't reach Moira, so she left him. She said it was only for an hour, but it must have been longer, because his body was cool by the time I got there. Sharon said she found him that way."

"Where was Moria in all this?"

Annette sighed like wind whistling through the last leaves of autumn. "We thought he'd died of natural causes. At least that's what we told each other. But when was it? Ten days ago? Word came out he'd been poisoned? I knew I hadn't done it. Moira claimed she hadn't. So we focused on Sharon. She also denied it, but she was the one coming unglued, calling us while we were working, crying and moaning. She was leaving a cell phone trail. I kept telling her to stop, but that just made things worse."

"Moira?" Barnwell said in her softest voice.

"I drove out to Sharon's house to calm her down. Had to leave work to do it. They don't like it when you take off. I've never missed a day." She seemed to think about it. "Sharon was lying on her bed, comatose. I found an empty pill bottle on her nightstand and a suicide note accusing both of us of killing Mike—Walker, I mean. The note claimed we were setting her up. 'They tried to kill me by pinning his murder on me,' she said, 'so I've left this earth. Let whoever finds this bring them to justice.' Something like that, anyway. She was still breathing. I worked to revive her. Once I had her sitting up, I called Moira to tell her what had happened. I was so angry with her."

"With Sharon?"

"With Moira. If Sharon denied poisoning him, it meant she'd done it."

Only Annette's heavy breathing broke the silence, to which she now added choking sobs. "By the time she got there, Sharon had slipped back into a coma. I showed Moira the note. She tore it up, denied she'd had anything to do with it. She accused me of killing Walker, when all I'd done was to go along with her scheme to get our money back."

She wrapped her arms around her torso and rocked back and forth as though cold. Her voice grew quiet as she recalled the events. "He kept insisting he'd gambled it all away, but Moira didn't believe it. I tried reasoning with her. 'It's gone,' I said. She wouldn't listen."

"Annette, who killed Sharon?"

"Moira. Didn't I just say that? I don't know what I've said." She shook her head in confusion. "She told me, 'We need to finish this. Sharon started it. Let's let her have her way.' I argued with her, but she paid no attention. The woman's stubborn. She said if we let her live, she'd find another way to implicate us. 'I didn't kill him. You say you didn't. That leaves Sharon. This whole thing is her doing, and she wants us to pay the price. We can't let that happen.'"

"So you helped hang her?"

She looked away and wiped her hands on her bluejeans as though she were Pontius Pilate. "I helped, but Moira did it."

———

AT TEN THAT NIGHT. Lydia and Calvin sat at the dining table, two empty pizza boxes between them. Calvin maneuvered the last two dozen pieces of the jigsaw puzzle in the puzzle's vanishing hole. Lydia sat rotating her wineglass as she spooned out the day's events.

"We kept hammering at Moira. We'd question her for twenty minutes, go away for ten, then come back with some new piece of information as though Annette had just revealed something else." She paused, smiling to herself.

"By that point, she'd admitted everything and was on her way to Second Avenue, but Moira didn't know that."

Calvin laid another two pieces in place and looked up to show he was listening.

"When we revealed we had her fingerprints on the beam and the ladder, she finally admitted to hanging Sharon. You should have heard the self-justification. 'She was going to do it anyway. She'd try to overdose, and it hadn't worked. It wasn't murder. We just helped her do what she wanted.' It was nauseating to hear her describe it so casually."

She paused and poured herself another glass of wine, something she rarely did. "I asked her why they'd removed his clothing. Do you know what she said? 'Have you ever tried to dress a stiff?'"

"So he was already naked?" Mayfield asked.

"Yeah, after he'd peed all over himself, they took his clothes and tied him to the commode. He sat like that for hours each day."

She paused, seemed to look past him, and bit her lip. "But?" he said as he pressed another piece into the disappearing gap. He'd become accustomed to her moods and knew there was more.

"Moira adamantly denies poisoning Walker. She insists Sharon did it, but Sharon's suicide note blamed the two of them. Annette insists she didn't do it, and that appears to be the case. We know from her manager she didn't leave her work until late in the afternoon, and the phone records show Sharon had already called her."

"So who killed Walker?" he said.

"I don't know. They both deny knowing Thorson. Annette says she was unaware he had a brother. It would have been easy for one of them to point the finger at him.

Neither did." She tossed her curls in frustration. "Jeffrey wants the DA to charge both of them and let the two sort it out in court."

"But that's not good enough for you," he said.

"It is not." She rose and poured the rest of her glass into the sink, then returned to pick up the empty pizza boxes.

While Calvin continued to work on the puzzle, she took out her notebook, edited a few entries, and added more.

> *1/18, Walker arrested*
> *1/19, Preliminary arraignment; released;*
> *    transfers funds for attorney; now broke*
> *1/2, Formal arraignment, Walker noshow*
> *1/25, Sharon writes on Neighborhood*
> *1/26, Women meet for breakfast, begin*
> *    texting and calling*
> *1/29, they lure Walker to Sharon's house*
> *2/5, Sharon returns home and finds*
> *    Walker dead*
> *2/6, The three leave Walker's body beneath*
> *    bridge*
> *3/3, They leave Walker's car at airport*
> *3/20, Cindy Thorson discovers body*
> *3/25, Sharon is murdered*

"A piece is missing," Calvin said.

"I know," she said, staring at the timeline. "Something we don't yet know."

Mayfield smiled. "That's not what I meant. There's a piece missing." He scooted his chair back and poked his head beneath the table. "Not here."

Lydia went into the back room and lifted Howie off his bed. She passed through the kitchen, tossed a few scraps of paper into the garbage, and returned to the table, holding the errant piece of cardboard. He reached for it, but she played Miss Liberty, holding it aloft like a torch.

"Who's that officer from Crafton you used to golf with?"

"Joe Ransombe. Joey," he said. "Are you keeping that?"

She lowered her arm and dropped the piece into his hand. "But you no longer play with him. Why?"

He snapped the piece into place. "Voila," he said and returned his attention to her. "Why do you ask?"

"Play along with me for a moment. This is important. Back when we were at Boyleston, you two used to go off together once a week. Last summer, you stopped and joined up with three cops from Carnegie. You guys now play whenever the weather permits. What happened to Joey? Why did you drop him?"

"I didn't drop him. He quit. He didn't play well, always slicing the ball into the trees or dropping it into a pond. We were playing so slow we were holding other—"

"Would you say he couldn't play?"

He shook his head in puzzlement. Where was this conversation going? "No, he just doesn't play well. I tried to get him lessons, but—"

"Calvin, would you ever say, 'He can't play?'"

"I wouldn't put it that way."

"What if the golf club barred him?" she persisted. "What if every course for a hundred miles said they wouldn't even allow him on the practice green?"

"That would be brutal," he said. "But yeah, I'd have to say he can't play. Satisfied?"

She tossed her head and looked off at a horizon only she could picture. "Very."

CHAPTER TWELVE

LYDIA AWOKE AT THREE. The suspicion she'd had four hours before bounced off the walls of her mind like a ping-pong ball. Calvin lay next to her, his breathing so light she couldn't hear it. He could fall asleep whenever and wherever he chose to. Not her. When an idea came to her, she couldn't put it to bed, let alone herself.

Her mind returned to the morning two weeks prior when Detective Carpenter assigned her to investigate what he believed was an accidental death. It proved to be much more than that, providing a chance to prove herself in her new job to the men who dominated the detective division.

Replaying the mental tape of her initial interviews, she saw where she might have gone wrong. It was a mistake she'd made before, taking a witness's statement at face value, letting her instincts overrule her judgment.

She knew she could never fall back to sleep until she'd formed the pieces into a new shape. She arose and brewed herself a cup of herbal tea, reviewed the timeline she'd built, and began making notes. The more she wrote, the clearer things became. She thought she knew what had happened and how.

If she was correct now, she'd been mistaken before. She understood why Inspector Andrew Morris had given her case to Lyle Jeffrey, though he'd never taken over, loosening the reins and giving Lydia her head. She'd galloped in the wrong direction, taking him with her.

At six, she switched from tea to coffee, ate a piece of toast, and dressed as quietly as possible. Still not quiet enough. Calvin rolled over, opened one eye, and said, "Going somewhere?"

"Yeah," she said. "To solve a murder."

He wished her luck and turned over. How that man could sleep.

---

WHAT HAD Ben Thorson told her? He and his brother had been raised in Louisville. How long had they lived there and when had Thorson moved to Pittsburgh? Stop it, she told herself. You're so tired you don't recall answering this question a week ago. He'd come here to attend Point Park University thirteen years before. Brad had followed him six year later, having dropped out of college in Kentucky and settled for an associate degree at a community college.

And when had Thorson married? Lydia found nothing in Pennsylvania state records, so she turned to those for Kentucky. There it was. He and Cathy had wedded in Louisville after his graduation, when he was still trying to break into an acting career. Another records search told her Cathy had graduated from the same high school as had Ben. They'd probably been sweethearts. Brad had attended the same school. The trio had known each other for years.

Lydia seldom had a second cup of coffee in the morning, switching to water after the initial jolt, but now she swilled it as she pawed through more records. Kentucky DMV. "Uh-huh," she said aloud. Then the Kentucky criminal court database. There it was. She leaned back and read the details of a nine-year-old case. What had happened, who had been charged and convicted, and why. "Gold," she said. "I've struck gold."

"What?" She turned to find Jeffrey standing at her door.

"I've found something." To his raised eyebrows, she said, "I don't want to say anything just yet. Let me talk to one witness, then I'll come see you."

"Okay," he said, tossing it off with a chuckle.

Should she handle this by phone? No, she needed to do it right. She signed out a cruiser, headed west on the parkway, and peeled off on Route 60, arriving in front of the apartment building twenty minutes later. She took the elevator to the third floor and knocked at 311. Greta Norland answered, still in her housecoat.

"I'm glad to see you again, but I wish you'd called. I'm—"

"Don't worry. This will just take a minute."

She held the door open, and Barnwell entered. "Have you arrested Cathy's husband? I know something's going on there."

"No, nothing like that," she said. "I need to ask a question about the kindness you've shown her."

———

"As we were escorting Thorson out after we did the formal interview," Barnwell said, "I mentioned his wife doesn't have a car. Do you remember his answer?"

"He said she doesn't drive," Jeffrey replied

"Not exactly. He asked why she would need a car. 'She can't drive,' was his answer. His exact words."

"What's the difference?"

"One is a choice. The other is a requirement."

Jeffrey said nothing, but his slight shrug amounted to, "So?"

"Nine years ago," she said, sliding into the chair at his desk, "Cathy Thorson was behind the wheel of a car that drove through a red light at high speed. She hit another vehicle driven by a 44-year-old mother of three and killed her. She was tried and convicted, but the judge gave her a suspended sentence on the condition that she is never to operate a motor vehicle. If she gets behind the wheel, she goes to prison. She literally can't drive."

"Okay." Jeffrey frowned. "That's a pretty light sentence."

"The judge found extenuating circumstances. Cathy's physician testified she'd had a blackout. She'd gone into diabetic shock."

"Ah," Jeffrey said. It took a beat, but daylight spread across his face. "Diabetics need insulin to stay alive."

"And they know how to use it. While Cathy is prohibited from driving, it turns out she does. She frequently borrows a neighbor's car. She used it four afternoons in early February."

"You're thinking Cathy killed Brad Walker? What was her motive?"

"If you'll have the District 1 question the TSA again, we may find Cathy was well aware they'd suspended her husband. If she knew that, she may also have learned the reason. Cathy has known both brothers all her life. They went to school together. And Brad has been a pain in the

derriere for years, sponging off his brother as he accumu-
lated gambling debts. He borrowed their life savings and
never repaid it. If Cathy learned this…"

"All right, genius. I'll talk to Inspector Whelan. What
else do we need?"

"Her cell phone records. We'll also need to re-interview
one key witness. And that may take a court order."

---

BEN THORSON HELD the door open for his daughter and
followed her into the North Fayette police station. Barnwell
greeted them at the security desk. "Hello, Cindy," she said,
extending her hand. The youngster looked up at her father
for permission, then accepted Lydia's handshake.

"Are you sure this is necessary?" Ben said.

"I think Cindy saw something that can help us solve
this case," she replied. "As I've told you, I can get a court
order, but if you're willing, we can clear this up with about
three questions."

"I don't know what more she can tell you," he said.

"If I'm mistaken, perhaps nothing," Barnwell replied,
"but that, too, will tell us something. What do you say?"

"I can be there while you talk to her?" he asked.

"I insist on it. It's vital you hear what she tells us."

He threw out both hands as though in surrender. "All
right. Are you willing to talk to this lady, honey?"

"Sure," she said. Did Barnwell imagine it, or did the girl
throw out her chest, pleased to be the center of attention?

She led them to a small office where Lyle Jeffrey waited.
The child tensed when she encountered the male detective.
"It's okay, Cindy. Mr. Jeffrey is a friend of mine. We work
together."

"Okay." She looked up at Ben again, who smiled and patted her on the back.

"Can I get you anything? A glass of water? Some lemonade?"

Her face brightened. "I'd like that."

"Is it okay, Ben?" Barnwell said, realizing that with Cathy Thorson having diabetes, this might be a rare and unwelcome treat.

"More healthy than pop," he said.

Barnwell withdrew a six-ounce carton of lemonade from the cooler bag she'd brought and began tearing the straw away. "I can do it," Cindy said.

Barnwell grinned and handed it over. "I'm sure you can." The youngster ripped the straw from the side of the carton, grabbed it by the wrapper, and plunged it into the table, ejecting the pointed edge from its plastic. She thrust it into the top of the carton and took a giant gulp. "Are we ready?" Barnwell said.

The girl nodded.

"Cindy, do you know your Uncle Brad?"

The child nodded as Ben's eyes grew wide. Barnwell had given him no clue why she wanted to question his daughter. He assumed it had something to do with the day she and her dog had stumbled on Brad Walker's naked body. This was not what he'd expected.

"When did you last see him?"

She looked at her father with what Barnwell took to be a trace of apprehension. Ben nodded. "Go ahead, honey. You can tell them."

"It was a while ago. After Christmas. We'd gone back to school for a couple of weeks. It was when we had to take all those tests."

Barnwell would check, but she suspected this placed the event in late January. "Did he come to your apartment?"

"Yeah. He knocked at the door real loud. Mommy answered it and asked what he was doing there. He said he wanted to talk to you." She turned to her father. "She told him you were at work."

"And what did he say to that?" she asked.

"'Work?' he said it like it was funny. He asked where you were working." Cindy again turned to her father. "Mom gave him this funny look and told me to go to my room."

"How did your mother seem?"

"When she first opened the door, she was angry. She said, 'What are you doing here?' But then, when they started talking about work, she seemed kind of scared. You know?"

"Yes, baby, I know," he said.

"You went to your room, and they—what? Continued talking?" Barnwell asked.

"Yelling. He shouted at her. She told him to keep his voice down, but she was screaming even more than he was. I was scared."

Barnwell longed to gauge Thorson's reaction, but she now focused her attention on the girl, smiling in what she hoped was a reassuring way, as though nothing she said was of great importance. "Did you hear their conversation?"

"I couldn't help it. Their voices came right through my door. Uncle Brad said he had to go away and needed money. He told her to go to an ATM and pull out cash. He promised he'd pay it back. 'All of it,' he said. He mentioned something about a loan. She asked him a few questions and started screaming even louder. I was worried the neighbors would hear."

"Did she give him any money?"

"No," Cindy said. "She said she didn't have any and wouldn't give it to him if she did. She asked what he needed it for. I couldn't hear all he said, but he repeated he had to go away. Then he said he needed a phone."

Barnwell heard a sharp intake of breath from Thorson and cast a glance his way. He was red in the face, his jaw clenched and his scowl so intense his eyebrows threatened to touch his nose. "What did she say to that?" she asked.

"She told him she had an old phone. She was supposed to save it for me, but by the time I was old enough, I'd want a newer one, she said. 'If that's what it takes to get rid of you, you can have it.'"

"And then what?"

"I heard her messing around in the closet. It's right next to my bedroom. She must have found it, because she said she'd lost the charger and it wasn't hooked up to anything. He said it didn't matter. They had a few more words. She told him not to show his—" She turned toward her father. "Can I say a bad word?"

"Yes." He spat the word out.

Cindy cupped her hand to her mouth so only Barnwell could hear and whispered, "Not to show his ass around there anymore. That's the word she used."

"Thank you," Barnwell said, also sotto voce. "So then he left?" She nodded her head, her blond bangs bouncing on her forehead. "And you haven't seen him since?" Her head turned from up and down to back and forth. Her eyes were wide.

"May I ask a question?" Thorson said.

"Of course."

"Why haven't you told me this, honey?" Her face crinkled as though she might burst into tears. "It's all right. You can tell me."

"Mommy said not to. She made me promise. She was real firm about it. 'You are not to mention this to your father.' You know how she gets."

"Yes," he said, his voice grave. "I do."

Lydia thanked the girl and asked Jeffrey if he had any questions.

"No," he said, "you've covered it all." He rose with them and clapped a hand on Thorson's shoulder as they made their way to the entrance.

He let his daughter through the door first, turned and said to the two detectives, "What happens now?"

Barnwell was lost for words. Didn't he know what his daughter's revelation meant? It was left to Jeffrey to tie a bow on it. "We're continuing our investigation."

---

BARNWELL BLAMED HERSELF. Cathy Thorson had depicted herself as an abused woman, psychologically, if not physically. Trapped at home by a domineering husband, isolated from friends and family, unable to get out on her own. All this when she was the dominator, the manipulator.

Not that Thorson was without fault. His lies contributed to his brother's murder.

But she had missed the clues. She recalled how, at their second meeting, Cathy had turned to look at something hidden in the folds of her sweatshirt at her hip. Lydia had taken it as a tracking device, assuming so because that was what she chose to believe. Instead, it was a glucose monitor. If she'd realized that, if she looked more closely...

"How shall we handle this?" Jeffrey asked, interrupting her self-flagellation.

There's a widely held belief that investigating officers play good cop/bad cop during an interrogation. While many do, hardened criminals are on to the trick. They know that when those playing the good cop role say they're only trying to make things easy on you, they're trying to make things easy on themselves. More often, the interrogators play tag-team, so one is fresh when the other wears down. What Jeffrey asked now wasn't how they planned to manipulate Cathy Thorson, but how they might outmaneuver her when, as they knew she would, she tried to manipulate them.

"She's met me," Lydia said. "You start with what we know. I'll dive in when she lies. It won't take long."

They watched her sitting alongside an attorney on the monitor. She seemed calm, her hands folded before her, looking neither left nor right, not engaging with the lawyer. Barnwell's purpose in leaving her alone wasn't to rattle her. Unlike the way the process is depicted on television, it takes time to process fingerprint evidence. They had taken Cathy's when she arrived, and the crime lab was working to match them against the unidentified prints found at Sharon's house. Matching the DNA sample would take more time. That could wait until later.

"Here we go," Jeffrey said. He printed the report, which Barnwell grabbed from the printer. They looked it over, shoved it into the growing case file, securing it with what Pittsburghers call a gum band.

"Afternoon," Jeffrey said as he entered the room, not suggesting it was a good one. He introduced himself. "You know Detective Barnwell." Cathy gave no sign of recognition, betrayed no emotion. He began the recording, gave the date and time, had those present identify themselves, and issued the warning.

"We're investigating the death of Bradley James Walker, the half brother of your husband, Benjamin Forrest Thorson. You were acquainted with Mr. Walker."

She stared at him, waiting for him to go on. When he did not, she said, "Of course."

"Went to high school with him," he said.

She nodded, and he asked her to speak up. "Yes," she said.

The preliminaries over, he began the interrogation. "On January 18th, we arrested Mr. Walker and two other TSA workers on charges of stealing cash, credit cards, IDs, and personal property from passengers as they passed through screening. Because your husband often supervised them during these shifts, he was suspended pending an outcome of the investigation. When did you first realize this?"

"My husband told me a few days ago." She stared at her folded hands as she spoke, refusing to look up.

"And not before that? Your husband was out of work for two months. You must have been aware of it."

"No," she said.

"We spoke earlier today with Daniel Othmer, Ben's former supervisor at the TSA. He says you called him on January 24th asking for your husband and he informed you he'd been suspended. Do you admit making that call?"

"No, it must have been someone else."

"He's certain it was you. He says you've spoken in the past."

"I don't know anyone by that name."

Barnwell withdrew a stapled report from the file. "We have the record of calls made from your cell phone. Here it is, 11:39 a.m., January 24th. From your phone to the TSA's private line. The call lasted four minutes and twenty-two seconds."

"It wasn't me," she said. "Someone else made that call."

"We know it wasn't your husband," she said, withdrawing another report. "He was working at Carnegie Distribution Center at that hour."

"There must be some mistake," she said. For the first time, she lifted a hand from the table and covered her mouth as she spoke.

It would have been simple for her to admit placing the call, saying, "I forgot," but that would have revealed she knew what Brad had done to her family, giving her a motive for murder. This, Barnwell thought, is the liar's dilemma. One fib leads to another, and you become entangled in your web. The only option is to keep lying, which was the course Cathy took.

She insisted she hadn't spoken to Brad in months, denied he'd come to their apartment demanding money, and claimed she'd hadn't given him the old cell phone. *She must wonder how we know*, Barnwell thought, but the woman didn't ask.

"Ben must have done that," she said, casually throwing her husband to the wolves.

The best was yet to come, and Jeffrey set it up. "We also know you used an iPhone app to trace Brad to the house where three women held him. You borrowed a neighbor's car four times during the week leading up to his death. We've traced your phone to that location."

"I know nothing about any house. I was never there."

A long pause, and Jeffrey allowed Barnwell to deliver the blow. "We have your fingerprints in the kitchen, living room, and wooden railing leading to the basement where they held Brad."

Barnwell had wondered why the attorney, pressed into service at the last moment, had allowed the questioning to continue. To find out how much they knew? Whatever her strategy, she now put an end to it. "My client has nothing more to say." She turned to her and said, "Don't respond to anything they ask."

Barnwell was undeterred. "Brad came to your apartment on January 23rd demanding money. He told you he'd been arrested, was running from police, and Ben had been suspended. You confirmed this through his boss the following day. In asking you to withdraw cash, he also let slip something he thought you already knew, that Ben had given him a substantial loan, one he'd never repaid. You were angry, screaming at him, but when he asked for a phone, you supplied it. Had you already added it to the iPhone app in anticipation of giving it to your daughter?"

No answer.

"You couldn't deal with Brad at that moment, not with Cindy in the next room, but using the app, you tracked him to his last location before his phone died. Using Greta Norland's car, you staked the house out. We know every day you were there. On the afternoon of February 5th, you saw Sharon Easterling drive away. Seeing no other cars on the property, you slipped into the house and found Brad tied up in the basement. Was he glad to see you? Did he think you'd come to his rescue?"

She saw a flicker of something pass over Cathy's face. Amusement? Contempt? She couldn't tell, but the attorney answered for her, repeating that she wouldn't speak.

"Instead, you administered a drug with which you prolong your life to end his. How many doses were in the vial? Three? Four? Five? How many does it take? Did you watch him writhe in agony or did you just leave, trusting it would do its job?"

No answer.

"No, you had to stand there, make sure the insulin did its job. Otherwise, who knows what would have happened to you?"

Again, she displayed no reaction.

"Do you want to tell us what parts of this I got wrong?"

Cathy snorted, looked up at her with a smile conveying pure hatred. But she said nothing.

---

"AND SHE NEVER CRACKED?" Calvin said.

It had turned cold again, winter's last gasp before releasing its grip on western Pennsylvania. Lydia lay huddled in a blanket before the fireplace. "Nope," she said. "We confronted her with everything we've learned. Walker was arrested at the airport on January 18th and arraigned the following day. He hired an attorney who got him released. He wanted to make a run for it, but had no money left. He turned to his brother, but he wasn't home that afternoon, so he tried to get money out of Cathy. That's when she learned her husband had been suspended and that he'd loaned Brad everything they had."

"That must have been a scene," he said.

"It was," she said. "She was so angry, it terrified her daughter. Cathy refused to give him cash, but did provide an old iPhone. He still needed money, so he turned to Sharon, the only victim with whom he was still in contact. Sharon grew suspicious. She posted a message on a social media platform that Annette and Moira responded. Over breakfast, the three women concocted a scheme. Sharon was to play along, get Brad to come to her house to collect money. He arrived to find all three waiting for him, taking him prisoner."

Calvin lay behind her and wrapped his arm around her waist. "Why did they hold Walker for so long? What the hell did they hope to accomplish?"

"I asked Annette the same thing. She couldn't give me an answer. 'We wanted our money back,' she said. When I asked why they continued holding him once they learned he'd gambled it away, she said Moira insisted on it. I asked how long were they going to keep this up. She couldn't tell me."

"They got into it and couldn't find a way out," he said.

"That's what I figure. The idiotic thing is, if they'd just let him go, what was he going to do? He could hardly report them to the cops."

Lydia described how Cathy had traced Walker's location and staked it out. "She entered the house, found Brad helpless in the basement, and shot him full of insulin." She paused for a moment, recalling some things that remained unsolved. "Did she mean to kill him or just torture him? Did she leave or watch him die? We don't know."

"She's not admitted to any of this?" he said.

"Not a thing. Cathy may go to her grave without confessing. But her prints place her in the basement of the house and her phone puts her there the afternoon he died. DNA will nail the coffin."

They lay side-by-side without speaking for a moment. After she'd killed Walker, Cathy was trapped. She now knew what her husband had been hiding from her all this time, but she couldn't confront him. She'd have to admit his brother had provided the information. This would have started a conversation that, once Brad's body was discovered, would point to her.

"How is Ben taking all this?"

"He was skeptical at first, but as his daughter recounted bits and pieces of the conversation she'd overheard, he accepted it. Cathy had been more skittish than usual over the past several weeks, and now he knows why. She couldn't understand why Brad's body hadn't been discovered. It was driving her crazy. Crazier," she said.

"And when Cindy discovered it..." he said.

"She became even more nervous. The slightest thing set her off." Lydia went silent for a moment, recounting her conversation with Ben after his wife's arrest. "He's remorseful. His lies and concealment set all this in motion. He's also realized he'll have to raise his daughter as a single parent. Welcome to the world so many women face. But he's not who I worry about."

"It's the daughter," Calvin said.

"Right. Cindy will live life knowing her testimony helped put her mother behind bars. First she discovers the body, then she identifies his murderer." Lydia gave an involuntary shudder.

He drew her more closely. "You're the only one who comes out ahead in this deal."

"Yeah, Jeffrey's given me full credit. Inspector Morris is issuing a commendation. No apology for doubting me, but it's something."

"You've shown the old boys a thing or two."

They lay together for a few moments, saying nothing to each other. Howie waddled in and nestled between their legs. "This reminds me," Calvin said. "There's something I've been meaning to tell you. It's about Tommy."

She flipped over to face him, Howie scrambling to avoid

being buried in the thrashing legs. "You're going to tell me he left the noose."

He drew back and squinted at her. "Did he tell you?"

"No, I kept wondering why he wouldn't take money for walking Howie. Then I figured it was guilt. How did you learn it?"

He planted his elbow on the floor, raised his head, and rested it on his fist. "I got his fingerprints. The crime scene investigators compared them with those they took from the window downstairs."

"Oh, no. Now they'll have a record of it."

"I made the lab destroy them. Told them it had all been a mistake." He chuckled. "Howie destroyed the only other copy the other night."

The dog, hearing his name, stirred between them. "I never confronted Tommy," Calvin said. "He came to me. It was his mother who called the cops the first time I came here, thinking I was a prowler. He took his cue from her. A kid at school told him he ought to hang that Black man. I'm sure that's not the term he used, but it's how Tommy replayed the conversation. The kid showed him how to tie a noose. Tommy broke in and left it. Then Anna told him she'd made a mistake, that I wasn't a burglar but a police officer. Walking Howie was his way of making amends."

"Anna's doing the same," she said. Lydia had found a loaf of bread and a jar of homemade jam, sugar free, at her door when she'd arrived two hours before.

"Tommy's a good kid," Calvin said. "He just needs a father figure."

"Lots of boys do. Many of them are Black," she said.

"I know." He lay back down again, turned onto his back and rested both hands on his stomach. "But you have to start somewhere."

# ACKNOWLEDGMENTS

This story grew out of a series of police procedurals, the Chief Novak series, set in a fictional borough outside Pittsburgh. Lydia Barnwell was one of the most popular characters to emerge from that trilogy. When I brought it to a close, therefore, it seemed logical to give Lydia a new role and her own series. This is the first of what I hope will be many cases for this talented police woman.

The story is a work of fiction. Unless otherwise indicated, all the names, characters, events, and incidents in this book are the product of my imagination. While many locations referenced in this story exist, they are used in a fictitious manner, and none of the people or events depicted in these settings are real. Any resemblance to actual persons, living or dead, or actual events is purely coincidental.

There are two exceptions. The theft by TSA agents of passenger baggage at Miami International Airport occurred. The terrorist attack at Pittsburgh's Tree of Life Synagogue took the lives of eleven innocent worshippers and is, as stated, the worst antisemitic attack in US history.

I wish to thank the dozens of law enforcement professionals who provided information to make this story as authentic as possible. I am especially grateful to Mandy Tinkey, Laboratory Director of the Allegheny County Medical Examiner for providing information and a tour of the facility. Any mistakes or liberties I have taken with law enforcement or forensic practices are my own.

James H Lewis has published eight novels, seven in the mystery genre and a historical novel set in World War II Canada. His short stories have been published by Mystery Tribune and in anthologies. He is a former journalist whose work has appeared in the Washington Post, on ABC News, PBS, and the Eurovision News Exchange. Lewis lives in Pittsburgh, PA and is a member of Mystery Writers of America, PennWriters, and The Author's Guild. Follow him at jameshlewis.com.

ALSO BY JAMES H LEWIS

THE CHIEF NOVAK NOVELS

Novak's Mission

Novak's Quest

Novak's Verdict

THE WORLD WAR II NOVEL

The Quadrant Conspiracy: The Plot to Kill FDR

THE ALAN RUDBERG NOVELS

Sins of Omission

Breaking News